The Ninth Circle

The Ninth Circle

Alex Bell

The right of Alex Bell to be identified as the author of
this work has been asserted by her in accordance with the
Copyright, Designs and Patents Act 1988.

First published in Great Britain in 2008 by
Gollancz
An imprint of the Orion Publishing Group
Orion House, 5 Upper St Martin's Lane,
London WC2H 9EA
An Hachette UK Company

This edition published in Great Britain in 2009
by Gollancz

3 5 7 9 10 8 6 4 2

A CIP catalogue record for this book
is available from the British Library.

ISBN 978 0 575 08465 0

Typeset by Deltatype Ltd, Birkenhead, Merseyside

Printed in Great Britain by
CPI Mackays, Chatham ME5 8TD

www.orionbooks.co.uk

The Orion Publishing Group's policy is to use papers that
are natural, renewable and recyclable products and made
from wood grown in sustainable forests. The logging and
manufacturing processes are expected to conform to the
environmental regulations of the country of origin.

For Robert.

'At times our own light goes out and is rekindled by a spark from another person. Each of us has cause to think with deep gratitude of those who have lighted the flame within us.'

Albert Schweitzer

8th August

My name is Gabriel. There – I have a name. So there's no need to be afraid. But I wish I could remember ... something more. Seven days ago I opened my eyes and stared at the kitchen floorboards stretching out before me – worn old floorboards that were stained with someone else's blood. And when I tried to lift my head, I found that my face was glued to the floor where the blood had dried there, sticking to my skin.

I'm only writing this down now because I – ah – don't want to forget it all again. If a man doesn't know who he is, he might cease to be a person altogether. I mean, he might just sort of ... *fade* ... right out of existence. So I'm making a record here in this journal. It's the sensible thing to do. I'm being rational; you see that I am being calm about this. I am not afraid. What good would fear be?

When I at last managed to get to my feet, the room tilted and the air went thin. I staggered, almost fell back down again. My tongue felt like sandpaper in my mouth, my lips were dry and cracked and my head was throbbing. I stumbled from the kitchen, half in a daze, wandering from room to room trying to get my bearings.

The apartment was small and shabby: just a kitchen, bathroom, lounge and small bedroom. The carpets were worn and drab and the wallpaper was threadbare and virtually peeling from the walls. But the furnishings and other possessions were clearly of high quality. The wine and clothes, the many books, the classical music collection, the fine artwork ...

I walked into the bedroom and sat down on the double bed. The sheets were crumpled as if they had been slept in, but the apartment was deserted. And completely silent. I sat there, staring at the wall, and it occurred to me that perhaps I was dead. It seemed a sensible explanation. This place couldn't be real. Obviously, I wasn't real either. Real people knew their names. This didn't worry me at first. In fact, I felt I could sit there for ever on the bed, untroubled by this surreal experience, half expecting it to fade away like some vaguely worrying dream.

But slowly noise began to filter through to me. The noise of traffic passing by outside somewhere. I got up and crossed to the window, drew up the blind and looked out, flinching instinctively at the brightness of the sun and shielding my eyes with my hand. I was about six floors up in a large apartment block. There was a main road not far away, and the noise from it had clearly been there all along. Now that I was listening, I could also hear people on the pavement below and the odd door opening and closing within the building. There was life, after all. This was not what came afterwards. Craning my head and squinting against the light, I could see that I was on the top floor. A city glinted dully below and around me. From my window I could see the Danube and the Chain Link Bridge. I think it must have been these landmarks that made a name suddenly come into my mind – Budapest.

I turned, frowning, from the window. Was I Hungarian? What language did I speak? What language was I thinking in right now? I searched my empty mind desperately for memories that weren't there, feeling more and more alarmed by the second.

'I don't know,' someone said hoarsely, and I yelled in fright and spun around, looking for whoever else was in the room with me.

I saw him at once, standing only a few paces away in a doorway that led to another room. About thirty years old – his hair was black, his face was hollow and his eyes were horribly sunken. There was at least a couple of days' growth of stubble on his chin. But what immediately caught my attention was the black bruise on the side of his head, stretching halfway down his face. And the blood that had dried a rusty red-brown, crusted to his skin and in trickles down his neck, staining his creased white shirt. He was visibly shocked at the sight of me.

'Who are you?' I demanded, shakily, trying to conceal my fear.

But he spoke at the exact same time, the exact same words, and I realised then that this was not another person and it was not a doorway. It was just my reflection in the full-length mirror. I stared, incredulous for a moment, amazed that the sight of him – *me* – did not cause even the faintest spark of recognition. It was like I had never seen that man before in my life. I crept cautiously closer to the mirror, tapping the glass with my fingertips to make sure.

I turned my head to one side and then moved it sharply back as if half-expecting to catch the reflection out; but after peering into the mirror from every angle for some minutes, I had to admit that the stranger looking back at me really wasn't a stranger at all. Or at least he shouldn't have been.

'Who are you?' I asked again softly, but the reflection stared back at me, equally mystified.

I was speaking English. Was I English, then? Yes, probably. This was good. I was getting more answers all the time. I would probably remember everything any second now. My reflection grinned at the thought, startling me into taking a hasty step back, for the smile made him look a little menacing. My eyes went back to the bruise on his temple, and for the first time I became aware of the blood beating painfully in my head, this incessant thumping ... Jesus Christ, it was unbearable. How could I have failed to notice it before?

I walked into the bathroom, opened the medicine cabinet in there and found a bottle of aspirin. My shaking hands fumbled with the lid, but finally I managed to take two of the pills, wincing as they scratched painfully at my dry throat. Automatically, I turned on the rusty shower tap over the bath, and then stood underneath the hot water for a while. But when I raised my hand to push my hair out of my eyes, my fingers came back into my field of vision with blood on them, and I yelled in alarm and somehow managed to slip over in the bath, jarring my already sore shoulders and back. It was only then I realised I'd forgotten to take off my clothes and that a soaking shirt was clinging to my back, and the trousers were equally ruined.

Stiffly, I got back to my feet, stripped off my sodden clothes and dropped them into the bath. I turned off the shower, wiped the steamed up mirror with a towel and carefully examined my face. The water from the shower had knocked the scab on my temple, causing it to bleed a little, but already it seemed to have stopped.

I opened the cabinet over the mirror once again and found a comb and a razor, which I grabbed at eagerly. Clean-shaven and with my wet hair combed back, I felt I was starting to look a little more normal. At least I could look at myself without feeling quite so alarmed. I was tall, and now that my clothes were gone I could see the toned muscles of my body. With my height, athletic build and dark hair I could be handsome. I should be handsome. And yet somehow I feel I'm not. There is something about my face – about the look in my eyes – that seems wrong even to me. I look ... cold, somehow.

When I returned to the bedroom and examined the expensive clothes in the wardrobe and in the drawers, I found they were all my size and, for the first time, it occurred to me that – perhaps – this was where I lived. Perhaps these things all belonged to me. Perhaps this was home.

Clean and freshly clothed, I walked back to the desk I had seen in the living room. There was a piece of paper folded on top of it, and when I picked it up I saw that it was a tenancy agreement leasing this apartment to a Mr Gabriel Antaeus. My first thought was that I must find some way of contacting him. He must know who I am; after all, I seemed to be in his home. But then I paused and it occurred to me that – perhaps – I myself was Gabriel Antaeus. This was my apartment. I was living here. I examined the signature on the document, picked up a nearby pen and decided to see if I could copy it. But as soon as I put pen to paper, the signature was curling out beneath my fist, an exact replica of the original, as if my hand instinctively remembered even if I did not.

'Gabriel Antaeus,' I muttered. The name was strange and unfamiliar in my mouth.

I put the pen down and walked back to the kitchen. And that was when I noticed the cardboard box, carefully placed in the middle of the small kitchen table. It was full of money. There must have been at least a hundred thousand pounds' worth of Hungarian forints wrapped up in a plastic bag inside the box. I sat staring at the money for a while, my fingers drumming on the tabletop. It was a lot of cash to be just left there … on the kitchen table like that.

This apartment looked like it was my home – but I couldn't remember it. I couldn't remember me. I got up and walked to the spot where I had been lying. There was a shelf on the ground nearby, one corner of which was stained with blood. And there was a chair positioned by the wall next to a row of already installed shelves. I had been trying to put up shelves. That must have been it. Somehow, I had lost my grip on this top shelf, it had swung forwards and hit me on the head, and I had fallen from the chair and knocked myself out. Yes! Yes, yes, yes! And now I was suffering from some kind of temporary amnesia. It was that simple. It was as gloriously simple as that. Just a stupid, stupid accident.

'Gabriel Antaeus,' I said again. It was definitely an English accent.

I suppose I should have phoned someone. The police, or the British embassy, or a hospital … I wanted to. I wanted to find someone who could help me. But there was a hundred thousand pounds' worth of Hungarian forints on my kitchen table. Would they believe that I couldn't remember stealing it? For that seemed the most plausible explanation, even to me. And I did not want to go to prison.

I found this journal in a drawer beside my bed. It was empty but for my name, which I'd written on the inside cover. I don't know why I started writing everything down like this. I suppose I'm just scared of forgetting it all again. And I don't know who else to tell.

12th August

It's been four days and none of my memories have returned as I'd hoped they would. But what is worse is that I have been unable to find anyone who can tell me who I am. There is no wedding ring on my finger and not a single photograph of anyone in my apartment. There is no address book, no telephone book, no letters from anyone. When I turned on the computer, all I found was spam mail; and there were no messages on my phone's answer machine. My mobile appears to be brand new, for there aren't even any numbers stored on it. Where is everyone? Where are my family, my friends? Where are my acquaintances? Where have they all gone? I mean, they can't all be on holiday, can they? I felt a thrill of panic at the thought. What if there was some big family reunion or something going on in some distant country, and I had volunteered to stay behind to water the plants and feed the fish? There could be dozens of fish slowly starving to *death* because of me! What would my family say when they got home and found their pets floating dead in their tanks because I hadn't taken care of them like I'd promised?

The thought filled me with panic, and it was this that finally overcame my fear of leaving the apartment. It took several abortive attempts, but I did at last manage to make it through the door. I seem to live in a fairly central, if somewhat rundown, area of the city; and after much searching I found a pet shop where I bought as much fish food as I could carry. Now I always have a box of fish food in my pocket so that the second I remember where my families' homes are, I can go there to feed their fish straightaway. I can't do any more than that, can I? I am sure my family will understand when they return.

When I got back to the apartment I realised that, in my pre-occupation with the fish food, I had forgotten to buy any supplies for myself. Until then I had been eating the food I'd found in the freezer and in the cupboards but it would run out soon. So I forced myself to go back out into the city once again.

I realised, travelling around Budapest, that the city is familiar to me. The faded elegance of so many old buildings, with weathered statues on their roofs or crumbling balconies or grand, dilapidated pillars reaching right down to the ground. I must have lived here some time because I can speak Hungarian fluently.

It occurred to me yesterday that if I've been here a while, then my neighbours must know who I am. Again, I had to gather my courage to leave my apartment. I felt safe there and vulnerable outside it. But at last I managed to step out and knock on the door opposite mine, pleased to think that I would find someone here who would remember me.

After a few moments, a pregnant teenager opened the door. She had beautiful coffee-coloured skin and a series of delicate gold hoops in one ear. Black Celtic symbol tattoos adorned one of her upper arms and a silver nose stud pierced one nostril. Her hair was black and straight with irregular streaks of pink and electric blue. I waited for her to recognise me – I think I might have been grinning in anticipation – but after a few moments when I didn't speak, she said in accented Hungarian, 'Yes? Can I help you?'

Can I help you? *Can I help you?* I stared at her, taken aback, the grin faltering uncertainly. It had simply never occurred to me that she wouldn't recognise me.

'Er … I live over there,' I said stupidly, pointing at my apartment door.

'Oh, you're the new tenant,' she said. 'You moved in last week, didn't you?'

'Er—'

'I'm Casey March,' she said, holding out her hand.

'My name is Gabriel,' I began, taking her hand, but then I faltered. Gabriel ... Gabriel *what*? What was my last name? What *was* it? I tried to picture the words in that notebook. It had been some French sounding name. 'Gabriel, er—'

'Are you all right?' Casey asked, and I saw her gaze move to the still-ugly bruise on my temple.

'Yes, yes,' I said quickly, dropping her hand and glancing over my shoulder at the beckoning safety of my apartment door. 'Yes, I'm fine. I'm just ... I just remembered there's something ... that I need to go and do ... Right now. Sorry.'

And I dropped her hand and rushed back to the safety of my apartment, aware that she was still staring at me. I had not been expecting *that* at *all*. She should have known me! She should have been a friend of mine, living right next door. How dare she just be a ... a stranger? What use was that? What *use* was that? To have lived here only a *week*! Of course, that is why I must have been putting up shelves. People do that sort of thing when they have just moved in, don't they?

17th August

I don't seem to sleep very much. No matter how late I go to bed, I wake up on the dot of six. And however little sleep I get, I never seem to become that tired. Nor do I ever have huge amounts of excess energy. I just function. It's the same with food. I never feel hungry. This unnerved me a little. I mean, it's not normal, is it? So I decided not to eat until I became hungry, just to make sure. But it was okay because after four days of nothing but water, I was feeling light-headed and sick all the time, so I know that I *need* food like everybody else. That pleased me. I am normal. I am normal after all.

19th August

I have reluctantly come to the conclusion that it will not do simply to *wait* for my family to return. After all, who knows how long that might take? I must find out about myself now. I hate to think that there might be something sinister in all of this, but ... there was this distasteful episode that occurred yesterday. I was in a park, not far from where I live. The day was bright and sunny, and there were families having picnics and going for walks and playing games out there.

A fat boy scampered over towards the bench where I was sitting. He must have been about six or seven. The sticky remnants of old sweets and ice-creams covered his grubby t-shirt, and there was a horrible eager glee in his little eyes. At first I didn't realise what he was doing as he pounced on something in the grass. But when he sat back triumphantly, I saw that he was gripping a large, beautiful butterfly in his plump hands. As I watched, the boy tore off the creatures' wings and several of its legs.

The strangled yell of pure horror that escaped my lips startled me as much as it did the kid, who dropped the dying butterfly to thrash and curl on the grass in dreadful spasms of silent agony. I don't know why the sight was so *nauseating* to me. After all, it was only a butterfly. But in one movement I stamped down on it as hard as I could, rounded on the brat and before I knew what I was doing, I had struck him hard across the face with the back of my hand, once, twice.

'Look what you made me *do*!' I hissed furiously, gesturing at the broken dead thing in the grass.

And as I stared at him, a savage desire rose up and rushed through me. The desire to hit him, to hurt him, to cause him to feel pain such as he had himself been happily inflicting only moments ago. He ought to know what it *felt* like. He was dribbling blood already from where his teeth had cut into his mouth, but it wasn't enough for me. I should have felt ashamed of that, shouldn't I? I should have been horrified. As it was, within moments the kid was screaming loudly enough to alert everyone in the park. Instinct took over and I ran from that place as fast as I could.

I couldn't get back to the darkened haven of my apartment quickly enough. Slamming the door behind me, I then locked all the locks, pulled across all the bolts and drew all the curtains over the windows with shaking hands. Then I folded myself into the small, dark gap between my bed and the wall, covering my head with my trembling arms. *How could you,* accusatory voices whispered to me; *how could you? What's wrong with you?*

When the whispers stopped and I at last looked up, the room was pitch black and my back and shoulders ached horribly. How long had I sat there, muttering to myself? Am I really dangerous? Do I belong in some kind of mental institute? Some kind of prison? Do I? After all, I didn't *really* hurt that boy. A couple of stitches and he would be fine. Everyone loses their temper sometimes, don't they? I mean, everyone does it. There will always be ugliness. It's not only me.

24th August

I still know next to nothing about who I am. It panics me sometimes; makes me feel like a shadow. But I'm not – shadows don't
have names. I have a name: Gabriel Antaeus. Gabriel, Gabriel,
Gabriel Antaeus. After all, I sleep, I eat, I *bleed*. That must mean
something? I knew I could bleed from the way I had found myself
here at the beginning of August but I cut myself with a knife the
other day just to make absolutely sure. There was blood, so that
cheered me. The sight of it horrifies me, though. It goes beyond
mere squeamishness; it is a true horror. I must just be one of those
faint-hearted people, I suppose. Probably because I have spent my
whole life around books. I have written books. One book, anyway.
I found the manuscript when I was going through my desk. It was
entitled *Dante's Hell: A Theological Study*. Skimming through it, I
saw that it was an in-depth study of the structure of Hell, complete
with references to demons and the nine circles of sin.

As I read through it, I remembered the subject matter. The
manuscript dealt with the depiction of Hell put forward by Dante
Alighieri in his poem *Divina Commedia*. But the manuscript I
found in my desk argued that it was no mere poem; that Dante
had really travelled down to the bowels of the Earth, through the
nine concentric circles of Hell right to the frozen core where the
Devil himself was held immobilised. The claim, of course, is quite
preposterous, and with such wild and unsubstantiated theories
it is no wonder that the script remains unpublished, assuming

publication was ever sought. It unsettled me to find my name in the top right-hand corner of every page of the manuscript – I hate to think that I might actually have written this fanatical work. But at the same time, it pleases me that I am a writer. What danger is there in that? What violence could there possibly be in that?

Neatly arranged in a file in one of the desk drawers, I found all my banking and tax records. Having studied these I can see that I am, in fact, a very wealthy man indeed. It's no wonder my rooms are filled with such fine things, although the state of the apartment itself puzzles me for I could easily have afforded something much nicer with my savings, not to mention the cash I'd found in the kitchen. It was nice to discover that I don't need to be concerned about my financial situation, anyway. I also found my passport tucked away in the bottom drawer, which confirmed that I am a citizen of the United Kingdom. For the first time, it occurred to me that perhaps my family were all still living in the UK? My hand automatically went to the box of fish food permanently in my pocket. Perhaps there were no fish? No one about to return from holiday?

But, God, what am I saying? No fish? No *fish*? There *must* be a holiday; there *must be* fish … otherwise why the hell am I carrying fish food around in my pocket like this? No, the fish are real – I know they are.

I found contact details for my landlady in my desk. When I phoned her, she seemed completely uninterested in speaking to me, and really wasn't of any use at all. My tenancy agreement is a standard one and began at the start of August. It was clear she knew next to nothing about me – she even called me by the wrong name more than once during the conversation. But then, why should she know me? I would hardly have poured out my life story to her when I arranged to rent the apartment.

I'd hit a dead end. There were no *people* around … at least, not until my family returned. In the meantime, I examined one of the few clues I had: my name. Gabriel Antaeus. I typed it into Google one day, stupidly thinking that a website may come up telling me all about myself. But there was nothing – not even other Gabriel

Antaeus's that I could search through. It's an unusual name, I suppose.

Having found the internet no use, I turned to the books on my shelves. Of course, the name Gabriel has very strong religious and biblical, in particular angelic, connotations. The Hebrew meaning translates as 'man of God' and everyone knows of the archangel Gabriel of the New and Old Testaments. My books are all stacked alphabetically, and I have several that refer to angels and their realm. Clearly this issue of my name is one that has bothered me before, for my books are heavily annotated with all references to Gabriel underlined or highlighted.

You'd think that being named after an angel would not have any negative, any frightening, connotations whatsoever. But you'd be wrong. For angels are scary. I have had nightmares about them. I found the internet to be of little use, for the websites all spoke of the 'new age' angels so beloved by hippies and self-proclaimed healers and psychics. These angels were forgiving and loving, and covered people in golden light and love, inspiring feelings of well-being and peace. I wish that I could find some angels like that here.

But the original angels – the biblical ones – are so very different from these modern creations. Gabriel spans several religions, being the highest-ranking angel of the Christian, Hebrew and Moslem faiths. According to Mohammed, Gabriel was the author of the Qu'ran. Mohammed was meditating in a cave when he was visited by Gabriel in a vision that so terrified him in its violence and hostility that it left him feeling suicidal. I find this story very disturbing. It's gone round and round my head. Angels should not be violent.

I've had trouble placing the origin of my surname, Antaeus. French, perhaps? But I know I'm British because of my passport. And my accent ... not that I ever really speak aloud, for I have no one to speak to and I don't talk to myself in the privacy of my own home the way some people do. My apartment is always silent, whether I'm in it or not. Perhaps I should start talking aloud as I write in this journal. I hate that my voice still seems unfamiliar to me, still startles me if I speak without thinking. Yes, I think I will start to do that. It is not enough to write; I want someone to talk to as well.

But I've reached a dead end anyway. So what now? I'm too afraid to go to the hospital. All this fear ... am I just the most terrible coward? I can't go to a hospital or the police because they'll ask questions, and I have a large and unexplainable stack of cash in my possession, now hidden away under the floorboards. What did I do to earn that money? I can't let them find it. I can't go to prison. Not now when I have so many fish to feed.

I hope I merely stole the money. I could live with being a thief. There are worse sins than thieving, although that crime in itself is disgusting to me ... I think I might just be suffering from stress. I mean, I've waited patiently, haven't I? It's been over two weeks now and I haven't remembered anything, and it's not fair at all! I hate being stuck with a stranger like this. But it can't be much longer before someone I know makes contact with me ... an old friend who wants to catch up, or borrow something, or ask my advice, or whatever. I can't go to them because I can't remember them. But, soon, one of them will find me and this whole ridiculous situation will be all smoothed out, and there will be a rational explanation about the money, and I will remember everything. In the meantime, I will keep to myself in case I hurt someone again. It is not right to hit children. It's not right. I shouldn't have done it. I will order food to the door and I won't leave my apartment until I know it's safe. Just for now, this journal will have to do until I can find some people from somewhere.

29th August

Five days have passed since I last wrote here. It's almost one o'clock in the morning. I'm dripping wet, my clothes are stained with splatters of blood, and there is a bleeding gash at the back of my head that is swelling up into a painful lump already. For four days I kept to my decision to stay inside the apartment. But this morning, I decided that I might have overreacted to the incident with the boy and the butterfly. And I was tired of takeout food. So I went to a nearby restaurant: the Pest Buda Vendèglö. I don't like eating alone – it depresses me. I ordered a Hungarian traditional speciality, *Libamàj Zsirjàban* – goose liver fried in its own fat – along with a glass of dry Pinot Noir. I don't have much of a sweet tooth so I would usually skip dessert, but the Vendèglö does the most delicious *Gundel Palacsinta* and I was reluctant to return to my apartment too soon, so I ordered the dessert to extend the evening.

I had been feeling almost content until the couple at the table next to me started to argue. Quietly at first, and then the man started to raise his voice and the woman was crying and other diners were looking embarrassed and pretending they hadn't noticed.

The man stormed out in the end, leaving the woman alone at the table, looking miserable and embarrassed. I should have felt sorry for her like everyone else. But all I could feel was *envy*. At least she had someone to argue *with*, the lucky bitch. They must surely care about each other a lot to argue so fiercely. I could have hated them for it.

I lost my appetite, and pushed away the remainder of the sweet pancakes— And then I saw her. She was staring in at me through the window from the dark street outside, her nose pressed up against the glass. She was a little distorted from the ripples of the window, but she was clearly shocked by the sight of me. And she recognised me. I know she did. Pure instinct made me jump to my feet in excitement. She was middle-aged. In her forties, I would say, with the most beautiful chestnut hair. She saw that I'd spotted her and turned away from the window at once.

I called out to her as she walked quickly off into the night, and made to follow – but then remembered the meal and hastily threw down a roll of notes, probably leaving far too much on the table before striding from the restaurant.

Once on the darkened street outside, I strained my eyes, hoping I was not too far behind her. My only thought was to catch her up and make her tell me what she knew. For she did know something about me, I was quite sure in my mind about that. I'd seen it when our eyes met. For a moment I thought I'd missed her. There were few people out and about at this time of night in this area, and there didn't seem to be anyone else within view as I stood there in the shelter of the restaurant archway. But then, by chance, I saw a head of chestnut hair disappearing down a side street and, with a strangled yell of excitement, I set off after her at a run. Thrills of anticipation rushed through me as I chased her. The mist hanging in the air clung to me and wet my hair and clothes even as rain began to fall in a gentle, hushed whispering that dampened out all other sound.

Within moments my clothes were soaked through. Feet sliding on the wet cobbles, I rounded the corner and set off down the dark alleyway behind the running woman. Anger flared suddenly and I was aware of a snarl curling my lips. Damn her, why did she run from me? I wasn't going to *hurt* her. I just wanted her knowledge. Information, memories, answers – that was all I wanted. She was fast, though, and seemed to know where she was going as she sped deeper into the maze of back streets that we were both now quite lost in. I'm very fit and a fast runner myself, but I always seemed to be just a few yards behind the chestnut-haired woman. It was infuriating. Several times I almost lost her in the rain and mist, the only light coming from the shadowed moon above and the soft, reflected light from elsewhere in the city.

She had been running with surprising speed, as if she was scared out of her mind. So I was not prepared for her to suddenly come to a dead stop in the middle of a darkened street. I, too, slid to a halt, panting and trying to get my breath back as she turned towards me, her face half hidden in shadow. She did not seem at all breathless, and for long moments we simply gazed at one another in silence, the rain falling around us, drenching the cobbles beneath our feet. I had been about to ask her who she was, her name, how she knew me ... but her expression stopped me. Deep, harsh lines were etched into her face, and there was raw fear in her eyes as she gazed at me in silence. And then she spoke, in a quiet, desperate voice, which somehow I managed to hear above the rain.

'*Eltévedtem.*'

I'm lost.

I stared at her. Rainwater ran down the back of my neck and down my face, dripping from my chin and the ends of my eyelashes. After a moment I took a step towards her. I would help her. I'd find a way to assist her somehow. But then I noticed a movement in the darkness and realised that we were not alone in the alleyway.

'*Tessék vigyàzni!*' *Look out!* I yelled as a man stepped out of the shadows at her back.

I made to run towards them, but pain exploded suddenly behind my eyes as someone struck the back of my head, hard. In my preoccupation with the mystery woman, I had failed to realise there were other men behind me. A broken cobble bit deep into my cheek and my teeth seemed to go halfway through my lip when I hit the ground, warm blood filling my mouth and running down my face. Someone grabbed my shoulders and twisted me onto my back, running practised fingers through my pockets. Rain fell into my eyes and the moon above me seemed to spin nauseatingly in the night sky. I was aware of the thief's crow of glee as he drew out my well-filled wallet.

Perhaps hoping to find more riches, the thief was still leaning over me when I spat a mouthful of blood into his face. He jerked back instinctively, and at the same time my hand whipped out and gripped his ankle. One swift jerking movement and he'd slipped over on the wet cobbles, sprawling on his back beside me. Others started running towards us.

Afterwards I counted five of them on the ground around me. They had hardly touched me, for all that they had attacked together. There had been no conscious thought involved at all. Some of them had knives and other makeshift weapons, but it had been an easy enough thing for me to twist their hands back round on themselves so that they couldn't help but drop their knives of their own accord, turning their strength against them, bones snapping like twigs so that I hardly even broke a sweat. The stronger they were, the easier it was. With the right movements, they would break their own bones *for* me. How painfully easy it was. Like shooting fish in a pond with a bazooka. There's no need for endless, energy-sapping punches and kicks when pressure applied to a certain place on a man's neck will render him unconscious before he's even realised what you're doing. You just have to know where to press.

I don't think the fight went on for very long. I was disappointed when they stopped getting up. It had been too easy. It had been far too easy! I was not ready for it all to be over yet. My heart was thumping in my chest with exhilaration, and I wanted more! I kicked one of them a couple of times, hoping it might incite him to get up, but all I got out of him was a muffled groan. They were all much larger than me, I noted with fierce pleasure as I bent and retrieved my sodden wallet from the ground.

It took me another moment before I remembered why I had been in the alley in the first place. I looked up sharply but, in all the turmoil and disorder, the woman had fled. The alley was quiet and deserted once more, save for the soft whisper of the falling rain. I'd saved her from being mugged or raped, or worse. She had escaped. I'd saved her from her own folly at running deep into one of Budapest's dark, deserted side streets – the predatory silence of a sordid, greedy night.

In that moment I didn't care that I was still without answers. And I have to say, I still can't find it in myself to care. They were no match for me! Those five large men, no doubt professional thieves, muggers and pickpockets – bulging with brute muscle and brimming with cowardly weapons. The euphoria of it, like rediscovering some old hobby that you had once taken such pleasure in, and finding your skill not at all diminished by time. Even now, back in the haven of my apartment, my senses are all tingling with a thrilling, heightened awareness. This has been, I am sure, one of the best evenings of my life. I wish I could do it over again every night!

1st September

What I wrote in this journal three days ago ... upsets me. It really scares me. I wish I was someone else. I wish I could be some other person. When I woke up the next morning, sprawled on my bed, my head was throbbing dully, the pillow was spotted with dark blood, but I still felt exhilarated as I showered and dressed. Exhilaration for some minutes before the fear. Fear that got more intense until I cringed just to see myself in the mirror. *What kind of a thing are you anyway?* It wasn't the fight itself that scared me; it was the fact that I hadn't really held back. It had gone beyond mere self-defence, somehow. And ... I couldn't remember all of it ... too clearly. I didn't use any weapons, though, did I? Only my hands, and how much damage can be done with them? I didn't *kill* anyone.

I hid in my apartment for the next two days, waiting, waiting for any news. I checked the Hungarian news on the internet and had local papers brought up to me from the shop below, opening the door a mere crack to snatch the papers from the boy and thrust the money at him. There has been no mention of any back street murders, which surely there would have been had any of the muggers not survived. So perhaps I am overreacting. No one died, so what's to be so upset about? Night-time crime will be rife in any capital city. All I really did was take five of those criminals out of action for a while. And they attacked me first anyway. Apart from feeding the fish, once I remember where they are, my life has no purpose at the moment. Perhaps the sensible thing to do would be to go out every night and *seek out* such criminals.

I know it sounds a bit alarming, but isn't that what the super-heroes do? The superheroes that children so love to read about – Superman and Spiderman and the rest of them. They have the means to take the law into their own hands to protect people, to *save* them. I like that. I could do that. I don't need sleep and food in the same way that other people do. I could be a superhero.

I can imagine the headlines now: 'Night-Time Crime in Budapest Mysteriously Drops by 80%!' I would very much like to do it. But I'm not naïve. I know what would happen. The police would view me as a criminal too – after all, I would be *attacking* people. I can't risk the police finding me. They wouldn't understand that I was only doing it to keep people safe. All they would see was this crazy man who went out late at night *looking* for people to beat up. I can't have that. Sadly, the community will just have to do without me.

What happened three days ago was bad enough, for I wasn't discreet at all. Once I was sure I wouldn't get any more fun out of my attackers, I ran through the streets to the metro station, jumping and whooping and yelling in my euphoria. God, what craziness – the police might have seen me. They might have arrested me. If there was anyone else in my carriage on the metro, they must have been appalled at the sight of me – this wild-eyed, dripping wet madman with blood running down my face and crusted in my hair; and I had probably still been sucking it from my teeth and gums. Bloody, bloody stupid thing to do.

But at least I saved the mystery woman. I gave her the diversion she needed to escape. But how to find her again? Budapest is a large city, and she could be anywhere. She might not even live here at all; she could be anywhere in Hungary. It was the most extraordinary bad luck that those thugs should have attacked at that moment. She knew me. I know she did. But with no name, no address, no personal details of any kind, I have no way of contacting her. All I can do is hope that I might stumble into her again; but really, in a city of this size, it was unlikely enough to happen once let alone a second time. It puzzles me, though – I mean, who *was* she? She couldn't have been a relative. A relative would have greeted me no matter how annoyed they might have been about my not feeding their fish. They would have greeted me even if only to berate me. I don't know; I don't know. Maybe she was, after all, just a crazy woman. God knows, there are plenty of those about.

2nd September

There is no denying it any more. I have been here like this, waiting for family or friends or colleagues or *someone* to turn up, for almost a month now. But no one has come, and I admit I am beginning to feel the pinch of loneliness. Though I hate to admit it, I do think there is a very real possibility that ... no one is coming back. I have only just moved here myself. Perhaps I was going to send a forwarding address to my friends and relatives once I got settled in, but lost my memory before I could do so? Perhaps I really don't know anyone here in the city. How long can I let this go on for?

I spent several hours today wandering round Budapest asking people if they had the time. I just wanted them to *see* me. I just wanted to actually talk to someone. But the exchanges could never go on for too long, of course, because someone would be bound to ask me something about myself that I could not answer, and I know I would panic and probably just start running back here. People wouldn't like that. It's not normal. I wish I could get a child from somewhere. Children don't ask awkward personal questions like that. They're not interested in where you've come from or what you did before this moment.

I like going to the park to watch them play. There is nothing inappropriate in it – nothing perverted or depraved. I just like watching. They're so ... new and unspoiled. They're so trusting and naïve and beautiful. The world hasn't had a chance to ruin them yet. But it doesn't look right for me to stand there, alone, staring at them for hours. It makes the mothers nervous, despite my expensive clothes and immaculate appearance. I suppose they don't think it natural for a man to be stood there, just staring, for so long; so if I go again, I think I must buy a cheap pushchair or something to stand there with, and then everyone will assume I am simply keeping an eye on my own child. I admit that I would very much like to take one of those kids.But I would never act on this. I can't abide criminals, and it's not right to take other people's children. I would never do something like that. I just hope that my own family, my own friends, will turn up soon. If there's really no one here, then I need to find someone else to talk to.

3rd September

I had an unsettling dream last night – of a nine-year-old girl who was promised to the church by her father. The monastery was her home from the age of nine until her death twenty years later. I dreamed that as a child, ordered to leave her family, she entered the cold stillness of the monastery – fearful and alone but for the other silent-footed nuns and the stone sculptures of the angels – the only world she would know for the rest of her brief, ascetic life.

I wouldn't have minded the dream so much if it hadn't been true. The girl's name was Princess Margit. Her father, King Béla IV, made an oath that if he was successful in repelling the Mongol invasion, he would offer his daughter to God. Unfortunately for the child, the Mongols were driven back and the King built a church and convent on an island in the middle of the Danube in 1251, and sent his daughter there. Today the island is named after her – Margitsziget, or Margaret's Island. I suppose it must have been the dream, and my own empathy for the princess, that made me visit the island today.

I caught the metro to Margaret Bridge and felt myself physically relax as soon as I stepped on to the island. It has had the honour of being a retreat for religious contemplation since the eleventh century, and is a strange, quiet little haven, nestled in one of Europe's busy, bustling capital cities – a halfway point between the once separate towns of Buda and Pest. Cars aren't allowed past a certain point, so most of the island is given over to bicycles or horse-drawn carriages. I like that. It's almost like going back in time.

It had rained the night before, and the air was sweet with the damp, leafy-green smell of well-nourished plants and grass. But as the day went on, the sun came out, glowing warmly on the peaceful island despite the unseasonable chill that still clung to the air. The crunch of my feet on the gravelled tracks was soothing, and the smell of fresh rain was invigorating, and I was glad that my dream of Princess Margaret had prompted me to come here today.

As I walked through the woodland, I became aware of stone faces watching me from behind low-hanging branches and realised that the area was scattered with stone busts of Hungarian artists and musicians – raised on plinths and weathered by age. They kept making me jump as my eyes found another and another, half hidden where the forest was almost growing over them.

I suddenly came out of the woods to find myself right outside a tall, thin church, so completely surrounded by trees you could easily walk right past it and never even realise it was here. The dappled sunlight of the forest became a strong beam of light that shone off the old stone walls. This was Michael's church, I realised as I gazed above the wooden doors at the familiar carved relief that depicted the archangel with his scales, preparing to weigh souls on Judgement Day.

Although Gabriel is probably the most well-known angel because of his prominence within the nativity story, Michael is the one said to have replaced Satan as God's closest and most trusted angel after Lucifer's fall from grace. And, theologically and hierarchically speaking, Michael is above Gabriel in the heavenly order. Somehow in that moment I felt sure that if only I stayed close to this church, I would be protected. That no harm would come to me here in this safe, secluded little green haven.

'Beautiful, isn't it?'

I jumped, startled, as a voice spoke behind me. I turned to see a young, slender, dark-haired man leaning against a tree, watching me. He had rather pale skin, intelligent eyes and a handsome, shrewd face. He was not very tall, some inches shorter than me, but he held himself well and his clothes, like mine, were clearly expensive.

'What makes you think I speak English?' I asked the stranger suspiciously, eyes narrowed, for that was the language he had addressed me in.

He laughed and gave a slight shrug. 'Your Bible gave you away.'

Following his gaze, I glanced down at the English Bible I was holding. I had hardly realised that I had even taken it out of my pocket. Frowning slightly, I replaced the book in my jacket.

'Where are you from?' the stranger asked casually, still lounging idly against the tree.

'England,' I answered.

'So what brings you to Hungary?'

'I live here,' I replied. 'Where are you from?'

'Italy originally,' the stranger replied. 'But I'm a traveller really. Always moving, you know.'

'Isn't English your first language?' I asked in surprise.

The stranger smiled. 'I grew up speaking Italian and English,' he admitted. 'I have a gift for languages.'

Something we had in common, then, for I knew from the collection of books I had at home that I was fluent in several languages. In fact, we had two things in common, for we were both foreigners here in Hungary. That pleased me. I didn't seem to have much in common with the average people I saw in the streets. In fact, this was probably the longest conversation I'd had with anyone since I started this journal. It's not that I don't enjoy writing in here, I do; and indeed sometimes I seem to have spent most of the day doing so ... It's just that it simply isn't enough. Writing in a journal like this is just one step removed from talking to myself. A book can't talk *back*. I don't think I had realised myself how lonely I was until I started talking to this stranger.

I realised that I was grinning at him stupidly. He laughed good-naturedly and held out his hand. 'I'm Zadkiel Stephomi.'

'Gabriel Antaeus,' I replied, shaking his hand and feeling pleased that – just like a normal person – I did not struggle to remember my last name at all this time.

'Antaeus?' Stephomi repeated.

'Do you know it?' I asked sharply, my grip on his hand tightening unconsciously.

'Er ... no, no I'm afraid I don't,' Stephomi replied, extricating his slender hand from mine and rubbing it absently. 'Should I?'

'No. No, it was just ... the way you said it ...'

'Unusual name, though, isn't it?' Stephomi said, looking at me with clear blue eyes. 'What's its origin?'

'Origin?'

'Yes, where does it come from?'

'Oh, er ...' I cast around desperately for a country. 'It's a French name, I think.'

'French?' Stephomi repeated. 'You don't think, perhaps, Greek?'

'I think it was French,' I said again desperately. 'But I really don't know much about my family history.'

I was enjoying talking to him, but these questions were making me feel awkward. Perhaps I should just have said that I didn't know; that I couldn't remember. But would he have believed me? I mean, it's not normal, is it, by anyone's standards? I thought fleetingly, and bitterly, of how easy such conversations must be for other people; not to have to struggle to make up plausible lies second by second. I felt a familiar panic starting to rise, just as it had done when I had tried to talk to my teenage neighbour. Was I even *capable* of having a normal, two-way conversation? What could I possibly talk *about*? My name is Gabriel. I know that, at least. It can't be all that bad as long as I know my name.

'What are you doing in Budapest?' I asked, trying to deflect attention away from myself.

'Sightseeing, really. And researching. I'm visiting the churches and cathedrals. I have a doctorate in religious philosophy,' he said. 'I used to lecture on the subject.'

'But not any more?'

'No, I'm afraid not.'

'Were your lectures too controversial?' I asked, knowing what a sensitive subject religion could be.

'Ha! Controversy wasn't the problem so much as the fact that I could prove a lot of my theories – or come close to proving them, anyway. People don't like that. Anyway, now that my lecturing career seems to have come to a premature end, I'm just pursuing a private interest in the subject.'

'Budapest is the right place for that,' I said. 'There are so many beautiful churches and cathedrals here.'

'There are indeed. And I'd better get on if I want to visit them all,' the young scholar said.

Don't go, I wanted to say. *Please … don't leave me here like this! I have no one.* I fingered the edges of the fish food box in by pocket. I was sick of waiting for everyone to come home. Although I had only had a very brief conversation with him, I instinctively liked this man. I wanted to be friends with *this* person right here. No one else would do. For a wild moment I even considered knocking him down where he stood and taking him back to my apartment, tying him up and keeping him so that I might have someone to talk to and live with. Someone who could maybe replace this diary for me. But people would notice me carrying him through the streets, and there would be a fuss when a bright young man went missing, and then police investigations, and I would risk unwanted official attention. And anyway, it is not right to kidnap people. So I would never resort to something like that.

'I'm sorry?' I said, realising that, preoccupied as I was with my thoughts, I'd missed what Stephomi had just said.

'I was just saying that we should meet up for a drink some time,' he repeated with a smile. 'I don't know anyone in this city, my Hungarian is not quite up to the standard of my English, and I admit I could use the conversation.'

'Really?' I blurted out, hardly daring to believe what I was hearing.

'If you're interested,' the scholar said with a shrug. 'I realise you must have your own friends here if you're living in the city but,' he paused and smiled slightly, 'I'm hoping you'll take pity on me as a friendless traveller.'

'I'd be more than happy,' I replied, pleased to note that I didn't sound at all desperate.

Stephomi pulled a card out of his pocket and handed it to me. 'Well, my mobile number's on there. Give me a call some time.'

We shook hands and he strode away, back into the trees, leaving me alone outside Michael's church. As I gazed up at the carved sculpture of Michael, I couldn't help but feel deeply thankful towards the church. It was, after all, our shared interest in God that had led Stephomi and I to meet in the first place. It will be nice to have an actual person to talk to.

I took the card out when I got home, and carefully placed it on the table by the phone. Then I stared at it for a while. I wanted to phone Stephomi right then and there. He had said to give him a call 'some time', but what exactly had he meant by that? How long did I have to wait? What would be a socially acceptable period? I wrestled with the dilemma for a few hours and, in the end, I decided that by 'some time' Stephomi had probably meant in a few days or a week or so. So I have decided that I will wait three days before contacting him. I don't think I could physically wait any longer than that.

There will be no need to kidnap anyone if this works ... Not that I would ever have seriously considered doing so, for I am quite clear on the difference between right and wrong. Besides, I'm okay on my own. I'm certainly not one of those people who are for ever *needing* others to boost their own sense of self-worth. Forever *needing* to be surrounded by friends and loved ones to tell them how wonderful they are all the time. That would be pathetic. No – mine is nothing more than a perfectly healthy desire to see another person every once in a while.

5th September

There are devils in my head. I've feared it for a while now. But I didn't want to record those fears here because it would have made them too real. Now I can't deny that they're there. And they hate me! They've prised everything from me with their bare, clawed hands, with the curled, bent fingers and leathery skin. They possessed me while I destroyed my apartment inch by inch, shattering and tearing and shredding in a sinful glut of destruction. They made me feel that all the violence and bloodshed in the world would not lessen the horrible rage that was thumping in my head or get rid of the bitterness that was rising like bile in my throat.

But now they have gone at last, the horned devils all scampering back to their hellish realm, and I am left with nothing ... Nothing but this great, aching *emptiness* within that will never be filled, no matter how much I give to it, no matter how long I wait, no matter how many boxes of fish food I buy. It almost makes me wish I were dead. Why is this happening to me? What did I *do* to make God *hate* me so badly?

8th September

I need to record what happened. I don't want to, I have avoided it ... but I'll have to write it down at some point.

The day I visited Margaret's Island, I went to bed quite late. But when I eventually slept, my dreams were full of fearful, disturbing images and whispering voices that tried to speak to me; but there were too many all trying to speak at once and too loudly and I could not make out any individual words. And there were people trying to show me things but not giving me time to look, and the shapes and pictures were blurred and shifting so that there was only the odd image that I was able to recognise – Michael's church; the lost and wandering mystery woman who had run from me in the alley, her eyes widened in fear; a carved stone angel crying tears of blood; a laughing Stephomi; naked demons that thrashed in flames, biting and fighting one another—

And then, quite suddenly, a sharp, crystal-clear image. A tall man with fire radiating from him and wet flames dripping from his clothes, walking through the streets of Budapest until he came to my apartment. He passed straight through the doors as if they presented no earthly barrier to him, striding into my rooms as I stood and silently watched him, his flames flickering over the walls and ceiling, throwing alternate patterns of dancing light and murky shadows throughout the room. And then he stood still, turning his head as though searching, his flames dancing and leaping about him. His eye fell on the card Stephomi had given me, lying on the table by the phone. He reached out a burning hand, picking it up and setting it alight with the tips of his golden, fire-edged fingers. My scream of desperate horror woke me and I leaped from the sweat-soaked bed and ran into the living room, flicking on the light and staggering over to the table where Zadkiel Stephomi's card had been mere hours earlier. It was gone, as I had known it would be. A wretched, dry sob escaped me and I swept through the whole apartment looking; looking even though I knew I would not find the card. And then, when I could no longer deny what I knew to be true, I destroyed my apartment inch by inch. If I hadn't found some way of venting my anger, I'm sure I would have suffered some kind of heart attack or brain haemorrhage.

I don't think I ever would have stopped if it weren't for the blue lights I suddenly noticed flashing down in the street outside. The noise I'd made had obviously caused one of the other tenants in the building to phone the police. I stared madly round in horror. What was I going to *do*? How was I going to *explain* this? I couldn't simply tell the officers that sometimes I became so consumed with rage, that I did things without meaning to. They'd lock me up for sure!

My first instinct was to run, but I had nowhere to go. And if the police searched my apartment, they might find the bag of money I had been so careful to hide. So when they started knocking at my door, I ran into my bedroom, which was as I had left it a mere half hour ago, and got into the cupboard. As soon as I could hear the police in my kitchen, I knocked my foot against the wooden door, hoping it would sound accidental. A moment later, when the cupboard door was flung open, I shrank back with a cry of false fear. After that it was an easy enough thing to convince the police that burglars had trashed my apartment while I had hidden in this cupboard, too scared to move. After all, why should they question my story? What kind of nutcase would do this to his own home?

But it wasn't a home, not really. The apartment was simply a set of rented rooms, that was all. As far as I know, I do not have anywhere that could be said even remotely to resemble a home. And, God, it makes me feel so bitter! It just isn't *fair* and I don't know what to *do* about it. I can't stand to be on my own like this any more. I desperately want to know where the bloody hell everyone else has *gone*.

I've since had people in to replace the broken windows. I have also replaced my computer. Some of my books I was able to salvage by patiently pasting the pages back between the covers and returning them to their alphabetical order on my shelves. The kitchen had been swimming in red pools of wine and broken glass from where I had hurled the expensive bottles around the room. I have replaced my stock, and once again arranged the bottles on the wine rack according to vintage and grape. Most of the fine artwork that had lined my walls had been in shreds throughout the rooms. Almost all of the furniture had been overturned but was still useable once I had put everything back into order.

I take back what I wrote before. I *do* need people. Right now I would even settle for enemies, never mind friends and family. It surely can't be right to be completely isolated like this. It almost makes me think that I should go to the police immediately, tell them everything, show them the money hidden away under my floorboards. When the story hits the papers, people who know me might come forward and I will discover who I was. There must be *some* people out there who know me. My passport clearly states that I am thirty-three. I must, therefore, have *existed* in some form before last month, even if I can't remember it.

But I must not overreact; I must remain calm. It is not the end of the world to have lost Stephomi's card. I have managed for several weeks on my own, and I will simply continue to do so. I must not be resentful. Bitter feelings will not lead me anywhere good. I know I left the card on the table, but perhaps the windows had been open before I smashed them from their frames; perhaps the card had been caught up in a freak breeze and swept out of the window. That was the only sensible explanation. And it was surely no more than a strange coincidence that the table, when I put it back together, seemed to have scorch marks on its surface.

Those marks were surely old ones, made long ago if only I could remember the occasion.

15th September

For the last week, I've wandered about the city, often visiting Michael's church in the hope that Stephomi might be there; but I haven't seen him, and I now doubt that I ever will.

I've toyed with the idea of trying to arrange another 'chance' meeting with some other person. I could look out for someone I liked the look of, follow them around for a while to learn their habits and daily routine, and then arrange for some mild disaster to befall them and I would then, of course, be on hand to assist them in their hour of need. There were certainly aspects of the plan that appealed to me. After all, some people are born lucky, and such things may happen to them without any prearrangement.

If I met and assisted someone in a moment of crisis, that would create some kind of bond, wouldn't it? I considered smashing in someone's car window so that I could help them when they discovered the vandalism; or, better yet, pay someone to rob a person in the street so that I might come to their aid and ward off their attacker as I had done for the mystery woman.

These ideas had merit, but they were unlikely to lead to any kind of real friendship. After all, what had been so incredible about my meeting with Stephomi was that we had things in common. I had warmed to him at once, and he had obviously taken a liking to me or he wouldn't have given me his mobile number. We had both been alone here, and so we might have relied on each other for companionship far more than any normal Hungarian residents would. And to top it all, we had both been foreigners, and both shared an interest in religious cosmology, oh God, even now I could cry with the loss of such a thing.

I find whenever I'm upset I *crave* beauty. Anything that might make life seem a little less pointless and sordid and ugly. One day I locked myself in my apartment and spent all day listening to the works of Mozart, Bach, Vivaldi, Beethoven, Tchaikovsky and other musical geniuses. The great composers must be turning in their graves at the way music has changed – garage and rap have replaced the great symphonies and sonatas … It depresses me and makes me wish I lived in their time instead of this one. But at the same time it comforts me that my tastes have remained the same despite my amnesia. I know I liked classical music before because there is so much of it here in my apartment. The fact that I continue to like it means I am not losing all of myself. I remain a part of the man I was before.

I like Mozart's scores the best. I like the idea that God was speaking through his music. It fits. It works. It makes sense to me. For I am sure that is how God would talk to us – the only way that we would be able to understand – music so perfect that it must have come from God Himself.

But Mozart was hounded by debt and died at the age of thirty-five. That's just two years older than I am. To make it even worse, he was given a pauper's burial in an unmarked grave. Wolfgang Amadeus Mozart! Where were the kings he'd composed for when he died? Where were the great emperors and the queens and the noblemen who'd enjoyed his music then? What a *disgrace*! I find it hugely upsetting that his final resting place was an unmarked grave in a plot reserved for the insignificant and the inconsequential. The bitter injustice of such a thing. It disgusts me – makes the anger start throbbing again in my head, if I think about it for too long; and then I have to distract myself with something else.

After going through the great composers, I moved on to the verses of golden-tongued poets such as Wordsworth, Byron, Blake, Coleridge and Shelley … But Keats is my favourite, with his gift for making sadness itself beautiful. How did he do that? The idea that beauty, joy and sadness are not so very different; not so very far apart from one another ... This soothes me somehow, and takes the edge from my loneliness.

Keats died young too – only twenty-five. It's not fair. There is little enough beauty in the world as it is. If Keats and Mozart had both lived to ninety, what more could they have done? I want to read the poems that were never written; I want to hear the music that was never composed! I feel like I've been *cheated!* But aside from the tragedy of the men themselves, their creations comfort me as no others can. The eternal nature of beauty that has survived for over two hundred years ... I don't think I need anyone else after all. If I could just be allowed to stay here in my apartment, reading these poems, listening to Mozart, I am sure that would be enough for me ... What more could I ever possibly want?

For a while, I thought about getting a dog. With a pet in the apartment, it might have more of a lived-in feel. There would be someone to greet me when I came home. Even a cat would be something. The thought of it curling up on my lap in the evenings, purring, sleeping on my bed at night, relying on me for all its food and wants ... They couldn't possibly compete with human companionship, of course, but at least there would be someone who had feelings for me, loved me, relied on me, *needed* me ...

But this isn't an option either, for animals don't like me. They're afraid of me. I first noticed it a few days ago when there was an incident in the park. Two children were walking their dogs; there was a girl with an Alsatian that she simply wasn't strong enough to control, and a boy with a Spaniel. As the two passed one another, the Alsatian snapped at the Spaniel, who retaliated, and soon the leashes had been ripped from the children's hands and there was the most hideous racket as the two dogs went for each other. The children watched in horror as their beloved pets did their utmost to tear each other's throats out. The yelping and howling was enough to attract the attention of several passers-by, but no one seemed to want to get between the two scrapping dogs. And I couldn't blame them – the two were an indistinguishable mass of teeth, spit, blood and jaws, and it looked very much as if the Alsatian was going to kill the smaller dog.

I got up from my seat on a bench, thinking I could escort the boy home with his dead dog and that I might then be able to meet his parents. They might invite me in for coffee, or something. But as I made to move, the thought occurred to me that if I turned up with their son and a rescued dog, I would be more likely to be welcomed into the family than if I had a dead pet in tow. Indeed, the more I thought about it, the less likely it seemed that I'd be invited in for drinks if there was a dead dog and a crying kid taking up everyone's attention. His parents were hardly going to hand him a shovel and tell him to get on with it himself, were they?

So I strode towards the fighting creatures, somehow grabbed each by the scruff of their necks, and pulled them apart. At once, the Alsatian rounded on me, snarling; but in another second it had recoiled and was cowering close to the ground, whimpering softly. The Spaniel was doing the same. Unsettled, I handed the dogs back to their respective owners. Although hurt, the Spaniel was not dead; and in another moment the boy's mother had rushed over, exclaiming over the dog and rushing the two of them back to their car to take it to the vets. She didn't even look at me, much less invite me back to her house for coffee to thank me for saving her child's pet. It's a thankless task, rescuing. The mystery woman never troubled to thank me either when I saved her from those muggers in the alley. Why are people all so selfish? Perhaps I am better off on my own.

Last night I came across a cat outside my building on my way home. I tried to stroke it, but when it saw me all its fur stood up on end and it hissed and spat, growling in the back of its throat. This thing with the animals upsets me, particularly the dogs. I had rather warmed to the idea of having a pet in the apartment. But I am also unnerved by this strange behaviour. What is it they see when they look at me that causes such fear? Perhaps they can sense my amnesia? I read somewhere that some dogs can sense epilepsy in humans. This must be a similar thing. I will get a pet one day. I just have to wait until I get my memory back, that's all.

A parcel arrived for me today for the first time. I was stunned to learn that someone had sent me something and for a moment thought there must be some mistake and the box was meant for another tenant living in the building. But it was my name – Mr Gabriel Antaeus – written clearly and carefully on the label on the front of the box. My heart was pounding with excitement, but for some minutes I simply sat in the living room, staring at the carefully wrapped parcel on the table. At last, what I had been waiting for – *contact* from someone. Someone who had known me before my amnesia. If they had enclosed a return address, I would be able to contact them; but even if there was only a name, I was bound to be able to find them eventually.

The stickers on the front told me that the parcel had been sent from Italy. Someone had my name, my address ... Here, on the coffee table, was a link to my life before all this. At last I leaned forward, picked up the box and, with exaggerated care, prised the cardboard flaps open.

I was intensely disappointed to discover that I myself was the sender of the parcel. I had placed the order some months before at an antique bookshop in Italy. The carefully wrapped book inside was indeed old, almost crumbling at the edges, and I could only imagine what such a thing must have cost. The cover was made of faded red leather, and emblazoned on the front in fine letters of gold was the title: *Demonic Realms*. It was a book about demons, I realised in disgust, complete with graphic paintings of writhing devils and endless tortures in the Hellish realms. Why had I been so interested in this horrible subject before? I would have simply tossed the book out – I already had more than enough books about devils and Hell on my bookshelves – but it was far too valuable to just throw away.

I laid the old book on the table, picked up my jacket and walked towards the door. I had been intending to go out, get some breakfast at a *kàvéhàz*, and then go and visit the Inner City Parish Church, one of the few churches in Budapest I hadn't been to yet. I like churches and religious places. They make me feel safe. And there is always the vague hope that, while visiting one of them, I might run into Zadkiel Stephomi. I had also half formulated a plan to go to a bar or something in the evening. People talk to each other in bars, don't they?

But as I placed my hand on the front door handle, I paused. The awareness of the book in the next room was burning in my mind, tugging insistently at me until I felt I really couldn't just go out and leave it there. At last I turned back from the front door, dropped my jacket onto a chair in the kitchen and walked back into the lounge to gaze down at the book, wondering why I had gone to such trouble to have it sent from Italy when I already had so many books about Hell. Stupid bloody thing, lying there, mocking me like that.

In the end, I sat back down on the couch, picked up the book once again and carefully turned over the front cover. I suppose it must have been about 9 a.m. when I first opened the book. It was well past midnight before I glanced up to check the time. I haven't eaten all day but even now I'm not hungry. I didn't read the book because I enjoyed it but because the knowledge inside it fanned some forgotten flame within me, possessing me with the desire to read on and on well into the night as dust was blown from buried memories, stamping them once again in the forefront of my mind.

So I've spent the entire day reacquainting myself with devils and the places they come from. It has been disturbing reading. The book refers to devils as 'fallen angels'. I don't like this. I really don't like it at all. Demons and angels should be opposites. I hate to think that demons were once angels ... that they ever had anything to do with Heaven. It seems blasphemous to me. But how can the idea be blasphemous when it is supported by the Bible itself?

The book refers to Lucifer, before he was known as Satan, when he was still God's most favoured and trusted angel ... until the day he refused to bow down before Adam and, as a result, was hurled from Heaven down to the Hellish realms deep within the Earth's core. Lucifer's wounded pride and bitterness consumed and ate away at him until there was nothing good or angelic left.

After Lucifer's fall from grace, other angels rebelled against God and fled to Satan's side. Even now, the battle between God's angels and Satan's devils continues, although most of it takes place at Hell's border. According to the book, angels are still being seduced to Satan's ranks and it's the angels patrolling the borders of Hell who are most likely to fall prey to him, due to their regular close contact with demons.

But it seems that this works both ways and the angels are sometimes able to win devils from the border over to their side as well. I find this idea utterly disgusting. Such intermingling should be absolutely forbidden. One being should not be able to flit between angel and demon in such a manner, forever crossing lines, becoming one then the other and back again. The very notion is deeply repugnant.

Worse still is the idea that some devils, like Satan in the book of Job, have special 'passes' to occasionally visit Heaven for duels of wits with the angels. Duels of *wits*! The sacrilegious, blasphemous frivolity of it!

There is one story in the book, concerning the demon Mephistopheles, that I find especially disturbing. Mephistopheles, or Mephisto, said to be the next angel after Lucifer to fall from grace, was made Satan's second in command and became one of the seven Princes of Hell. The etymology of his name is unclear, but the most common meaning appears to be 'he who destroys by lies'. While Lucifer's rejection of God was born from pride and jealousy, it would seem that it was Mephistopheles' passion for sardonic wit and sneering cynicism that caused him to turn from God to find more entertaining pastimes in the form of relentlessly pursuing human souls on Earth. What it came down to was that being an angel *bored* him. He was said to be the most adept at causing humans to stray from the divine path of righteousness into sin and damnation, for he was the cleverest and slyest of the devils and could tempt people in subtle and cunning ways.

The story in question concerns Mephistopheles venturing into Heaven and making a bet with God regarding the scholar, Faust.

The demon claimed that he would be able to tempt the scholar onto the path of sin if only he was allowed the chance; and God accepted the challenge, granting Mephistopheles permission to interfere in Faust's life and insisting that, even in his darkest moments, Faust would not stray from the path of righteousness. But ultimately Faust did succumb to the wiles of Mephistopheles and, as the demon had predicted, the scholar ended his life with blood on his hands.

There appears to be a broad consensus that Faust never wanted or imagined the horrors that came to befall him and those he cared about; that he did not instigate these disasters, and that they would never have occurred at all without the sly manipulation so cleverly exercised by Mephistopheles as the demon posed as the man's friend.

After reading of Mephistopheles and his corruption and seduction of Faust, I was so repulsed that I was going to put the book aside and get out of the apartment, which suddenly seemed heavy with claustrophobia. But then a name caught my eye. It was my own, the name of the archangel Gabriel; and just seeing it on the page, surrounded by the names of devils, demons and Princes of Hell, made me feel nervous and uncomfortable.

As I read I remembered that there was a subclass of fallen angels known as the Watchers, who were sent to Earth to supervise the development of the human race but tried to give mankind secrets for which they were not yet ready. And then, worst of all, the Watchers fell in love with the daughters of men and procreated with them. A race of giants was produced that drained the Earth of its resources and cast a blight of famine and misery over the land. So God decided to destroy his creation by sending a great flood and starting anew ...

But there is something wrong with this, isn't there? I mean, the people were praying to God because they were hungry, because they were *starving* ... and he answered their prayers by drowning them all. I am sure that this cannot have been the help everyone had in mind when they kneeled down to pray ... I'm sure our ancestors must have got this story very wrong indeed ...

Angels were sent to round up the Watchers and imprison them in the Third Circle of Hell, where they were told of God's plan to obliterate all that they had helped create on Earth – but not until they had been forced to watch their children destroy each other. Gabriel was instructed to incite war between the giants so that they might all die vicious deaths at one another's hands, before the great flood swept through the land destroying all else. The Watchers appealed to God for mercy on behalf of their children and themselves, but their pleas were coldly rejected, and Gabriel did as he'd been told and stirred up such venomous savagery in the giants that they tore each other apart in a brief and bloody war. And now the Watchers hate Gabriel for what he did. But, of course, I don't believe a word of this – angels do not have sex with humans. And even if it did happen, there must have been a damn good reason for God's furious response. He's not evil – He wouldn't kill people over love affairs. But the book frightens me, even if it is a pack of lies, so I have hidden it away under the floorboards with the money. I am going to pretend that it is not there. That I never even saw it.

To reassure myself, I opened one of my other old books about archangels – one that portrayed them in a much more accurate light – describing their goodness and compassion and mercy to all of mankind, and their desire to save as many souls as they could. It was then that I made two discoveries. Like all my other books, this one was heavily annotated with highlighting, underlining, and the occasional note pencilled in the margin in my own slanting handwriting. Two angels in particular were covered in pencil marks. One, naturally, was Gabriel. Written in the margin in tiny script were the words: 'Heroes' Square, Budapest – Gabriel's Millennium Monument.' I've never been to Heroes' Square but I intend to go there tomorrow to see the monument for myself.

The second discovery I made was in the form of the second most heavily annotated archangel – Zadkiel, angel of memory, mercy and benevolence, and one of the two standard bearers who closely follows Michael into battle. I felt a horrible ache as I realised that here was a fourth thing I shared with Zadkiel Stephomi – we both shared names with angels. And we were both somehow linked to Michael, greatest of the archangels and God's most trusted servant. It had been his church beside which we had met that day. I think I must have some kind of special *connection* with angels. My name is Gabriel. Everyone knows that that is an angelic name. I saved a woman who stupidly ran off into a back street alley at night ... Oh, yes, and I've also saved children's pets that would otherwise have killed each other. In some ways, *I* am like an angel. I save people. I rescue them. I am here ... to *help* people.

16th September

God is with me. Truly He must favour me, for once again angels have led me to the most extraordinary good fortune. It's very late but I'm not tired at all. I was reacquainted with Zadkiel Stephomi today. What are the chances? Really, what are the *odds* of chance meetings happening twice like that?

I wrote before of my intention to visit Heroes' Square and the Millennium Monument, with which Gabriel had been linked in my own notes in the margin of one of my books. When I got up this morning, the weather was so miserable outside that I was tempted not to go out at all. The sky was choked with heavy, forbidding storm clouds, and rain was rocketing into the windows, shaking them in their frames as a vicious chill crept in through the floor-boards and the cracks in the doors. I thought about turning the heating up and crawling back under the covers of my bed, since I had no responsibilities to co-workers, employers, friends or relatives to draw me from my dry apartment into the thundering gale outside.

But the silence of this shabby, grotty little hovel depresses me. So I took the metro to Heroes' Square, huddled in the small carriages with other wet, disgruntled passengers who pushed and shoved at each other. Despite the rain, I longed to get out of the station with its damp, fetid smell of old rainwater and rotting leaves that had been blown in by the wind. But at the foot of the steps leading outside, I hesitated, realising for the first time that I hadn't brought an umbrella with me.

I briefly considered turning back to my apartment. But the book of demons from the night before was still unsettling me. Especially what it said Gabriel had done ... Not that I believed it for a moment, of course. But I still couldn't throw off the vaguely worrying feeling that had descended on me since the night before. If I could only see Gabriel in association with something good, I felt that these fears would be allayed. The Millennium Celebrations of 1896 opened in Heroes' Square and marked a high point in the development of Budapest. I wanted to see Gabriel associated with such a time of progress and hope, in order to dispel the bitter taste in my mouth that had been there since reading the book.

So I trudged up the stairs and out into the rain, not sure how far I'd have to go before I came across the Square. But as soon as I got to the top of the steps, I stopped and stared. Hösök Tere Metro Station is only just across the road from Heroes' Square, and I could see even from there what an incredible sight the Millennium Monument was. I crossed the road, dodging cars to reach it. The place was deserted – not surprising as the rain had reached torrential levels, and water was inches deep in some places on the stone pavestones, reaching up to my ankles and soaking straight through my shoes and socks. Thunder rumbled dully in the distance as I walked closer to the monument. And as I stood there staring up at it, with icy rain running down my neck and dripping from my hair and the ends of my fingers, I was immensely grateful that I had, after all, ventured from my apartment on this foul-weathered day.

The monument consisted of a towering central column, with two colonnades curving round behind it. I hardly noticed War and Peace in their huge stone chariots, or the Hungarian heroes, leaders, statesmen and monarchs stood within the colonnades beneath, for the crowning glory of it all was the grand 120-feet-high Corinthian column at the centre, upon which Gabriel stood holding St Istvàn's crown in one hand and the apostolic cross in the other, great feathered wings spread behind him. I could feel all my unease and bad feeling from the night before melting away, to be replaced with this calm, deeply spiritual peace, even as rain cascaded down to the ground around me and storm clouds gathered in the sky overhead. It was almost as if the angel was *talking* to me. He knew that I was there, somehow; I was sure of it. He recognised me even if no one else did.

Water ran down my neck, soaking my shirt beneath my coat as I gazed up at the stone angel, surrounded by statues of Hungarian heroes instead of devils; presiding over an era of progress and advancement rather than bloody, violent war. It was so *big*; somehow I hadn't been expecting the monument to tower over me like that. Gabriel himself must have been visible for miles around. Rain dripped from the great hooves and rolling eyes of the huge stone horses at the base of the column and the heroes all gazed down at me with expressions of grim nobility and an almost pained pride ...

'Happy looking bunch, aren't they?' a familiar voice remarked behind me, somehow clearly audible over the roar of the approaching storm. 'It's a serious business, heroism.'

I turned round sharply, wrenching my neck painfully, to face the man standing mere paces behind me; and then my mouth fell open, amazed at my good luck. 'Stephomi?'

'Hello, Gabriel,' he replied. 'Come to visit someone?' He nodded towards the angelic statue. 'I must say, you picked a fine day for it.'

'I—' I broke off for a moment, turned away from the monument and took a step closer towards him. I had to resist the urge to grab him in case he should slip through my fingers once again. 'I lost your number,' I said at last. 'That's why I didn't—'

'Doesn't matter,' Stephomi interrupted, with a wave of his hand. 'I see I'm not the only one stupid enough to come out in this weather without an umbrella. I wanted to see the monument too, but ... Well, to hell with culture when it's pissing it down like this. Do you want to go and have a drink somewhere?'

And that was how I met him again. Who would have believed it? We left the heroes to the rain and found a small *sörözös* just a short walk away from Heroes' Square. It was unusually busy, full of others who had ducked in to avoid the bad weather, but luckily there were still some free tables at the back near the crackling fires. There were also warm, orange lamps giving the place a cheerful glow, and people talking animatedly over their drinks around us as barmaids edged through the throng with trays of beer balanced on the flats of their palms.

We each ordered a pint of *barna* and, as we had missed lunch, a dish of smoked knuckles as well as an order of *pogácsa*, made delicious with crackling, cheese and paprika. And then we talked, thankfully about neutral topics that I did not have to lie about. He almost seemed to be going out of his way not to ask me any personal questions this time, and I was grateful for that. Instead he seemed quite content to talk about himself, and I was more than happy to listen.

The time went quickly; in fact, I was amazed at just how fast the afternoon disappeared. Time moves much slower when I am here in my apartment by myself. At last, Stephomi glanced at his watch and my heart sank as he pointed out how late it was.

'I'm sorry, Gabriel, we've been here for hours and I've hardly asked you anything about yourself. It's one of the unspoken requirements of being a teacher, you know – you have to love the sound of your own voice. Why don't we move on to a restaurant and you can do the talking this time?'

I hesitated, pushing down that familiar panic. I didn't want to do the talking. I didn't know enough about myself to be capable of talking for any great length of time. *My name is Gabriel ...* ? I mean, how long does that take to say? And he knew anyway, I had already told him so more than once. It occurred to me that perhaps the sensible thing to do would be to quit now while I was ahead.

'Er ... I'm not sure that I—' I began.

'Please, I insist. It'll be my treat.'

The rush of panic increased. What if he asked me something I couldn't answer? What if he asked me where I'd grown up or how many siblings I had or something? What if I panicked and ran away again? *Get a grip ... get a grip ...*

'It's the fish!' I blurted out.

'I'm sorry?' Stephomi asked, looking taken aback.

'Er … I'm supposed to be looking after someone's fish,' I mumbled, my hand automatically going to the fish food in my pocket. 'I don't mind, though!' I added hurriedly. *What was I doing? Urghh, why was I talking to him like this?*

'Someone else's fish?' Stephomi asked, looking puzzled.

'Yes! They're not mine. I just … it's just a favour … until they get back from holiday—'

'Gabriel,' Stephomi said, mercifully cutting me off in mid-flow before any more damage could be done. 'Don't take this the wrong way but sod the bloody fish. You can go and see them tomorrow; I'm sure they won't starve overnight. And I can assure you that my conversation is much more stimulating than that of any fish …' He paused. 'Although, depending on how much I might have to drink, I can't make any promises.'

I laughed. All at once the panic disappeared. The fish were important but, right now, Stephomi was more important. If he asked me any awkward questions, I would just say that I'd rather not talk about my past. Problem solved.

Outside we found that it was no longer raining, although the sun was beginning to set. We walked back past the monument and a little way down Állatkerti Street until we came to Gundels, the most famous restaurant in Hungary. Stephomi was shocked I'd never eaten there before although I had, of course, heard of it. It was housed in a large old building with panelled white ceilings, old paintings on the walls and polished walnut pillars standing throughout the spacious room. A pianist was playing over in one corner, and soft lighting gleamed off the rich pillars and the elegant old crockery on the tables.

Once we were settled I asked Stephomi about his name, as much to deflect any personal question he might ask me as anything, and he arched his eyebrow at me in surprise when I mentioned the archangel Zadkiel.

'You do know your angels, don't you?' he replied. 'Isn't Zadkiel supposed to be the angel of …what was it … *memory*?'

I jumped at his emphasis on the word and knocked my wine glass over.

'Oh dear, how clumsy of you,' Stephomi said lightly, calling over a waiter to help clean it up.

He couldn't know ... He couldn't know about my problem ...

'Are you okay?' he asked once the waiter had gone to get me another wine glass.

'Yes, of course I am! I'm in perfect health, why? Why do you ask?' I replied in a panicky rush.

Stephomi gave me an odd look. 'You just seem a bit jumpy, is all.'

'No,' I said, running a hand through my hair agitatedly. 'No, no. I just—'

'You're not diabetic, are you?'

I couldn't stop the slightly nervous laugh. 'I hope not.'

'Well, the food will be here in a minute, anyway,' Stephomi replied.

With a tremendous effort, I pulled myself together. As the evening wore on, I switched to non-alcoholic drinks. Sighing wistfully, Stephomi agreed that there had been enough alcohol for now and, with a twisted smile, proclaimed that I was good for him indeed. It wasn't that I had anything against drinking; it was just that I needed to stay alert in case Stephomi asked me something that I would need to quickly lie about. I couldn't risk ... I don't know, having too much to drink and then blurting out the whole truth to him, or something equally awful. Although with such a sensational story, I suppose he would probably have taken it for drunken rambling anyway.

At one point, somehow, the topic of music came up and Stephomi mentioned that he owned a beautiful, priceless, old Italian violin – a Grand Amatis, in fact, made by Andrea Amati, who had himself been the teacher of the great Antonio Stradivari.

'Violin?' I asked sharply.

'Yes, do you play?'

'Er, no, I don't think so.'

'Don't think so?' Stephomi asked, looking amused. 'Well, I'm sure you would remember something like that.'

I laughed it off hurriedly. 'Isn't the Devil supposed to play the violin?' I asked, remembering one of the paintings I had seen in my book.

Stephomi raised an eyebrow at me. 'I believe there are certain myths that portray the Devil as a supernaturally accomplished violinist. Hasn't there been a song about it or something? A bet made between the Devil and a fiddle boy as to who could play the greatest? The boy wins in the song, playing for his soul; but if legends are to be believed, then Satan's skill with the violin is unrivalled, in this world or any other.'

The amusement in Stephomi's voice told me clearly that he did not believe any of the myths he was repeating, but still they made me a little uneasy.

'And then, of course, there was Giuseppe Tartini's *Devil's Trill Sonata*,' Stephomi said, leaning back in his char. 'The inspiration for which came in a dream Tartini had in which he gave the Devil his violin and heard it played on a level he hadn't thought possible. Although the *Devil's Trill* was seen as far superior to Tartini's other compositions, he maintained that it was nothing but a pale reflection of the music he'd heard Satan play in his dream.' Stephomi tilted his head at me slightly and grinned. 'Perhaps I should give it up and play the heavenly harp instead?'

At last it was time for the restaurant to close and, when we could no longer ignore the pointed looks of the staff, we retrieved our coats and stepped back out into the cool night. I was going back to the metro station and Stephomi was catching a bus a few blocks away. We paused in the archway of the restaurant as we buttoned up our coats.

'You have my card safe this time?' Stephomi asked, turning to me.

'Yes, and you have mine,' I replied. 'Don't worry. I won't lose it again.'

Indeed I won't – it's lying on the table beside me as I write – but I spent the journey home committing the number to memory anyway. No being alive will be able to take it from me this time. Nothing short of a renewed bout of amnesia will tear the digits from my grasp.

19th September

I have been savouring the memories of my hours with Stephomi these past few days, rarely leaving my apartment but simply sitting, staring at the walls for hours. I had almost been feeling content. Which is why I am irritated that something should have occurred to mar my pleasure.

It was because of the antique book I had received from Italy. The one so concerned with *Demonic Realms* that I had hidden away under the floorboards with distaste. But, over the last few days – as I have been spending so many hours within the apartment – the book has been calling out to me. Almost as if the hateful thing really did have a voice. Its presence burned in my mind with white heat, imprinting its image there even after I had closed my eyes. I did not wish to have such a thing in my home. I had quite enough books with devils dancing through the pages as it was, so I decided to send this one back to the Italian bookshop so that it might be re-sold to some other person.

I walked down the street to buy some brown paper and tape, which I took back to my apartment, already feeling the beginnings of relief. Once home, I retrieved the volume from its hiding place beneath the floorboards and placed it firmly face down on the sheet of brown paper I had laid out ready on the kitchen table. I began to fold it carefully, and then ... hesitated. This was dangerous, I suddenly felt. I should not be sending the book away like this. I would make it angry.

I shook my head impatiently and thumbed all the way through the old pages, just as repulsed by the vivid images and descriptions as I had been before. As I gazed down at it, I saw that a corner of the yellowing parchment had come unstuck from the red leather back cover and was curling forwards. Frowning, I pressed my thumb over the paper, but it curled back again as soon as the pressure was gone. Then, looking more closely, I saw that the cover had been repaired before – rows of neat, black stitching pinned the yellow paper to the leather back.

It's hard to explain what happened next without sounding like a madman, which I know I most certainly am not. I even shocked myself when, with a yell of fear, I leaped to my feet and stumbled several steps backwards, my chair clattering to the floor, sliding back along the floorboards. Something about the book had bothered me from the very beginning. I had assumed that it was merely an aversion to the repulsive subject matter. But now I know that it was more than that. There was some palpable evil radiating from the book in invisible waves, pummelling into me as I stared fearfully at the horrible thing. It would harm me. I knew it would. There were real devils living in those innocent pages and they *hated* me and would be only too pleased to destroy me given half a chance. Well, they wouldn't have it. I wouldn't give it to them. I pulled open one of the kitchen drawers, grabbed a carving knife, whirled back to face the book and with a strange animal-like sound somewhere between a snarl and a sob, I drove the knife through the book to its hilt. My own strength surprised me – the knife went through the volume and well into the wooden table beneath as easily as if I were slicing the blade through butter.

And then, to my horror, there was a call at the door. 'Hello? Gabriel?'

I recognised that voice, and even as I looked I saw that I had not shut the front door properly on my way in. When the visitor knocked, it swung open easily, leaving Stephomi's slender figure framed in the doorway. His eyes swept the room and I saw him take in the red book, pinned to the table by the large carving knife, the overturned kitchen chair, and me, backed up against the kitchen units and struggling to look like a calm and rational human being rather than a depraved and dangerous one.

'I'm not mad!' I said at once, eager to reassure him.

But I shouldn't have said that. Most people don't need to defend their sanity. I should've just laughed it off. Laughed it off and made a joke of it. But my mind wasn't working quickly enough for that.

'Mad, Gabriel?' Stephomi asked with a smile. 'Why, whoever said anything about being mad?

'I—' I began, having no idea what I was going to say but feeling the pressing need to say something, anything, to explain.

'Don't tell me,' Stephomi said holding up his hand and taking a step into my apartment. 'The author was a narrow-minded bastard? I've sometimes had the urge to impale such works myself, although I must say,' he said with a grin, 'I've never actually acted on it.'

I laughed, I hope not too hysterically, relieved that Stephomi was not pronouncing me a lunatic and leaving my home with haste.

'I'm sorry if I've . . . come at a bad time,' Stephomi said, glancing at the book with an amused expression. 'I just wanted to return this.' He held up a slip of paper and I saw that it was my weekly metro ticket. I had missed it when I went to board the metro after our dinner and had needed to buy a single ticket to get home.

'There are still some days left to run on it so I thought I'd better return it. It must have been left on the table when you took your wallet out, and I picked it up by mistake with the receipt.'

'Thanks,' I said, taking the ticket from him. 'Will you stay for a drink?' I asked, even as I spoke realising that I only had wine or water to offer.

'Not today, thanks. Some other time, though.'

And with one last quizzical grin at the speared book on my table, Stephomi walked from my apartment, closing the front door firmly behind him.

Although not as bad as it could have been, this incident was enough to convince me that the damn book really had to go. I could not have it in the house a moment longer. Once Stephomi had gone, I grasped the knife by the handle and pulled, but I could not wrench the bloody thing free, it was so ingrained in the table. I couldn't believe I'd driven it in as forcefully as all that; really it should be a simple enough matter to pull the knife free again. I redoubled my efforts, grasping the handle of the carving knife with both hands and heaving on it as hard as I could; but, although I lifted the whole damn table from the floor, still the blade wouldn't come loose. That book ... was *mocking* me!

At last, in a fit of desperation, I tore it through the knife in order to free it, virtually cutting the old volume in half in the process. As I pulled the book free, something dislodged from the back cover and I bent to pick the pieces up, thinking it was a page the blade had sliced in half. But, no, it couldn't be a page, could it? It was never going to be just some harmless, meaningless old page. Some innocent thing that couldn't hurt me. That would have been too easy.

When I bent to retrieve the pieces, I realised that they were actually two halves of a photo. My heart sank when I saw what the photo was of. Slowly, I lowered myself to the floor, held the two halves together and gazed at it in dismay for a while. Later, on closer examination of the book, I saw that the photo had been concealed in the back cover, covered over by the stitched yellow parchment I had seen ... those neat little rows of tiny black stitches that had caused me to lash out so violently.

The photo was of a woman. She was walking down a street somewhere, although it was impossible to tell where. The camera lens had zoomed in for a close- up shot of her head and shoulders, taken from slightly above her. She was in her forties with an intelligent face and long chestnut hair. There was no mistaking her – she was the running woman I had encountered some three weeks ago. The woman who had run blindly away from me into the back alleys of Budapest, and then quietly slipped away while I was occupied with the five large men all doing their best to bash my head in.

I carefully taped the split photo together, and then sat there staring at it, hoping if I only did so for long enough it might make sense. The photo was a little scratched from its concealment in the book, but other than that it was in good condition and was obviously fairly recent. When I turned it over, I saw that there was English writing on the back, printed in neat capitals and written in red ink –

NEVILLE CHAMBERLAIN'S WEEPING WILLOW IS WEEPING STILL.

Also printed on the back of the photo was the name of the film developers. It was an English name. The photo had been developed in the United Kingdom, been concealed in the back of an antique book in Italy, and was now lying on a table before me in the centre of Budapest. I was at a loss. I could not even begin to explain it. I had seen this woman three weeks ago. She had run from me, as if she was scared of me, but I am sure that must have been some kind of misunderstanding. I know nothing about her. I have no name, no nationality, no occupation, no address … But she spoke to me in Hungarian, and I saw her in Budapest – I suppose that, in itself, suggests that she must be Hungarian.

As for the reference to Neville Chamberlain and a weeping willow printed on the back, I couldn't even begin to imagine their relevance to the woman in the photo. The words seemed so utterly irrelevant that I wondered if they were, in fact, unrelated and had been written on the photo back by accident.

Was the photo meant for me? If not, it surely is the most incredible coincidence that I saw this woman only weeks ago. She knew me, once. I think she might be in trouble. I want to help her. And I would if I could. But I don't have the slightest idea as to how to go about finding her.

21st September

I have pored over and over the photo in vain. I have sat and stared at it for hours. I found the card that had been in with the package, giving the address and phone number of the Italian antique bookshop. When I phoned the number, the elderly owner of the shop answered the phone and recognised me at once, greeting me warmly – firm proof that the book had indeed been a costly purchase. I spoke to him in Italian for some minutes about the book, and am confident that he knew nothing of the picture. For one thing, when I suggested that something had happened to the back cover that had necessitated its repair, he sounded quite alarmed and assured me that he had not had any need to repair the book. I learned that he had one young man who assisted him in the shop, so I suppose it's possible that this assistant could have placed the photograph inside the back cover for some strange reason – but it would have had to be a strange reason indeed. When I asked where the book had come from, the shop owner said he had purchased it from a private collector over ten years ago. For some reason, the book had been difficult to sell.

I was sure that the photo was not ten years old – for one thing, the woman had looked the same as when I'd last seen her, which meant that the photo must have been hidden in the book while in the possession of the dealer. The only reason I could see for perpetuating such a childlike prank would be to perplex and disturb the buyer of the book. Perhaps, after all, it was nothing more than a coincidence that I had seen this woman a few weeks ago; but I find that difficult to believe.

I didn't know anything about any weeping willow but, of course, I knew who Neville Chamberlain was. I can't help but feel for the man. It was hardly his fault that Hitler was a nutcase who couldn't be reasoned with. The holocaust wasn't his fault any more than it was Churchill's or Roosevelt's, or any other of the world leaders during that time.

While reading about the Second World War on the internet, I came across something that referred to a Holocaust Memorial in Budapest, so yesterday I went to see it. I stood staring at it in perplexity for some time, for it takes the graceful form of a weeping willow. It's in memory of the 600,000 Hungarian Jews killed by the Nazis during the war, so why would anyone refer to it as Neville Chamberlain's tree? Surely, if the tree belongs to any one man, that man is Adolf Hitler?

There is something poignant and sad about the elegant fronds of the aptly named tree, immortalised in honour of those who fell prey to Hitler's demon-driven sins. I stood and gazed at it for a while, feeling regretful and ashamed on behalf of the human race in general. Then I went home.

How was the mystery woman mixed up in all this? The image of the weeping willow, and the history that had caused its tears, depressed me and I found I was unable to shake the bleak mood that was haunting me. I had no appetite and I did not feel like going out, so for once I decided to break my usual routine and go to bed early.

It didn't work. Nightmares ruined any hope I might have had of shaking this unsettled frame of mind. I dreamed I was at St Stephen's Basilica, seeing the sacred building overrun with Nazi soldiers. The flickering light of flames from elsewhere in the city danced through the windows of the church, and distant screams and shouts were carried in on the night air. There were monks running, sobbing ... Mephistopheles was playing the huge organ and three Nazis were exclaiming in delight over the size and value of the huge old bell that had just been taken down from the bell tower. A monk was begging, pleading with the soldiers not to take it. One of them looked round and shot him in the head before turning back to the bell, and I recoiled in horror as he fell onto the stone flagstones, blood staining his robes and spreading in a pool around him. What madness was this? Jesus Christ, it was just a fucking *bell!*

And then a tall man, dripping with flames, walked into the church, past the engrossed Nazis, and gazed down at the fallen monk. He looked up, gazing right at me, and I flinched instinctively from the hatred in his eyes. Then he was gone, to be replaced by the mystery woman from the alley. I yelled at her to get out of the church before the Nazis saw her, but it was as if she couldn't hear me over the screaming and the deafening music Mephistopheles was playing on the organ. To my horror, she walked up to the soldiers and asked them to help her find her way home. I braced myself for the ringing gunshot and the thump of her body falling down lifeless next to the deceased monk, but it never came. The Nazis turned to the woman kindly and assured her that they would help. And, although I screamed at her not to trust them, I was unable to move and was forced to watch, helpless, as the soldiers became devils, surrounded the woman, and took her out into the burning city. When I woke up this morning, I was even more restless and unsettled than I had been last night. I washed and dressed, then took out one of my books on Budapest and read about St Stephen's Basilica. There was the by now familiar sensation of memories being brought to the surface as I read that the cathedral had indeed been looted by the Nazis in 1944. After the nightmare, I decided to go and see it for myself, in an attempt to shake the horrible air of foreboding that had clung to me ever since I drove a kitchen knife through the old red book.

It was bright, sunny and warm again today, and the white cathedral was a beautiful sight. It's unusually shaped, with two towers rising on either side at the front of the building, and in the centre a 300-foot Neo-Renaissance dome that is visible from all over Budapest.

When I climbed the semicircular white steps at the front and went inside, I was *stunned* by the richness of the interior. The ground plan is shaped like a Greek cross and the walls, floor and ceiling are all covered in blue marble and gold and bronze and mosaics and paintings and murals. Tall white candles stood in golden candlesticks attached to square red marble pillars; white angels curved over the top of gold studded arches and pink marble pulpits, which had fat, white cherubs perched on top, gazing down at the congregation. The final glory was the many stained-glass windows speckling it all with so many different colours. It was stunning and I couldn't help but feel sickened at the idea of Nazis desecrating this beautiful place with their presence – greed-ily looting its treasures to line their own filthy pockets. And for what? What was that bell to them but so many Deutschmarks? Money to be spent on women, alcohol, and the pursuit of other disreputable prizes.

There's an observation point at the top of the bell tower, and I stood savouring the view from it for some time. I could see the Hungarian Parliament building and the old palace and, every now and then, part of the Danube weaving through the splendour. Held above the city in such a way, leaning on the wall with a gentle, warm breeze stirring my hair, I felt relaxed and at peace in a way I haven't known since losing my memory. What did it matter if I could not remember who I was? God knew.

The bell now hanging in the bell tower was bought by German Catholics as a replacement for the one taken by the Nazis. Such a thing pleases me. The Germans who paid for the new bell were not the ones who stole the old one and I admire them for putting right a wrong that they were not responsible for.

After a while, I turned back for the stairs. There are two stair-cases through the hollow dome – one carries on all the way to the ground, and one leads back to the elevator. For one wild moment, as I took the stairs leading to the ground, I thought I glimpsed the mystery woman standing on the staircase opposite leading to the elevator; but when I looked back sharply I clearly saw that there were only two elderly men making their way down the stairs to the lift. My mind is just playing tricks on me. The photograph is upsetting me. I think the best thing will be to hide it away under the floorboards in my cupboard along with all the other things I don't want to think about. I do not remember this woman. There is nothing I can do. If she needs my help, she will have to come and ask me for it herself.

3rd October

I am starting to fear that there might be something wrong with me. I went out to eat in a new restaurant this evening, and the waitress asked if I would like my steak *angolosan* – cooked rare. I said that would be fine and after about twenty minutes, the meal was delivered to my table. I had planned to eat and then walk back to my apartment block, taking in the cool evening air before going to bed.

But the steak was very rare indeed, still a light pink colour; and, as soon as I sank my knife into the tender slab of beef, some red blood oozed out of the sides, staining the plate and running into the vegetable juices, collecting in clotted pools and swirls. I cannot do justice to the strength of my utter revulsion in that moment. Suddenly, my appetite was gone, and I felt sick at the sight of those scarlet droplets splattered across my plate and dripping from the end of my knife.

Before I knew what I was doing, I had jumped up and over-turned the entire table with a yell. Christ – I cringe now at the spectacle I must have made of myself. The china plates and cutlery fell to the floor with a room-silencing crash, and nearby customers shrank back in alarm as the staff rushed over and implored me to calm down. But my mind kept replaying the memory of my knife plunging into the pink flesh and the scarlet blood that had bled onto the plate.

I can't explain why the sight caused me such horror, but I was suddenly quite sure that I was going to be sick. I pushed the staff aside and just managed to make it outside before folding over double and retching there on the pavement, much to the alarm of various passers-by and an old couple who had been looking at the menu. They left pretty quickly. I suppose the sight of a man sprinting out of a restaurant to throw up is not the highest recommendation.

I would like to think that it hadn't been the steak. That it had perhaps been something I ate earlier that day. But the nausea came upon me so suddenly. There wasn't any warning. If there had been, I certainly wouldn't have been vomiting in the street where all those people could stare at me. There seems to be a pattern emerging here. Sometimes ... I almost seem to lose my mind ...

The way I see it is this: either I truly am a madman, or else these episodes are triggered by my subconscious in response to some event that occurred before I lost my memory. And I know, I *know* I'm not mad. So this scares me, all this. I wish it would all stop. I walked home quickly last night in case the restaurant called the police or something equally alarmist. I just kept my head down, cheeks burning with shame, and carried on walking.

When I got back to my apartment block, I paused outside it and drew out the battered box of fish food from my pocket. I glared at it for a minute in the weak light of the street lamp, hating it. Then I dropped it into the nearby trashcan and went upstairs to bed.

4th October

Stephomi contacted me a couple of days ago to arrange to meet for a drink in the wine bar of his hotel. I had been pleased to make these plans at the time, but this morning I didn't really feel like seeing anyone. I missed feeling the fish food in my pocket. I realised how pathetic that was so I didn't let myself rummage around in the trash for it. I didn't take a new box from the stack in my cupboard, either. But I'm sure that my family are not returning now – after all, I've been here for two months. Holidays do not go on that long. There really are no fish. I must have moved to Budapest on my own. My old life could be anywhere, and I have no idea how to find it. Perhaps, after all, I should go to the police with this ... I had half made up my mind to do so this morning, but now I am not so sure.

I tried to cancel my plans with Stephomi – I just wanted to stay at home by myself today. But his phone was just ringing out so in the end I had to go, although I'm glad I did now. I was impressed when I located the Hilton – the hotel in which Stephomi had been living for the past weeks. It's situated on the other side of the Danube, in the Castle district – I had to walk across the Chain Link Bridge to get to it – and is one of the most luxurious hotels in Budapest. The hotel building incorporates parts of both a Gothic church and a Jesuit monastery, and the views of the Danube and the Pest cityscape are magnificent.

The wine bar in which I was to meet my friend was set in an

authentic medieval cellar built beneath the hotel. I admit I was disappointed not to drink in one of the bars upstairs, looking out over the Danube. It seemed a shame to be drinking in an underground cellar when the view from above was so beautiful. But Stephomi was waiting for me downstairs so I followed the signs to the wine bar, expecting only to have to walk down a few stairs before I came to it, but instead I had to go down several flights of stairs scattered across the hotel before I came to another door with a sign for the wine cellar. When I opened it and stuck my head through, I stared in surprise at the sight of a stone staircase carved out of the rock, twisting down in semi-darkness and illuminated only by the occasional soft orange lamp. For a moment I wondered if I was still in the Hilton, or whether I had in fact come across some kind of underground monastery. I looked back over my shoulder, but the sign definitely pointed to this door. So I shrugged and crept inside, half expecting to be told off for going through, although there was no one else to be seen.

The uneven rock was cold to my touch and there was that unmistakable musty, slightly damp smell that only truly ancient places have. I followed the twisting staircase down until I saw it reached a short corridor, at the end of which was a stone archway to the wine bar. I froze in alarm when I saw it, for the twisting black words above the arch clearly read: *Faust Wine Bar*.

I jumped when someone spoke below me. 'You're late.'

I strained my eyes and saw that Stephomi was waiting for me at the bottom of the twisting stone stairs, leaning against an archway with his hands in his pockets, virtually hidden in the shadows cast by the soft light.

'I, er ... had some trouble finding it,' I said, still staring down at him from the stairs.

'Yes, it can be like that the first time. I think most of those tourists upstairs don't even know it exists. They get distracted by the panoramic windows in the modern bars upstairs. Come on, this bar is far better, I promise you.'

I hesitated, feeling almost childishly afraid to go down the steps and join him. It was the name of the cellar: *Faust* ... the once honourable man that Mephistopheles had so cleverly managed to corrupt and disgrace.

'Is something wrong?' Stephomi asked, when I didn't move.

I wanted to ask if we could go back upstairs to one of the sunlit and tourist filled bars, but Stephomi was obviously keen to show me the cellar, and I knew it would sound odd ... so I walked down, and followed him as he led the way through to the cellar.

It was very small, with only enough room for six tables or so in a long, thin room, with the wall and ceiling forming a semi-circle above the floor. Apart from the odd light built into a rocky enclave, the whole room was lit by candles, illuminating the many bottles of wine stacked in the old wooden wine racks against the walls. When we got there, the cellar was empty but for the waiter stood behind the small table outside. Soft cello music was playing from somewhere, although I couldn't see any speakers. Stephomi ordered a bottle of Szekszárdi Merlot and we sat down at one of the corner tables in creaky old wooden armchairs padded with cushions.

'How long have you been living in this hotel?' I asked, once the soft-footed waiter had brought out our wine and retreated to his area outside, leaving us alone in the dim cellar.

'Since I arrived in Budapest. A few weeks, I suppose. I came into some inheritance a few years ago and now I'm lucky enough to be able to travel the world at my leisure.'

'What about your family?' I asked glumly, still brooding over the loss of my own.

At once, Stephomi's face darkened and he gave a bitter laugh. 'I'm afraid I'm rather estranged from my family,' he admitted.

I knew such things happened, of course. I knew that families could tear apart and life-long feuds prevented relations from speaking to each other for years and years. But I still couldn't help but cringe at Stephomi's words. What a *waste*! At least he *had* a family.

'It wasn't my fault,' Stephomi said, doubtless seeing the look on my face. He paused, then added with a smile, 'Well, mostly not my fault, anyway. It started off as a small thing – you know how it is. But somehow the situation just –' he waved a hand around, searching for words, '– escalated. Now even when I do go home, my father and brothers won't speak to me. Won't even see me.' He grinned suddenly and gave a lazy shrug. 'I think the situation could have been salvaged if only I hadn't proved them wrong about something some years back. The one thing they can't forgive, really. So what about you? Do you get on tolerably well with your family or do you avoid Christmas reunions like the plague?'

Christmas reunions ... ? I couldn't help but grimace. I had never thought about Christmas, only two months away now. What was I going to do on Christmas Day? Sit in my apartment by myself wondering what my parents might be doing? What my siblings might be doing? What my ... *wife* ... my *children* ... might be doing? I felt suddenly desperate for them – for these people that I no longer knew. What if they had given me up for dead already?

'I'm sorry, Gabriel, I didn't mean to pry,' Stephomi said quietly, misinterpreting my silence.

'No, no,' I said. 'Don't apologise. The truth is I ... I don't know my family. I can't remember them.'

'You don't say?' Stephomi murmured, eyebrow arched. 'You were adopted?'

I could have said yes right there. But Stephomi was my friend now – my only friend, in fact. He was a clever man; he might be able to suggest some solution to this problem. He might be able to *help* me somehow. He might know of some way to fix this without going to the police.

'There's no fish,' I said suddenly. 'All this time I thought they were real but ... there's no one here but me. And I'm not even sure who I am.'

So I told him the truth. I told him that I had woken up lying on the floor of my kitchen some months ago, and that I had no memory of my life before that day – no clue as to where I might have lived or who I might have been.

But I didn't tell him of the incident in the back streets of Budapest late at night when I had been unable to stop myself from beating up five Hungarian muggers. I didn't tell him of the utter horror that had risen up sharp and vicious within me at the sight of the dead butterfly, the antique book or the bleeding steak. Nor did I say anything about the strange mystery woman who had fled from me. I did not want to scare away the one person I felt I could trust.

I was afraid that he might be astonished and horrified by my predicament, or else denounce me on the spot as a compulsive liar. But Stephomi merely sat for some moments after I had finished, twirling the stem of his wine glass between his slender fingers and frowning slightly, as if contemplating an interesting puzzle.

'Amnesia?' he said at last. 'Most unusual. And all this from hitting yourself with a shelf and falling from a chair?'

'Well, as far as I can tell.'

'And there is nothing in your apartment that gives you some clue as to what your life was before? No one has been in contact with you?'

'No, but that's because I've only just moved in. I don't think anyone knows where I am. I don't know what to do about it!'

'You're right. It's a bloody mystery, Gabriel. But I'm sure the amnesia won't be permanent. These things usually aren't. You'll just have to wait it out.'

'Wait it out?' I asked, appalled. 'But I could go on like this for years!'

Stephomi shrugged. 'The only other thing to do is go to the police. There's nothing to stop you doing that if you want to.'

I could see him watching me closely. I hadn't told him about the large stash of cash I had found in my apartment, and had no wish to let him know of the sinister elements I had deliberately left out.

'I'd rather not do that ...' I began uncertainly.

'Well, if your family aren't in this country, then there's probably little the Hungarian police could do anyway. I'd wait it out, if I were you. I mean, your friends and family must have known that you were moving to Budapest. I expect one of them will seek you out eventually, even if they don't have your address. There can't be that many English people living here. It's only been two months, Gabriel. I'm sure everything will resolve itself eventually, just give it some time. And if your family is anything like mine, then be prepared for the ribbing of your life when they find out that you managed to knock yourself out with a shelf within days of moving in.'

His attitude made me feel so much better. I wouldn't always be in this situation. It was just a matter of time. It was not something to become hysterical about. I'm glad that I trusted Stephomi with this. Perhaps, in time, I will be able to tell him about the other things. I'm sure he would be able to come up with a rational explanation for everything else that has happened to me too.

When I returned to my apartment after meeting Stephomi at the Hilton, I sat thinking for a while about what he'd said, replaying the whole meeting in my mind several times, feeling much calmer about the situation than I had done this morning. I lost track of time and when I at last glanced at my watch, it was too late to go out for dinner. It had started to rain and large drops splattered against the darkened windows. It was not until then that I realised I had been sitting in darkness on the couch in my living room for some time. Reaching out a hand, I turned on the nearby lamp, bathing the room in a pale glow. The apartment was silent but for the rain falling outside. I gazed into the mirror hanging opposite me on the wall and watched the second hand of the reflected clock ticking round in anti-clockwise circles – an oddly discordant sight.

And then, quite suddenly, he was there without my even seeing him arrive. A man standing behind me in the mirror, next to the bookshelf, cold aversion on his face as our eyes met through the reflected glass. I recognised him. I had seen him twice before, both times in dreams. On the first occasion, he had walked into my apartment and destroyed the card given to me by Stephomi. On the second, he had been there in St Stephen's Basilica when the Nazis were looting the bell. And now, once again, flames flickered around the man and dripped from him like water.

'*Traitor!*' he hissed hatefully. '*Go back where you came from!*'

I could not place the language, although I could understand the words. His voice was deep, with a steely hard edge. I tried to say something but my mouth wouldn't open, my limbs wouldn't move. The suddenness with which he pulled a large book from my bookcase and hurled it at me, sparks spitting from its cover, shocked me out of my paralysis and I instinctively threw myself to the floor, hands over my head, as the burning book flew towards me ...

I woke with a start, still sprawled on the couch, my heart beating quickly. The living room was filled with shadows. I must have nodded off – but such a thing is most unlike me. I just don't get tired. I reached out my hand and turned on the lamp for real this time. Unable to resist, I glanced over my shoulder at the bookcase. There was no burning man standing there. There was no burning book on the couch beside me.

The evenings are worse. Much worse, somehow, than the days. That is why I usually eat out in the city and return to the apartment late. I find the silence and the emptiness oppressive, and it's the evening, more than any other time, when loneliness throbs inside me, even though I know this is only temporary. It will not go on for ever; I will eventually be reunited with all those people I knew. But for now I have no memories to return to. I'm not greedy; I wouldn't expect to get them all back in one go. But I'd like to have just one of those golden ones ... You know, something you find yourself thinking about for hours, revisiting a moment that once made you so happy. A memory that can distract you from any present bitterness. Sometimes I think even unhappy memories would be better then nothing. They would make me feel less like a ghost, an invisible man, a no one. If nothing else, at least there would not then be this terrible, vast *emptiness* that eats away at me like some sort of cancer from within.

I stood up, stretched stiffly, and wandered to the bookshelf. All the books were lined neatly on their shelves, and everything seemed to be in order. But then I looked again and realised that one book was not in its rightful place. As I've mentioned, I keep my books arranged in alphabetical order, and one book entitled *Keepers of the Circles* should have been filed under K but was at the front with the Bs. Clicking my tongue with disapproval, I pulled the book out by its spine. Like so many of my books, this one was old and well worn and when I removed it from the shelf, a page fell from it. I bent to pick it up and then paused as a familiar name on the page caught my eye. Then I felt my lips curving in a grimace. Reluctantly, I walked back to the couch, the book and loose page in my hand.

When I first began to try and find out who I was, I had examined the name Gabriel in some depth. But I had never got very far with Antaeus, never even been able to trace its origin. Now the name gaped at me from these pages. This book was yet another one about Hell – Jesus, I really had been completely obsessed with it – the nine circles of sin contained within the centre of the Earth where the condemned are forced to wallow for eternity in atonement for their earthly crimes. The circles are concentric, each one representing a greater evil, culminating in the centre of the Earth where Satan is bound in a great sphere of sparkling ice.

Each circle represents a different kind of sin, and each circle's tortures are different, corresponding with perfect symmetry to the crime committed. These punishments are dreadful to read of, turning the stomach and the soul with horror, and one can see why religion and the threat of an everlasting Hell used to inspire such fear in more religious days gone by. The Heretics of the Sixth Circle are condemned to an eternity of confinement within burning tombs. The Violent of the Seventh Circle are doomed to the eternal agony of being submerged in hot blood, the rim of this Circle guarded by centaurs that will shoot any souls who attempt to rise. Those who committed suicide are condemned to the Seventh Circle where they are turned into thorny black trees, their own human corpses hanging from the branches. The Sowers of Discord of the Eight Circle have their bodies ripped apart by demons, only to heal and be ripped apart again and again in a never-ending cycle of agony.

Each Circle is hidden deeper within the Earth's core, and some of the outer Circles are separated by rivers such as the Styx and Phlegethon, with Ferrymen keeping watch over the rivers and transporting sinners and demons between the different levels of the Hellish realms. The Ninth Circle is the centre of Hell itself – the deepest, filthiest, most agonising and tortuous realm of them all, especially reserved for those worst and most unforgivable of sinners – the Traitors. The most disgusting of men's sins – betrayal of family, friends and loved ones. Betrayers of Lords and benefactors, and betrayers of one's country and God. The punishment for this sin is to be held completely submerged in ice in the centre of Hell alongside Lucifer himself, the cold scarring and burning the skin with a white heat that far surpasses that of fire.

But it's the proximity to Satan that's said to cause the most suffering. Once the highest and most trusted of God's angels, his nature then mutated into something that even other demons fear to look upon. He's said to have three gaping mouths, with bloodied, matted black fur covering his lower body and three pairs of leathery, bat-like wings ... wings that have long since lost every single one of the white dove-like feathers that had once graced the highest ranks of Heaven itself. The three ultimate traitors – Judas, Brutus and Cassius – are held in each of Lucifer's three mouths, their bodies eternally consumed by the Devil, while his three pairs of wings send forth freezing blasts of impotence, ignorance and hatred.

I liked my first name and its connotations. As for my second one, I had assumed that Antaeus was just an old French name or something. But, no, the name doesn't come from France. Stephomi's guess had been correct – Antaeus was of Greek origin. He was the giant of Greek myth who killed passers-by without reason or mercy, building caves from his victims' skulls until he was at last slain by Hercules. Upon his death, he was brought to hell by Mephistopheles himself, and forced to guard the entrance to the Ninth Circle, standing aside only to allow sinners and demons to pass through.

I know I said before that I wasn't scared but ... I wasn't scared then because, if nothing else, at least I knew my *name*. Gabriel

... Gabriel Antaeus ... Perhaps I'm just being overly paranoid ... but the thought does occur to me now that perhaps, after all, Gabriel Antaeus is *not* my real name. I know it sounds sensationalist, putting it like that. I'm sure I'm probably just letting myself get carried away. But no one can deny that it's a very unnatural coupling – a name from Heaven, a name from Hell ...

'Is this a reality TV show?' I said aloud, thinking I'd worked it out and staring suspiciously around the living room for any hidden cameras. 'All right, I've worked it out, very funny, game over.'

But no camera men came bursting in; no TV presenter came to shake my hand and tell me I'd won ... I was so convinced that was the answer for a minute that I even turned on the TV and flicked through all the channels, half expecting to see myself on the screen. But that was stupid. They would hardly allow the show to be broadcast on my TV, would they? I can't seriously believe it's a reality TV show but ... government experiment, maybe? An experiment exploring the effect of isolation and fear on the human psyche? I may even be putting myself in grave danger just by writing down this suspicion. The government have eyes everywhere. They might find out. But I can't afford *not* to write it down in case I lose my memory again and have to start from the beginning once more. I should start hiding this journal when I go out. I cannot risk it falling into the wrong hands. And I can't shake the feeling that someone – whether a TV audience or the government or somebody else – is watching me.

6th October

When I look at what I last wrote in this journal – when I read of my first discovery of the murderous, Hell-bound Keeper, Antaeus – it's hard to believe that was really only three nights ago now. I feel I must have been a different person altogether when I made my last entry, for I didn't know *anything* then. At least now some of the secrets are no longer secrets.

The first thing was that I saw the mystery woman again. Or rather, a child did. Yesterday, still very early, I was troubled by what I had learned about Antaeus and decided to go to St Stephen's Basilica again before it became more crowded. Spiritual places and holy buildings have always calmed me in the past, but not this time.

The morning was cool and still. Soft, white-gold light tinted the sky and a gentle breeze blew through the air. But as I approached the church, all I could think of was my dream of the Nazi invasion. The fear and the shouts and the sobbing and the fires. Some of the Jews never even left Budapest: they were just shot and thrown into the Danube. The blood of children, grandparents, wives, fathers and mothers running through the river, forever staining the city with a shame that would surely never come out. Was that really only sixty years ago?

The Basilica didn't open until nine o'clock so, when I reached it, I sat on the edge of one of the fountains to the left, where I could sit and look up at it while I waited. It was cool at this time of the morning, with an early, dew-laden freshness that was more befitting the vast countryside than the inner circles of a capital city. A few pigeons fluttered about at my feet, cooing softly to each other in the great shadow of the cathedral, and the hush of early morning settled softly like a smooth, cold blanket.

I had not been there for very long when I felt a hand tugging insistently at my sleeve. Glancing down, I saw a boy stood before me, no more than six or seven. His head was bald and about his face and in his eyes there was that pinched look of illness. He was dying. Leukaemia, perhaps. A quick glance across the square showed me that a couple about my age were a few yards away, lost in fierce argument in front of the Basilica, and I guessed that these were his parents and, in their distraction, they had not noticed their boy wandering over to me.

I felt guilty as I looked at him. Why should I get to live so much longer than him? What had I done to deserve it? What was health to me? It was this terrible, disgraceful *waste* and I felt a bleak shame as I looked at him. I wished that I could take the illness out of his body and into my own. I would have done it if I could.

'She's still lost,' the boy said, one hand still grasping my sleeve as he gazed up at me. 'Can you help her?'

I gazed down at him in alarm, my mind at once filled with thoughts of the mystery woman. 'Who?' I asked hoarsely.

'The lady. She left when she saw you coming. She said the Ninth Circle took it all from you and now you can't help her. Can't you? She's scared, you know. She's really frightened. Isn't there anything you can do about it?'

You've known your share of fear, haven't you, little boy? I am sorry for that.

Out of the corner of my eye, I saw the boy's mother suddenly glance around in panic and then, spotting her son, she and his father started walking towards us with relief. Quickly, I pulled the torn photo from my pocket.

'Was this the woman you saw?'

The child took a look and then nodded. 'Can you help her?'

My answer seemed to mean a lot to him somehow so I just nodded in silence as his mother came up and took him by the hand.

'I told you not to wander off, Stephen. I'm sorry, sir, I hope he wasn't bothering you.'

I smiled at the couple, trying not to let raw, painful pity show on my face as I assured them that the child hadn't bothered me. Part of me wanted to run after the family, as they walked away, and get the child to tell me all he knew of the mystery woman; what exactly she had said to him and in which direction she had gone. But I didn't want to frighten them, and I especially didn't want to frighten the little boy. I watched him walk out of sight, standing between his parents as they each took one of his hands. When he died ... there would be this huge hole left in their lives. Would they ever be able to fill it? Would they ever be able to pretend it wasn't there for long enough to be happy? My disappearance must have left such a hole in the lives of my own family. I wondered if they missed me as much as I missed them.

When the family had disappeared from view, I found it easier to rid my thoughts of them and turn my mind back to the mystery woman. How strange that she should have mentioned the Ninth Circle. She surely couldn't have been referring to Dante's Ninth Circle of Hell. *She said the Ninth Circle took it all from you* ...The Ninth Circle ... My mind raced with the possibilities. Could the Ninth Circle be some kind of organisation? Or was it a place? Had something dreadful happened there, causing me to lose my memory?

Could the Ninth Circle be a person or a code name or a book or a thing? A valuable possession, perhaps, that I had stolen and sold, hence the large amount of money hidden under the floorboards of my apartment? Had the child simply been making it all up? Was he a compulsive liar with an attention-seeking problem? But then he would hardly need to be a liar to get attention, would he? That's the grand thing about dying: you can have all the attention you want. No, I'm sure he really did see her. And, in the light of what I have since found out, that in itself is extraordinary.

I waited until the Basilica opened and then climbed the steps to the top of the dome again. I was the only one up there and had the whole place to myself. For at least an hour, I just stood and gazed at the city, feeling safe and protected in a way I never felt when on the ground. Everything seemed so beautiful from that height. It was only at closer range that you could see the filth and the muck, but from the dome, everything was golden and dripping with clear sunlight. The cathedral was solid and safe at my back and beneath my feet, and I felt that, if only I could live here in this tower, everything would be okay. Everything would be fine and my existence would be bearable if I could just stay up here. Usually I enjoy human companionship ... but sometimes, peoples' eyes seem to burn into me and their very presence is painful, like acid on my skin. And all I want is to be alone.

I returned to my apartment in the afternoon, earlier than usual. I'd hoped that the visit to St Stephen's Basilica would lift my spirits but, if anything, the outing had only intensified my feelings of foreboding. The encounter with the dying child, and the news of the mystery woman in particular, had served to unsettle me even further.

But I wasn't prepared for what I found at home. I was not prepared for the sickening wrench of betrayal that wracked me upon the discovery. The bitterness of it cramped my whole body with pain and for long moments I simply stared at the photo, shaking with shock.

Like the photo of the mystery woman, this one had also been concealed within a package. This time the order was for a case of French wine and when I phoned the supplier I found once again that I had placed the order myself some months ago. There was nothing in the case to give any clue as to where I had been living at the time – the only address was my current Hungarian one on the label. So I unpacked it and proceeded to stack the wine according to vintage on the wine rack in my cupboard. As I took out the last bottle, a photo that had been concealed at the bottom beneath the bottles was pulled out, fluttering to the floor.

The photo was of Stephomi and I talking in a hotel room. We stood facing each other before large bay windows, a city visible through the glass behind us. And there, rising above the other buildings, was the clear outline of the Eiffel Tower, tall and majestic, piercing the sky with its tip.

I couldn't remember ever being in a hotel room with Stephomi. I couldn't remember ever being in Paris. I'd always assumed that our first meeting had occurred a few weeks ago, beside Michael's church on Margaret's Island in the middle of the Danube. But the awful truth in all its hideous and grotesque reality was that Stephomi and I already knew each other, before we ever met again in Budapest. Stephomi knew who I was, yet had given no indication of having seen me before in his life. On coming across me on Margaret's Island, he must have guessed or somehow already known about my amnesia. Perhaps our meeting had not been an accident at all.

How could he not have told me? How could he have so brazenly and coldly lied to me like that? *How could he?* It didn't make any fucking sense! At our last meeting I had even admitted to him that I had amnesia and didn't know what to do. He could have helped me then if he'd wanted to. He was using me. Somehow, in those moments, I was sure of it. Just as sure as I was that he was bloody well going to answer to me for what he'd done. I wasn't going to take one more lie from him.

I phoned Stephomi and asked him to meet me that evening. A painful anger had replaced the initial hurt and now all I could think of was getting the truth from the treacherous bastard. My hand shook on the telephone receiver and I was astounded by how normal, relaxed and friendly my voice sounded when Stephomi answered his phone and I invited him over to share a bottle of wine with me that evening.

In the hours before he arrived, I examined the photo very carefully, trying to get as much information from it as possible. I couldn't tell which hotel it was since the room was of a standard type and seemed to have no distinguishing features. I could see no personal possessions or baggage and couldn't even tell if the room was mine or Stephomi's. He looked much the same as I had always seen him: calm, at ease – one hand in his trousers pocket, the other being waved before him as he spoke. But yet there was something different. Something I had not seen in him before. Was it my imagination or was he speaking with a hint of … a hint of … gravity? Vehemence? An uncharacteristic seriousness, perhaps? Although there was that omnipresent smile lingering about his mouth still.

But it was my own face and posture that alarmed me more. I was staring at Stephomi coldly and I looked … wary. Stiff. This was no relaxed and amiable friendly chat. My heart sank as I came to these conclusions. Why hadn't he told me the truth? What did he want? I was not cheered when I turned the photo over and discovered that this one, too, had writing on the back:

'Always forgive your enemies – but never forget their names.'
Robert Kennedy.

And for the first time, it occurred to me that whoever was getting these notes and photos to me might be an unseen friend rather than a taunting enemy. That they might be trying to warn me of some unseen danger. But the two photos had come from different countries altogether. Could someone really have travelled from Italy to France to post the clues, to ensure I could not trace them? And why not send everything together? And why did everything have to be so fucking cryptic, damn it? Why not come to me themselves with what they knew? Because they physically couldn't? Because they feared to?

I stifled the urge to start smashing things up in frustration. What a total bloody mess this was! Well, I'd get some answers from Stephomi, that was for sure. As for the letter sender – for now I could only assume that I had a nameless friend out there somewhere. A friend who, from the quote, also seemed to know that I was suffering from amnesia.

I decided before Stephomi arrived that I wasn't going to hurt him. I wouldn't act in a savage, uncivilised manner. I would just confront him with the photo and see what he had to say for himself. After all, it wasn't as if he could deny it. He'd have no choice but to tell me the truth. But when I opened the door to him that evening and he walked in to my home, greeting me easily, carrying an expensive bottle of wine ... it was like having salt rubbed into a raw wound. I'd trusted him and he'd done nothing but lie to my face since we met. I felt like some jilted lover who couldn't help but fly into a passion, words being totally inadequate to express just how furious they were. He had made a fool of me, and I had let him.

Once he'd walked into my apartment, I slowly closed the door, softly drew the bolts across while he prattled on about something behind me. Then I slowly turned around ... and hit him really hard across the back of the head. I don't agree with violence but it was incredibly gratifying to force him to the floor, place my knee in the small of his back and twist his arm behind him in a grip that would break the bone if he tried to resist – all before he'd even had time to utter more than a startled yelp. I had him. It didn't matter which of us was the stronger now that I had him like this: he only needed to move a little to snap one of the bones in his arm. The bottle he'd been holding had fallen to the floor in the scuffle, and broken glass was floating in the spreading pool of red wine, staining his expensive white shirt as I held him to the floor.

'*Why did you do it?*' I hissed. 'Answer me, answer me, *answer me!*'

His other hand was pinned beneath him and, although I felt him shift slightly, he was quite unable to free himself – not without breaking his arm, anyway. I heard him make this strange little sound, somewhere between a laugh and a groan. 'Perhaps ...' he gasped, his voice muffled from where his face was pressed into the floor, 'if I knew the question, Gabriel ...'

I broke his arm then, in my mind. Revelled in the sound of the crack, as the bone snapped, and the scream of pain that came with it. Oh, I wanted to do it in real life, I wanted to. But I stopped myself. You see, *I* am the one who is in control here, not him. Not him!

'You knew me before I lost my memory!' I growled. 'If you dare deny it, I'll break your arm right now, I swear it. You get one warning, that's it.'

'Well, yes, I did know you before, you're right.'

I gaped at the back of his head in amazement.

'Aren't you going to deny it?'

'You just told me not to.'

'Do you think this is a game?' I shouted, forgetting myself and twisting his arm a little further, noting the harsh intake of breath with a grim satisfaction. 'Why didn't you tell me the truth from the beginning?'

'Because ... because you asked me not to,' Stephomi gasped. 'For God's sake, Gabriel, let go of my arm before you really do fucking break it! You're making a mistake! I've never been anything but a friend to you!'

I hesitated. He'd spoken so earnestly that the first doubtful butterflies began to flutter uncertainly inside me.

'I'll happily explain it to you if you'll just let me go,' Stephomi offered stiffly. Reluctantly, I released my hold on his arm and slowly got to my feet. With a sigh, Stephomi did the same and turned to face me.

'Well, I never liked this shirt anyway,' he said, a smile twisting his mouth as he glanced down at the dusky red wine staining his shirt, dripping like blood from his sleeve cuff and the tips of his fingers. The hand that had been pinned beneath him was bleeding and I could see small pieces of the broken bottle embedded in his palm. The same feeling of revulsion rose up in me as on the day of the rare steak incident – I could feel the bile rising in my throat and averted my gaze hurriedly. There were even a few flecks of wine down one side of his face and in his hair. He was gazing at the remains of the bottle sadly and, when he glanced up at me, there was a reproachful look in his eye. 'Really, Gabriel, was all that necessary? If you wanted to know something, you only had to ask. I, er ... admit I haven't been completely truthful,' he said frankly. 'The fact is that I have known you for years. I followed you that day to Margaret's Island and the second time to Heroes' Square. I just wanted to make sure you were all right, that's all.'

'How very altruistic of you! Now can you please explain to me why you've been acting like a compulsive liar?'

'Well, let's not get carried away,' Stephomi replied, looking mildly amused. He moved his hand to brush his wine-dampened hair from his eyes, and winced. Holding up his palm, he examined the shards of glass embedded in the skin. With a sigh, he let his hand drop back down to his side and glanced up to meet my uncertain gaze.

'Look, the truth is you didn't want me to tell you about your past. You made me promise that I wouldn't. I'm not even supposed to be here.'

'That's ridiculous!' I snapped. 'I don't believe a word of it! Just tell me the fucking truth! Is Gabriel Antaeus even my real name?'

Stephomi hesitated a moment and then nodded. 'Yes, it is.'

'And how did we know each other before?'

'I told you, we were friends.'

'What about this, then?' I asked, throwing the photograph onto the kitchen table.

Stephomi picked it up and I saw his mouth tighten with displeasure as he took in the quote on the back. A glint of irritation came into his eyes and he tossed the photo back onto the table.

'We don't look very friendly to me, Stephomi.'

'I was telling you something you didn't particularly want to hear at the time, I'm afraid. I'd like to answer your questions, Gabriel, but I made a promise to you and I have no intention of breaking it.'

'Who is this?' I asked, drawing the photo of the mystery woman from my pocket and holding it up.

'Where did you get that?' Stephomi asked sharply.

'What does it matter? Do you know her?'

'Don't worry about her,' Stephomi said quietly. 'Throw the photo away, Gabriel.'

'You know who she is, then? You do, don't you? You know

everything about this … this Godforsaken mess! Do you know how I lost my memory? Do you know where my family is?' I asked, desperately. And then, when he remained silent, 'Do you know who took the pictures? Do you know who sent them?'

'I have a fairly good idea.'

'But you're not going to tell me, are you? You're not going to tell me anything I want to know at all!'

'No, Gabriel,' Stephomi said with a wry smile. 'Because you don't really want to know it.'

I glared at him furiously, maddened by his attitude. How badly I wanted to hurt him in that moment. I could have beaten the truth from him, of course. After that back street incident with the Hungarian muggers, I was sure I would have been physically up to the task; but the thought of it chilled me, not least because it sprang so readily to my mind. That was not how civilised people behaved. That was not something a civilised person would think about doing.

'You're thinking about beating it out of me, aren't you?' Stephomi asked, with a smile. 'It won't work, you know.'

'Don't push me!' I screamed at him. 'For your own sake, don't give me a reason!' He couldn't know how perilously close I was … but I was determined not to lose control this time … I wouldn't let him force me into doing anything wrong. 'Get out,' I whispered.

He hesitated for a moment and then, with a shrug, he moved past me to the door and I heard it click softly shut behind him. I stood there for a minute after he'd gone, staring at the table and feeling more helpless, more completely alone than when I had first woken up, weeks ago, on the floor of this very kitchen.

The thought of not being in control is disgusting to me. Almost as if the aversion has been ingrained into my soul through years of disciplined habit. So after Stephomi had gone, I sat down at the kitchen table and calmly poured myself a glass of wine in an effort to stifle the urge to destroy my apartment again as I had done the night I'd lost Stephomi's card. I was even briefly tempted to go out and find some muggers to attack. After all, they were only muggers. The desire to do violence to *something* strengthened until it was more a *craving* than a desire. I regretted letting Stephomi walk away like that – perhaps I should go after *him*? I knew where he lived ... But it was no good, not in the mood I was in. It's a terrible thing to say ... but I was frightened that if I let myself give in to these feelings I might go too far.

So I did the responsible thing and took control of the situation and poured myself another glass of wine. And then another and another. Soon I was opening a second bottle ... The truth is that I drank myself senseless, but it's not as bad as it sounds. It was *intentional* ... *I* was the one in control. It was a logical solution to a problem, that was all. It's not like I intend to do it again – it's not healthy, for one thing. But alcohol is sometimes useful. If you're patient ... if you drink enough of it ... then there is a sort of heaviness, a paralysis that creeps into your limbs so that your fingers go numb and you drop the wine glass with a splintering of broken glass ... your head falls back, the chair tips over ... and you end up lying there senseless on the floor for the rest of the night where you won't be able to do any damage to anything ... or anyone.

I was woken up at about 10 a.m., rather suddenly, by a lot of very cold water being thrown into my face. I jerked awake, blinking water from my eyes and coughing it out of my mouth. At once, pain started throbbing dully through me – through my head, my neck, my shoulders – my whole body – from the combination of having slept on the hard floor all night and the alcohol that was still coursing through my system. 'Oh good,' Stephomi said, some of the concern fading from his face as he looked down at me, 'you're not dead after all. Careful, you've been lying in broken glass all night.'

I glanced down and saw that he was right. There were jagged pieces of glass all over the floor from the bottle of wine that Stephomi had dropped and the wine glass that I had broken later. The spilt wine from the bottle had soaked into my clothes, staining my shirt and making me smell like an alcoholic tramp.

'Luckily you don't seem to have cut yourself too badly,' Stephomi said, eyeing me critically. 'Let me give you a hand up.'

I didn't want to take his hand but standing up would have been difficult and – let's face it – undignified otherwise, since there was nowhere on the floor I could put my hands without cutting into them. So I took his hand in silence and let him pull me to my feet.

'What do you want now?' I asked thickly, carefully brushing crushed glass from my clothes.

My throat felt like sandpaper, my tongue seemed to be stuck to the roof of my mouth, and the light beyond the windows hurt my eyes, forcing me to shield them with my hand. There is, after all, a downside to too much alcohol.

'Oh, a great many things,' Stephomi answered cheerfully. 'But for today I'll settle for not seeing you drink yourself to death. It's lucky you weren't sick or you might have choked on your own vomit, you know. You would've done better to drink with me last night.'

'Oh, shut up! I know what you're thinking but I was in control the whole time. I told you to get out. Why have you come back? What do you want?'

Stephomi sighed. 'I phoned you a while ago and there was no answer,' he said quietly. 'I was afraid that something might have happened.' I gazed at him for a moment, water dripping from the ends of my hair to the floor where he had drenched me. I had meant it last night when I'd told the scholar to get out of my apartment. I'd really wanted to hurt him. And I was still angry with him. Angry for the deception, angry for his spiteful refusal to help me, and angry for his stubborn silence. But yet ... I was pleased to see him. Who knows what true loneliness is?

'I thought about it last night, Gabriel,' Stephomi said, still watching me warily, 'and I think there are some things I might be able to tell you without breaking my promise. If you want to go and dry your hair and change your clothes, I'll wait for you.'

'No,' I said at once. 'Tell me now.'

'All right,' Stephomi replied, following me as I stalked through to the living room.

I sat down on the couch, trying to avoid getting any red wine stains on it, wishing my head were a little clearer. Stephomi dropped down onto the other chair.

'For starters,' he began, 'the money that was in your apartment ... is it still here?'

I narrowed my eyes at him and forced myself not to glance at the cupboard in which I had hidden it.

'All right, don't tell me,' Stephomi said hastily, seeing the look on my face. 'All I was going to say is that it's yours. You didn't steal it or anything. I'm assuming that's what you suspected? But rest assured the money belongs to you fair and square.'

'And what did I do to get such an amount?' I asked.

Stephomi grimaced apologetically. 'All I can tell you is that the money is yours. You were a writer by profession.'

'A writer?' I thought back to the typed manuscript I had found in my desk. 'A less than popular one?' I asked, realising that if I had ever succeeded in publishing anything, my works would surely grace my own bookshelves.

Stephomi shrugged slightly. 'Mozart himself was before his time, my friend. Look, I can't really tell you very much. You can go on hating me if you want and scream at me to get out again, but I just want to emphasise first that ... you didn't do anything to deserve this.'

'You said that I asked you not to tell me about my past,' I said, staring at him. 'Are you saying that I knew I was going to lose my memory? That I somehow did this to *myself*?'

'Yes.'

'Why? *How?*'

'I don't know,' he said simply.

'Where is everyone?' I asked desperately. 'Where are my family? Where do they think I've gone?'

Stephomi was looking uncomfortable now. 'I really can't say any more, Gabriel. Faith is part of friendship,' he said softly, looking at me closely. 'You asked me to trust you when I promised not to give you these answers, and I did even though I didn't like it. I believe you must have had a good reason. Now I'm afraid you're going to have to trust me when I say I can't tell you any more. I know it doesn't make sense, that you have nothing solid to put your trust in here, but that is the meaning of faith.'

I wanted to trust him. I didn't want to be completely alone here for the rest of my life, spending my evenings counting and recounting the boxes of fish food in my cupboard that I still hadn't been able to bring myself to throw away.

With a last uncertain, apologetic grin, Stephomi stood up to go, but paused in the doorway to the kitchen and turned back. 'Please don't push me away, Gabriel. Leave the past alone and build a new life now.'

I laughed miserably. 'I want to believe you ... but faith isn't enough for me. How do I know that everything you've told me isn't lies?'

Stephomi paused, considering my question. 'What can I say? I'm afraid faith will just have to be enough for now because that's all you've got. But what reason would I have to lie anyway? "*The liars and those who distort the truth must perish ... and then there may be room for a freer, nobler kind of humanity again.*" To quote Captain Wilm Hosenfeld.'

The name was familiar to me but Stephomi was almost at the front door when horror made me leap to my feet as I suddenly remembered who the man was.

'You quote a *Nazi* to support your cause?' I asked, striding to the doorway to stare at Stephomi in disbelief.

Once again, Stephomi turned about to face me, a small smile on his face. 'Ah, Gabriel, why do you assume that following Hitler and being a good and brave man must be mutually exclusive?'

'Listen to yourself!' I said, appalled. 'Are you trying to be funny or something? Evil and Nazi are synonymous. To suggest anything else is ... it's blasphemy!'

'Then, forgive me, by all means,' Stephomi replied, tilting his head as he gazed at me. 'But I assure you there was no sin intended. You expect too much from humanity sometimes, Gabriel.

We can't all be perfect, you know. Why don't you ask Wladyslaw Szpilman about it?'

Stephomi's initial words had been soothing. I had begun to feel comforted by what he was telling me. But he had ruined it with that quote at the door. To even suggest that a German officer of the Second World War was anything other than a scheming, plotting, greed- and sin-driven demon made me feel utterly sick. Stephomi had described him as a 'good and brave man' ... What on Earth could have moved him to speak such depraved words? Perhaps he didn't know the full extent of what the Nazis had done? Perhaps he didn't know about the families murdered in front of each another; the husbands and wives who had been forced to dig each other's graves before being shot into them; the golden teeth and fillings that were ripped from Jewish mouths before their owners were shot like dogs; the families who had shuffled onto trains together, clutching the one suitcase they were allowed to take, full of their most precious possessions, hoping against hope that, somehow, everything would still be all right and Europe would not soak in its own blood – only to have their cases torn from their fingers before they were shipped off to slaughter houses like cattle ... To suggest that anyone even remotely connected with such atrocities had nothing to feel shame for ... to even *suggest* it ... disgusts me beyond words.

The name of Wladyslaw Szpilman was vaguely familiar to me and, running a quick gaze down my bookshelves, I saw that I owned a book written by him called *Śmierć Miasta*, translated as *Death of a City*. It was written in Polish, which posed no problem for me. Indeed I hardly even realised it wasn't in English until I was halfway through it. Szpilman was a Polish Jew; a survivor of the Holocaust who wrote about his experiences mere months after the war had finally ended. It was later renamed *The Pianist*. The memoir is quite a slim volume and, after showering and picking all the tiny pieces of glass out of my skin with tweezers, I sat and read it all the way through that day.

The story disturbs me greatly. It appals me, in fact. For the truth of it is that Captain Wilm Hosenfeld was indeed a good and brave man. Can I say that? Is it blasphemy? Or was Stephomi right? Hosenfeld saved Wladyslaw Szpilman's life at risk to his own, and was ashamed to be German at the realisation of what was happening. He was ashamed of himself for not doing anything about it. He was a schoolteacher by profession, with a love of children, and he absolutely deplored what was being done to the Jews. He deplored it. And he cursed himself for a wretched coward and he cursed his lack of power to do anything. But, really, how very illogical of Hosenfeld to feel that way, for he would have been quite unable to do anything to influence the war even if he'd wanted to.

Six million Jews died during the Second World War. Six *million* of them. Captain Wilm Hosenfeld's actions saved Wladyslaw Szpilman's life. And so what? Six million dead. Hosenfeld saved one. In the grand scheme of things, what difference did it make ... ? All the difference in the world to Szpilman himself, one supposes.

Captain Hosenfeld, like all other citizens of Hitler's Germany, had been bombarded with anti-Semitic propaganda for years: the Jews were the cause of all Germany's problems; the Jews were the cause of all economic crises and political instabilities; the Jews were a *subhuman* race, who would pollute the purity of German blood if they were given the chance; the Jews were a *disease*, an *infestation*, a *cancer* that would have to be removed from the Earth's gut. God, what utter madness that anyone should ever have *accepted* such nonsense. But people love to hate other people and pain comes easier when there is someone to blame.

When Wladyslaw Szpilman's hiding place was discovered by a German officer, the Jew was convinced that the man's appearance meant death for him, convinced that he would be shot in the head, as had so many others he had known. But instead of shooting him in the head, this German brought Szpilman food, wrapped up in current newspapers so that the Jew might see the war really was nearing its end. He ordered Szpilman to hold on just a little longer. Soon this will all be over and everyone can go back to being human beings again … He even brought him blankets to protect him from the bitter cold of his attic hideaway. Why did he do that? Why did he?

Szpilman wrote in his memoirs that, had it not been for this man's assistance, had it not been for the newspapers he brought that talked of imminent German defeat, had it not been for those things, then he might have taken his own life before the war was out. He might have killed himself, unable to go on with the constant fear, the constant misery of what his life had become … when only a few years earlier he had been a respected and admired Polish pianist who played on the radio for a living.

When Hosenfeld went to visit Szpilman for the last time before he left Warsaw with his detachment, the Jew tried to persuade the German to take his watch – the one remaining treasured thing he owned – to show his gratitude for what the officer had done; but Hosenfeld refused point blank to take it. A Jew's watch, a Basilica's bell … how do these things become so important at a time when they should be so utterly insignificant? Why do they *matter*?

So what of the German captain? Was he *born* heroic? Nazi Germany surely wasn't the ideal environment in which to foster heroism, so was the man simply *born* that way? A simple enough matter of a genetic predisposition towards bravery and decency? This story frightens me. I like black and white. I am comfortable there. Nazis should not be heroes. Just as angels should not be devils. It's not right. When I look at some of the photos of renowned Nazi war criminals, they do not all look evil. They do not all look depraved. They do not all look soulless. Some of them look like human beings. This is not right – monsters should look like monsters; they should not be allowed to wander round among other people in such a flawless disguise.

It must have been about 9 p.m. when the note was shoved under my door. I'd just finished reading Szpilman's memoirs and had gone into the kitchen for a glass of water when I heard the faint sound of a folded piece of paper being slipped under the door. I turned and, even as I did so, I could hear footsteps treading rapidly along the corridor. I crossed the kitchen in moments, flinging open the door and gazing out at the now empty corridor. Slamming my door behind me, I ran down to the end, just in time to see the elevator doors closing although I couldn't see who was inside. My apartment is several floors above street level and there is only one lift so I had no choice but to run down the flights of stairs, sliding and occasionally tripping in my haste, reaching out to steady myself on the twisting steel rail.

Who the hell knew where I lived? The only person who knew my address was Stephomi, but I couldn't believe he had shoved the note under my door and then run off down the corridor to the elevators like a child playing a prank. If nothing else, he was a clever man, and if he really wanted to torment me I am sure he would have found subtler and smarter ways to do it.

By the time I got down to street level, I was too late. There was no one. I had not been fast enough to beat the lift for it was now standing empty. The foyer was deserted but for a small, dark-skinned boy who was hovering by the front doors. I had been about to ask him if he had seen anything when a girl I recognised came into view.

I did not see much of my neighbours; probably because of the unsociable hours I kept, leaving the apartment early in the morning and not returning until late at night. But this was the pregnant girl I had tried to talk to a couple of months ago. What had she said her name was . . ? Casey March? I had since seen her going back into her apartment at hours similarly late to mine. I had been too afraid to talk to her after the spectacle I had made of myself before, and I hid when I could if I saw her coming.

It made me wince just to look at her as she scolded the boy for keeping her waiting, took his arm and walked out into the city. I hated seeing her coming in late at night. I got the impression that she had a late job in the city somewhere, although I didn't know what she did with the boy while she was there. She couldn't be his mother as he must have been at least eight. My guess was that she was his sister. I had never seen anything of any parents. It seemed it was just the two of them. I had wanted to introduce

93

myself properly but after the grand job I'd made of it last time, she probably thought I was some kind of nutcase ... this man who couldn't even remember his last name.

I watched the two of them leave the building and then, as there seemed to be no sign of my mystery postman, I turned and took the elevator back up to the top part of the building. I trudged back down the corridor and let myself into my apartment, bending to retrieve the piece of paper from the kitchen floor and moving to the table with it. It was a plain, white sheet of A4 paper, folded once. I sat down and unfolded it. Then I sat and stared for some time. As with the photos, the words had been written in neat capitals so that it was impossible to make out any handwriting style. The message was in Latin but, being another language in which I seem to be fluent, I could understand it perfectly. How very much I wished that I had caught up with whoever had delivered this note. The words read:

> *Facilis Descensus Averno:*
> *Noctes Atque Dies Patet Atri Ianua Ditsis.*

I recognised the phrase from Virgil's Aeneid. Translated into English, it reads:

> *The gates of Hell are open night and day;*
> *Smooth the descent, and easy is the way.*

Beneath the quote was another phrase, also in Latin, the translation of which reads:

> *The Ninth Circle can't hide you for ever.*

I dropped the note on the table, put my head in my hands and slumped forward in my seat, my whole body shaking with dread. *This wasn't fair!*

So there it is ... I was beginning seriously to consider the possibility that I was going mad. There was fear again, always fear. My sleep that night was restless – filled with Nazi soldiers, murdered Jews and red, shining circles of blood in which angels were bound. These nightmares woke me in the middle of the night and I went into the bathroom to splash cold water onto my sweating face and shoulders. I was leaning over the sink when I heard the noise behind me – the unmistakably powerful sound of roaring flames. When I slowly straightened up, cool water still running down my skin, I could see two people in the mirrored reflection of the bathroom behind me. One was the burning man I had dreamed about before. The other was the mystery woman from the alley. And they were both on fire. Neither one of them moved. They simply stood there. Staring at me. While great orange and white flames danced about their bodies.

Of course, I only gazed into the mirror for a moment before spinning round with a yell of horror. But there was nothing there when I turned. Just the sound of my own frightened breathing as the cool drops of water burned on my hot skin, splashing down onto the cold tiles. Perhaps I had a slight fever. Perhaps I was simply still half asleep. But I was beginning to genuinely fear for my sanity. My whole existence began to seem surreal to me. Why on earth hadn't I gone to the police when I first woke up here? Why didn't I go *now*? What was it, hidden at the back of my mind, that kept me from doing so? I couldn't go to the police. I couldn't do that. But although I knew this for the undeniable fact that it was … I couldn't remember the reason *why*. And it is that ignorance that scares me more than anything else.

9th October

If only I could have known that night that I was to find the answers to those questions a mere three days later ... I thank God that I now know the whole truth about my past, for at least now I don't have to live with the doubts. Just the sadness. My past was always going to be a sad one, wasn't it? How could it possibly ever have been anything else? But at least now I *know*. I know it all.

I decided to count the money – that was how it began. I decided to count the money I had hidden away so that I might know exactly how much was there. It was unsafe to keep such a large amount in the apartment and I was considering opening other bank accounts to distribute the cash. So I retrieved the sack from under the floorboards and, making sure that the door was locked and the blinds were drawn, I emptied the money out onto the floor and started to count it. And then I found something in among the bundles of notes that shouldn't have been there. It was a key. A safety deposit box key. The writing engraved on its face showed that it was from a Hungarian bank here in Budapest, deposit box number 328.

I sat back on the floor and gazed at the key in my hand for a while. I couldn't help but feel apprehensive at the sight of it. After all, if I was content to have a hundred thousand pounds sitting on my kitchen table in my apartment, then what on earth had I deemed so important that it must be hidden away in a vault?

I went straight into Budapest on the metro with the intention of stopping at the bank, but by the time I got there it had closed for the day. So I went first thing this morning, after a restless night of anticipation and unease. It was one of the larger banks in a busy part of the city. When I got to the entrance and saw that the doors were open, I hesitated. There could be any one of a number of terrible revelations waiting for me inside that building. Perhaps it would be better not to know? The anonymous note was going round and round in my mind. *What was* the Ninth Circle? The dying child had passed on the mystery woman's statement that the Ninth Circle had '*taken everything from me*'. The anonymous letter deliverer had written that the Ninth Circle would not hide me much longer. And Antaeus, the murderous giant of ancient Greek mythology, was the gatekeeper to the Ninth Circle of Hell itself ... But then perhaps, after all, there was no bad news waiting for me in the bank. Perhaps the deposit box would just give me answers, maybe even tell me where my family were ...

With an effort, I emptied my mind. I detached myself from the scene so that it was some other man, some stranger, who went and asked to visit his vault. I was shown to box 328 and left alone there. My hands did not tremble as I turned the key in the lock and drew out the slim, harmless looking drawer. I sat down at the table, removed the lid and ran my gaze over everything in the box. Pain twisted inside me as I realised the truth – the truth that had been eluding me for so long and was now all here in this little box, unable to hide from me any longer.

There was no money. No weapons, no ominous, suspicious objects as I had been half afraid that there might be. Instead, there were documents and papers and a letter. It hurt me, what was inside. First I saw the marriage certificate. Then the birth certificate. And my heart lifted. But then I saw the death certificates. There was one for a Nicola Antaeus, aged thirty. And a second for Luke Antaeus, aged four. Their names were unfamiliar to me. And yet I was listed on both as the next of kin. Husband of Nicola Antaeus ... father of Luke Antaeus ...

'No,' I said, staring at the two innocent pieces of paper. *This wasn't fair! This wasn't fair at all!*

'No!' I said again, thumping my fist on the table.

Cause of death ... car crash ... London ...

I rummaged around for something else in the box. Something that might take the sting out of the two death certificates lying on the table before me – as if anything could. But there was nothing to take comfort in here. I uncovered a letter I'd written to an aunt that had never been mailed. I realised why when I found a solicitor's letter informing me of my aunt's death and the fact that she had left all her wealth to me. That explained the money hidden under my floorboards, anyway ...

I stared at the letter until black spots winked across the page. I shook my head, pinched the bridge of my nose, tried again. My heart sank as I read the opening line: *'As the only relation I have left, I'm just writing to let you know that I'm leaving London ...'* My *only* relation? *Only* one? Surely not. *Surely* there must be someone else left? *'I can't stop thinking about Nicky and Luke ... I can't stop seeing them ... I'm moving to Budapest to concentrate on my writing ...I don't want to see anyone, I don't want to talk to anyone ... I don't know when I'll be back ...'*

'*No!*' I cried again.

I felt the strong urge to tear all these dreadful papers into shreds, but at the same time I wanted to preserve them as the one link I had to my life before. And my anger faded quickly, leaving behind this aching, empty *longing*, which was worse. Energy drained out of me and I sat there until one of the staff came and knocked on the door, asking me if I needed any help. I realised I couldn't stay any longer and hastily piled the contents of the box into my bag to go.

I suppose I must have caught the metro back home but I don't remember the journey. I'd feared that what was inside the deposit box would upset me, but I had been unprepared to receive such devastatingly bad news as this. The worst news I could have got. And now I suddenly had the most *thumping* headache, pressing in behind my eyes, throbbing relentlessly with every pulse of my heartbeat. I got into the elevator inside my apartment block and pressed the button for my floor. Then I put a hand to my head, fingers massaging my temples, trying to relieve the pain. There were tears pricking my eyes. I could throw the rest of that fish food away now. I was never going to need it. Everything was ruined. Everything was totally ruined. I couldn't even *remember* them! I couldn't even see their *faces* in my head ...

'Are you okay?'

I dropped my hand and glanced up, realising that the elevator had come to a halt on my floor and the doors were open. My neighbour, Casey March, was stood there gazing at me. She was wearing a barmaid's uniform; her dyed hair tied back; a satchel on her shoulders.

'Are you okay?' she asked again. 'It's Gabriel, isn't it?'

I glanced round fearfully but there was no way to avoid her. I couldn't leave the lift without walking past her. Anyway, she had seen me now.

'I'm fine, I'm fine,' I said, desperately trying to pull myself together long enough to get past her and back to my own apartment.

Casey hesitated, glancing at my shaking hands. 'Do you want me to call someone for you?'

'No, I'm okay,' I said, stepping out of the elevator. 'I ... I just got some bad news, that's all.'

'Oh, I'm sorry,' she said, looking like she meant it.

I nodded, and the movement seemed to almost split my head in two. I couldn't help but cry out and instinctively jerk my hands back to my head again. *What was this?* I hadn't been drinking! Where had this agonising headache come from? Why was the light suddenly *blinding* me? Why could I taste bile rising at the back of my throat?

'What?' I asked, realising that Casey had just asked me something.

'I said do you suffer from migraines?'

'Migraines?'

I automatically went to say that, no, I'd never had a migraine in my life, but then I hesitated. How could I know? How could I *know? I don't remember anything!* The pain was so bad I thought I was going to throw up.

'It looks like a bad one. My brother gets them. You can have some of his medicine if you want.'

I would have eaten a poisoned apple at that point if I'd thought it was going to help.

'Thank you,' I managed.

'I'll just get it for you.'

I followed her back to her apartment and waited outside until she came back with a foil strip of tablets in her hand.

'The adult dose is two tablets every four hours,' she said. 'It might help if you draw the curtains in your bedroom and lie down for a while. That's what I do for Toby. Anyway, I'd better go or I'll be late for work. I hope you feel better.'

10th October

Casey's advice worked. Although the pain lingered for a good twenty-four hours, it only felt unbearable for a few of those. I've never known anything like it. If Casey hadn't realised I was having a migraine attack I would have thought I was dying – having a brain haemorrhage or something. I checked my cupboards the next day and found migraine medicine in there, so I clearly have had migraines before. I don't know how often I have these attacks but I sincerely hope they don't occur often.

I couldn't even sleep. I wish loneliness could be the way it's portrayed in romantic comedies. When the lovely heroine feels lonely, she goes to her best friend for comfort, the friend gives her a tub of ice-cream and this very often seems to quickly solve the problem. I wish real loneliness was like that; I wish it really could be solved with ice-cream. Since I remember neither Nicky nor Luke, you'd think I wouldn't miss them as badly as I do.

What will happen when I am an old man, unable to take care of myself any more? There will be no children, no younger relatives to come to my aid. There will be no one. I will have to move myself into an old people's home. Still, at least I would be living with other people again; I wouldn't be on my own any more … But that's many years away yet. Perhaps I should ring some retirement homes and find out what the minimum age of admittance is, to know how long I will have to wait before I can go to one. But this is hardly the attitude, is it? I'm sure that, by then, I will have married again. I will have other children and grandchildren to care for me by that time.

I slept in late this morning, not getting out of bed until gone nine o'clock. By the time I had showered and eaten something, I was feeling much better so I caught the metro to the Castle District and walked to the Hilton. Of course, I didn't know if Stephomi would be in when I got there. But it was still quite early, only just gone 10 a.m., and there was the chance that he would still be in the hotel. I wanted him to fill in the blanks for me about my family. I wanted to know what Nicky, my wife, had looked like, how we had met ... I wanted to know about my son ... I wanted them to be real to me so that I could grieve for them, say goodbye to them, and move on. Only Stephomi could give me that.

It wasn't until I arrived at the Hilton that I realised I didn't know which hotel room Stephomi was staying in. I went to reception and asked if they could ring to Zadkiel Stephomi's room and let him know I was there. The woman behind the reception desk typed something into the computer, fingers flying over the keyboard before her.

'I'm sorry, sir, but Mr Stephomi has a Do Not Disturb request on his room. I can't phone up to him.'

'But I need to see him!' I said agitatedly, running my hand through my hair in frustration. 'Please, isn't there any way you can get a message to him? Or give me his room number?'

'I most certainly can't give you any of Mr Stephomi's private details, sir,' she said, looking alarmed. 'And I can't phone his room until the Do Not Disturb request has been removed.'

I argued with the woman for a little longer, even though I knew it was useless.

'Oh, all right,' I said in the end. 'Can you take a message for me and pass it on to him when you can? Can you tell him that Gabriel Antaeus wishes to—'

'Antaeus?' the woman broke in sharply. 'Why didn't you say? Mr Stephomi left orders that we might bypass the request for privacy if it was on your behalf. He is in the presidential suite at the top of the hotel, sir. I'll just phone to let him know you're coming, shall I?'

But I was hardly listening to her. I was already striding for the elevators with my bag firmly clamped under one arm. But as I got off the elevator and approached the room, I was surprised to hear thumping and muttered cursing from within.

'Stephomi?' I called, hammering on the door.

The scuffling abruptly stopped and the door was pulled open a bare few inches, showing half of Stephomi's face as he peered at me from behind the door. There was stubble on his chin and dark rings under his rather bloodshot eyes.

'What the hell happened to you?' I asked in surprise.

'I'm sorry, Gabriel, but this really isn't the best time.'

'What's going on?' I asked. 'There isn't somebody in there with you, is there?'

Stephomi gave a wry smile and swung the door open wide for me to see the empty living room within. 'No one here but me,' he said.

'Well, I need to talk to you,' I replied, pushing past him and striding into the room.

It was large and spacious with a cream couch and matching armchairs, a low polished wooden coffee table, a wide-screen TV and a dressing table. Another door led to the bedroom and en suite bathroom. I threw my bag down on the couch and then turned to face him as Stephomi resignedly closed the door.

'Why aren't you dressed?' I asked, only just realising that Stephomi was wearing a Hilton bathrobe.

'I only just got up. The receptionist's phone call woke me.'

'But it's almost eleven o'clock!'

'Yes, I know. I had a late night.'

And that was when I noticed some of the odd things about his room. There was a great crack down the centre of the large mirror over the dressing table, and strange, jagged grooves, almost like claw marks, in the wooden edges of the couch and coffee table as well as ripped tears running down the fabric of the curtains. A broken wine glass lay on the floor with a red wine stain on the carpet beneath it, and the room had a strangely chilled air. There were signs of black fur on one of the cream armchairs, as if a large, black dog had been allowed into the suite, and a slightly acrid scent hung about the room. And there ... on the floor against the wall, lay the broken pieces of what had once been a rather beautiful violin.

'What happened?' I asked, staring at the instrument. It looked as if someone had taken the violin by its neck and shattered it forcefully against the wall. Even with my distaste for violins in general, I found the sight of the broken instrument upsetting.

Stephomi sighed and ran a hand through his tousled dark hair. 'Visit from an old friend,' he said with a shrug. 'He's not too happy with me either, it seems. I lost something of his, that's all. And,' he gestured towards his broken Amatis, 'as you can see, he shared your dislike for my instrument of choice.'

'I'm sorry,' I said, gazing at him anxiously, remembering what he had said of his love for the instrument and the monumental level of its financial value.

Stephomi shrugged, but I noticed that he couldn't bring himself to look directly at the shattered violin. 'Really my fingers are too long for violins anyway,' he said. 'I'd be better suited to a viola. So what can I do for you today, Gabriel?'

My gaze fell on the coffee table once again and I saw that there was an expensive bottle of red wine standing on it, one glass placed alongside. The wine inside the glass was frozen. Frozen solid. I leaned down, picked up the glass and tipped it over. The frozen liquid inside remained glued to the glass.

'What the hell is—' I began, but Stephomi walked over and took the glass from my hand, picked up the bottle and moved them both to the nearby dresser.

'Look, I hate to sound impatient, Gabriel, but what is it exactly that you want? Like I said, this isn't the best time and I—'

'How did that wine get like that?'

Stephomi sighed. 'The wine cellars of the hotel are kept under ground and apparently the generator malfunctioned last night and the temperature in there dropped to well below freezing.

Hence ...' He waved a hand at the frozen wine. 'The steward who brought it up last night didn't notice. Now, what can I do for you?'

'Well, I ... I just came to tell you that I know everything.'

Stephomi smiled wryly as he dropped down into one of the cream armchairs, crossed one leg over the other and leaned back in it, somehow managing to look elegant even when wearing only a bathrobe.

'Everything, Gabriel? Well done. You've achieved what mankind have been trying to do for centuries. Will you let me in on these secrets of the universe?'

'I meant that I know what happened in my past and why you tried to keep it from me,' I said. 'Look I'm sorry about everything I said to you before. I understand now that you really were just trying to be my friend.'

He continued to regard me in silence and I could tell that he didn't completely believe me. Perhaps he thought I was trying to trick him into telling me about my past.

'I know about Nicky and Luke,' I said, to prove that I was telling the truth. I threw my bag over to him. 'It's all in there. I know that I inherited the money from my last surviving relative. I know about my wife and son. It was a car crash. There's no one here because there's no one left. All the people I cared about are dead.'

I sat down on the couch while Stephomi flicked through the papers in my bag.

'I'm sorry,' Stephomi said at last. 'How did you find out?'

I explained about the safety deposit key. Apart from the birth, marriage and death certificates there had also been an envelope full of rejection letters from agents and publishers for the book I had found in my desk as well as others. I really was a writer, or at least a would-be writer.

'Well, I'm sorry you had to find out that way,' Stephomi said again with a sigh.

'I'm sad that no one else is coming,' I said. 'But at least I won't be waiting for nothing now. At least I know for certain. I can

... I can throw away the fish food. I can start to make some new life for myself here now. Maybe one day I'll marry again. But I can't grieve for strangers. I need you to make them real for me, Stephomi.'

He looked uncomfortable at once. 'I'm not sure that I can.'

'Please. Give me something. I can't say goodbye to people I don't know.'

'I'm a traveller, Gabriel. You were only married a few years. The truth is, I never saw all that much of your family. All I know is what you told me in your letters.'

'Just tell me anything you can remember,' I pleaded. 'Just one or two personal things about them are all I need.'

'Well ... Nicky was a teacher of religious studies. You met at a religious lecture. One of my lectures, actually. She had dark blonde hair and so did your son, Luke. You told me once that she liked walking outside when it was raining and her favourite drink was an apple martini. What else ...? Well, she was Christian, of course. I think you said she could play the piano ... I'm sorry, Gabriel, I can't think of much more, I only met her a few times. As for Luke, I saw even less of him, but I remember you being very indignant when he was cast as the goat at his nativity play last year. You thought he should have been starring as Joseph. And he wouldn't eat spaghetti unless it was Postman Pat spaghetti, as I remember. Is that enough, Gabriel?'

'I suppose it'll have to be. Thank you.'

'That's the trouble with constant travelling – you don't always get to be in the lives of your friends as much as you'd wish.'

'How did the car crash happen?' I asked.

'That I can't tell you,' Stephomi said. 'You couldn't talk to me about it at the time.'

'But you must know *something* about it,' I pressed. 'Was it an accident?'

'Of course it was an accident!' Stephomi said sharply.

'Was I driving?' I asked.

Stephomi hesitated.

'Oh God, I was, wasn't I?'

'Look, it's not what you think. It wasn't your fault. Someone drove straight into you. They were speeding. There was nothing anyone could have done about it. The roads were icy.'

'Well, you seem to know a lot about it, given that I wouldn't talk about it,' I challenged. 'You're just making it up to make me feel better, aren't you?'

'No! I've told you the truth.'

'But how do you know if I didn't tell you?'

Stephomi sighed. 'I was with you when the police came a few weeks later and I learned about it from them.'

'Why were the police there? I thought you said it was an accident?'

'It was,' Stephomi said. 'But the police still have to investigate these things, Gabriel.'

'What did I do about this other driver?' I asked.

'What do you mean?'

'Did I kill him? Did I make him *pay* for it?'

'No,' Stephomi said patiently. 'You'd hardly be sat here like this if you had, would you? Although I admit that for a while I was worried that you might be moved to try and do something like that. There will always be pain, Gabriel. There's no way of avoiding it unless you become a monk or a hermit.'

'Did you come to their funeral?'

'Of course I came. The rest of your family were there to support you too but you, ah ... weren't well, you see, and I had to take your place with the pallbearers.'

I felt shame at that, of course, but at the same time I felt incredibly lucky to have someone like Zadkiel Stephomi in my life, and the gratitude I felt towards him in that moment was something I would never have been able to express with words.

'Thank you,' I said, trusting he could hear in my voice what his friendship meant to me. 'I'm so sorry for the way I treated you before, Stephomi, when you wouldn't tell me what had happened—'

'Don't apologise to me,' Stephomi said hastily. 'Please, Gabriel. I know you would have done the same in my place.'

Now that I know the truth, I feel worn out. Burned through. But, at the same time I feel better than I have since all this began. It's exhausting, coming to terms with the truth like this. But now at last I know, and it is a relief to know, to hit rock bottom knowing I won't stay there. Not with a loyal friend like Stephomi to help me up again. Nicky and Luke are gone. There's nothing I can do to bring them back. Now that I know about them, I can move on. And I don't need to fear myself any more. There's nothing sinister about me. I'm a writer, an academic ... that's all. Now I know who I am, where I stand and why, I am free to continue with my life.

11th October

Oh, God, to look at what I wrote in these pages yesterday. If only it could all be as easy as that. I felt at peace when I went to bed last night. The ghosts of my wife and son saddened me but I had decided to say goodbye to them and start again. And now grim foreboding has settled upon me like a cloak that I can't shake off.

Last night I had the most disturbing and unsettling nightmare. I dreamed that Casey was giving birth at the top of the snow-covered bell tower of St Stephen's Basilica. She was lonely and afraid but I was with her, helping her, reassuring her, keeping her safe. When the baby was born, a tiny, perfect little boy, I reached for a white blanket to wrap him in; but when I turned back, the baby had become a writhing black demon, sticky with blood, tiny batlike wings furling and unfurling as it thrashed around, lashing out with its claws, hissing and spitting and baring its sharp, pointed teeth at me. I shrieked and suddenly there was a dagger in my hand and I knew what I must do. My teenage neighbour screamed with horror as I drove the knife into her Hell-spawn baby, staining the white blankets with thick, sticky, black blood.

I looked up, gasping for breath, and the burning man was stood there staring down, the usual orange flames blazing all around him, the shimmering red light of the condemned, his fierce blue eyes taking in the weeping mother, the murdered remains of the twisted black newborn devil on the ground, and me hunched over it with the dagger in my hand, thick, black demon blood still dripping from the blade.

'Welcome back to the Ninth Circle, Gabriel,' the burning man said steadily, staring down at me with quiet approval.

I woke up screaming, quite sure that the heat from the blazing man's flames was still scorching my skin. I had leaped from the bed and was out of my apartment and in the main corridor, hand raised to start hammering on my neighbour's door before I checked myself hastily, forcing myself to stop. It was the middle of the night. I was wearing only a t-shirt and shorts. I couldn't knock on her door at this time of night, I'd frighten her. She might even call the police. But I had to see her. I couldn't wait until morning to see if she was all right. I thought of a hasty excuse and then knocked on her door as loud as I dared. I didn't want to risk waking the whole building. After a few moments, I heard movement from within the apartment. The walls were thin and I clearly heard the girl sharply telling her brother to go back to his bedroom and stay there. Another moment later, the door opened on the security chain and Casey was peering out suspiciously. She looked surprised when she saw me, and not entirely comfortable.

'What is it?'

Her words threw me for she had spoken in English, although she quickly corrected herself and repeated the question in Hungarian. I suppose, having been woken up in the middle of the night, she had used her first language unthinkingly.

'Aren't you Hungarian?' I blurted out in surprise.

'American,' she said, staring at me.

'I'm English,' I said, feeling pleased.

'Oh ... Okay, then. Well, goodnight.'

And she started to close the door.

'Wait!' I said quickly. 'You remember me, don't you? My name's Gabriel Antaeus, I'm your neighbour, you helped me when I had a migraine attack the other day. Look, I'm really sorry to disturb you at this time of night but I just got up to go the bathroom a few minutes ago and I saw someone outside the building next door being mugged. There's no credit on my mobile and I have no phone in my room, so I was hoping to borrow yours to call the police.'

She was still gazing at me a little suspiciously. I suppose helping a neighbour in broad daylight was something altogether different to letting him into your home alone in the middle of the night.

'Or perhaps you could call them, if you wouldn't mind,' I said to reassure her.

'How good is your Hungarian?' she asked.

'I'm fluent.'

'Then you'd better do it. I only really know enough to get by.'

She closed the door and I heard the chain being pulled back, then she swung the door open and held it back for me.

'The phone's just over there,' she said as I walked in.

Her apartment was similar to my own in terms of layout and design, but smaller. There did not seem to be a lounge, but rather the kitchen was a little bigger with an old couch in the corner, letting the room serve as a living room as well. While my apartment was furnished with good quality and expensive furniture, in addition to the couch, hers only had a couple of cheap chairs round a table, and a threadbare rug lay on the damp floorboards. The phone stood on the kitchen worktop and as I crossed over to it, one of the doors leading off from the room opened and a boy stuck his head out. His eyes widened when he saw me and he turned to his sister uncertainly.

'Casey—?' he began.

His sister turned sharply to him. 'Go back to bed, Toby! Everything's fine. Mr Antaeus is just using the phone and then he's leaving.'

'I'm sorry about this,' I said with an apologetic smile.

She smiled back at me uncertainly and took a cigarette from a packet on the worktop, watching me carefully as she lit it, before checking herself and putting the cigarette out with a regretful sigh. I dialled the number for the police and then reported the so-called mugging in the street. I altered the details, though – slurring my words, I told the police I thought I'd seen a man being mugged in the street outside by invisible goblins. The officer I was speaking to brusquely told me to lay off the bottle and go to bed and then he hung up.

As I spoke, I glanced surreptitiously at Casey. She was wearing a large, oversize nightshirt and was leaning against the kitchen worktop, fiddling with the cigarette box, still watching me closely. She seemed quite unharmed. Seeing her in such a way relaxed me and helped chase away the clinging shreds of my nightmare. I wanted to ask her if she had anyone to help her or whether she was alone here. I wanted to ask if she had made arrangements for when the baby came and what was going to happen to her brother while she was in hospital. I wanted to tell her not to go out into the city late at night. I wanted to ask her if there was anything I could do. I wanted to plead with her ... *beg* her to let me help her. But I had to be careful. In a world such as this, she would be a fool not to suspect ulterior motives from such a stranger. And the last thing I wanted to do was frighten her. The world doesn't make it easy to be kind.

'Thanks,' I said, turning from the phone once I'd replaced the receiver in its cradle.

She nodded again and I could tell that she felt vulnerable now, that she was probably regretting ever letting me in and that perhaps she now feared that she wouldn't be able to get me out. So I abandoned any half-formed plans of staying and talking to her for a while, deciding that the best thing would be to leave at once, having been allowed to use her phone as I had asked.

'Again, I'm sorry to have disturbed you so late. Thanks for your help.'

She smiled then, in relief I suppose, as she saw that I really was leaving. 'Goodnight, Mr Antaeus,' she said, accompanying me to the door.

'It's Gabriel,' I said, stepping out into the corridor. 'Good night, Casey.'

I want to get closer to God. I feel safe inside churches and other holy buildings. I couldn't sleep after checking on Casey. I was too scared that the nightmare might return. So I took my coat and stepped out into the cool night air. It was about three o'clock in the morning and dew sparkled on cobbles and mist hung about the streets in ribbons, as if the city had been decorated by phantom hands during the night in preparation for some ghostly wake. As the metro and tram lines would not be open for almost two hours yet, I had to call an all-night taxi service and order a taxi to pick me up outside the apartment block.

The driver had most likely been expecting to take me to the airport, and I didn't want to draw attention to myself by asking otherwise. So I explained that I was going on holiday with some friends and was meeting them at their house where we would then be driving to the airport together in my friends' car. I directed the driver to a street near Margaret's Island, paid him and then watched him drive out of sight before turning and striding off in the direction of Margaret Bridge.

I paused when I reached it, looking down at the angelic sculptures that adorned its columns, painted silver by the moonlight. They were old, these angels – created by the great artist Adolphe Thabart during the nineteenth century. I wished I could get close enough to touch them – close enough to trace one of those great, feathered wings with my fingers. I was suddenly painfully aware of this powerful yearning to be near angels, near Heaven, near God.

I trudged slowly across the quiet, moonlit island, feeling miserable and alone, missing my family even though I'd never known them. I thought of Margaret herself, condemned to this place for her short, cheerless life. Then I thought of Wladyslaw Szpilman hiding in his attic on the outskirts of Warsaw, desperately lonely while at the same time knowing that if any people did come his way his very life would depend on hiding from them. In his memoirs, he compared his existence to that of Defoe's Robinson Crusoe and pointed out that Crusoe at least had the cherished, precious hope of coming into contact with another human being. A hope that kept him going day after day. Whereas Szpilman, hiding in his tiny attic and longing for human contact, knew he would have to stay hidden from any passers-by if he were to live.

There was not even that miniscule drop of hope in the sea of utter loneliness in which he found himself drowning.

The island was beautifully quiet at night. I could even hear the faint sloshing of the Danube as it lapped against the banks. The smell of lush, living greenery filled the air with its healthy scent as I walked on in the semi-darkness. I was halfway across the island before I noticed the flames. They rose far above the treetops, a huge cloud of smoke billowing out over everything. I couldn't understand how I could have been unaware of it for so long as the flames seemed to light up the whole island and the smell of ash was strong even from here.

I started to run, crashing through the trees – the cold, empty eyes of stone busts telling me exactly where I was, and which building was on fire. By the time I stumbled out into the clearing, Michael's church was *engulfed* in spitting fire, smoke pouring out from gaps in the pointed roof. The heat was sending up fierce convection currents that rocked the bell in its tower, making it ring out in agonised peals.

I skidded to a halt before the church, staring at the old building in horror as flames leaped and roared against the still darkened sky. With the noise the old bell was making, it would surely not be long before other people arrived on the scene – after all, the island's hotel was only a few minutes away.

Then I realised that I'd better leave – and quickly. I didn't want to be found alone here with a blazing church. I would be jailed for arson within seconds. Even as I thought how lucky it was that this should have happened at night when there were no people inside, the wooden front doors burst open in a shower of sparks and two men tumbled out, falling in the dust on the ground. My mouth dropped open in pure horror as I realised that one of the unfortunate men was *on fire*! I hunted round manically, looking for something with which to put him out. I couldn't see anything so I stripped off my jacket, hoping it would be enough, and started to run towards the two men. And then stopped short in astonishment. One of the men was still hunched over stiffly on his knees, but the other had risen to his feet. The man on fire was simply standing there, silently, gazing at his opponent. There were no screams of agony; he was not writhing on the ground as surely he should have been with those flames caressing his skin.

And then I realised that I recognised him, although up until now I had only seen him in dreams. I had seen him in a dream less than two hours ago, looking on while I killed the newborn devil in the bell tower of the Basilica. He looked just the same now – enveloped in flames yet seemingly unaware of it, his blue eyes burning with a fierce light of their own.

He was holding a long, bejewelled sword in one hand and as I watched he approached the other man, still huddled on his knees on the ground, head bent. And then the burning man started to raise the sword over his head and I ran forward unthinkingly with a yell of horror. He looked up in alarm as he heard me and I saw his eyes narrow angrily. I reached out, grasped the kneeling man by the shoulder and yanked him back, ignoring his cry of pain. And then darkness fell like a cloak and I blinked in surprise as orange flashes winked before my eyes. The fire was gone, as if snuffed out like a candle, and the suddenness of the darkness left flaming imprints on my eyeballs. Amazed, I reached out a hand and brushed the wall of the church. It was cold to my touch. There was not even the slightest hint of warmth. It was as if the building had never been alight at all.

As my eyes adjusted to the watery light, I turned my attention to the man beside me and sucked in my breath in surprise. I knew this man too. It was Zadkiel Stephomi. There were scorch marks on his clothes and blackened ash and soot stained his skin. One hand was pressed over the deep gash slashed across his lower ribs, blood running through his fingers alarmingly. Cursing, he tore a piece of fabric from his shirt and tried to quell the bleeding with a trembling hand. Then he glanced up at me, brushing sooty hair from his eyes and leaving more smears of grime on his face in the process.

'Gabriel? What are you—?' he began hoarsely.

'What *was* that thing?' I interrupted, kneeling down beside him. 'What happened to the fire?'

'The fire was never really there.'

'But there's ash all over your clothes! I *saw* the church in flames! What was that thing with the sword?' I asked again, somehow dreading the answer.

Stephomi hesitated for a moment before replying. 'He was a devil, Gabriel.'

Welcome back to the Ninth Circle, Gabriel ...

'*What*? *What* did you say?'

'You heard me.'

'Are you *mad*?'

'Ha, ha. Mad. Yes ... perhaps I am ...'

He swayed suddenly and I caught at him in alarm.

'Are you all right?'

His breathing sounded shallow, sweat was running down his face, and I could feel that he was trembling.

'All right?' Stephomi choked out a disbelieving laugh. 'Only you would say that to someone who's just been hacked at with a fucking huge sword, Gabriel!'

'You need to get to a hospital,' I said, glancing at his blood-stained shirt. 'We've got to get you to the nearest one right now!'

'No, no, no. Don't start panicking.'

'*Panicking*? That wound needs to be stitched or you'll—'

'Does it?' Stephomi asked. He removed his hand and I stared in disbelief, for the skin beneath was already starting to heal where the sword had pierced the skin. Although it was now blistering and burning in a most painful looking way, it was no longer bleeding. 'Demon swords don't create permanent injuries.'

'How ... how is that possible?' I demanded. 'That wound ... I mean, the sword went right through!'

'Never mind the wound – it'll just be a scar by morning,' Stephomi said dismissively. 'It's the blood loss that's the, er ... that's the problem right now—'

'But it was deep before!' I protested. 'Just two seconds ago it was an open, bleeding—'

'Just shut up and listen, this is important! I'm, ah ... going to pass out. Don't want you to freak out and do something stupid. I just have to find back ... get back home, okay? Just unconscious, Gabriel, not dying. Please ... no hospitals ... all these awkward questions. Afterwards I'll explain ... tell you ... explain it all, I promise ...'

And then, with a sudden shudder, he crumpled against me, getting blood all over my once clean shirt.

I have to say the whole thing completely pissed me off. He'd put me in a really awkward position. The Castle District wasn't far away in a car but it would take far too long to walk there uphill, and we couldn't get on any of the late night buses looking like this. The only thing I could think to do was phone for a taxi and ask that it pick us up from the hotel just a few minutes walk away, relying on the dark to disguise the large amount of blood on Stephomi's clothes.

'My friend here's had too much to drink,' I said to the taxi driver in a lame attempt to explain why I was virtually carrying him. 'He's, er ... he's getting married tomorrow.'

The taxi driver grunted as if this explained everything, and drove us to the Hilton in silence. I shook Stephomi hard when we got there and after a moment, to my relief, he groaned and tried to push me away.

'Come on, we're at the Hilton!' I hissed, shaking him harder. 'Wake up! I can't drag you through the reception area like this, bleeding all over the place! *Stephomi*—'

'All right, all *right*, I'm awake! Stop shaking me, damn you! *Christ*, Gabriel!'

I hauled him out of the car before the taxi driver could catch on to the fact that anything was amiss, and was relieved when the car at last drove off.

'You're going to have to help me,' Stephomi muttered.

I glanced round and saw that he was leaning against the wall, looking like he was about to throw up. I stripped off my coat and handed it to him.

'Put this on,' I said. 'It'll hide your shirt. Hopefully no one inside will notice your hands if we move through the lobby quickly.

They'll just think you're drunk. And dirty,' I added, glancing at the soot in his hair.

Stephomi eased himself stiffly into one of the armchairs once we were at long last back upstairs in the suite.

'I need a drink,' he said, waving his hand in the direction of the well-stocked bar.

'What do you want? Water?' I asked, walking over to it.

Stephomi scowled and ran his hand through his hair. 'Gabriel, if you bring me water, I'll throw it at you.'

I glanced at the many bottles lined up on the shelf and took down the whisky. It seemed like quite a good idea so after I'd poured Stephomi's, I turned round holding a second glass. 'Do you mind?'

He shrugged. 'Not at all.'

I poured myself a drink and then walked back to the chair and handed him the whisky, but I hadn't even sat down before he'd knocked it back and was holding his glass back out to me.

'Again.'

'Are you sure that's wise?' I asked.

'Just get me the damn drink, Gabriel. On second thoughts, bring me the bottle.'

'Look, you can get drunk later!' I said irritably. 'But right now you owe me an explanation! And no lies! I want the truth.'

'You don't want much, do you?' Stephomi snapped. 'You know what, Gabriel? I feel fucking awful and the last thing I feel like doing right now is having this particular conversation with you. I'll do it because I said I would, but you are going to have to *shut up* and give me a minute, all right? Now either get me that bottle or bugger off.'

I opened my mouth to carry on arguing but checked myself when I looked at him, for he did still look awful – hunched awkwardly in the chair covered in blood and ash and wearing a coat that was too big for him, his face horribly white. If I hadn't been so upset by what I'd seen that night, I'm sure I would have been more patient. As it was, if ever a man looked like he needed a drink it was Stephomi, and I could afford to wait a few minutes.

'You're right,' I said. 'I'm sorry.'

I handed him the bottle and bit my tongue for the next few minutes. The alcohol quickly returned some of the colour to his face and it wasn't very long before he set his empty glass down on the table and said, 'What do you know about the Antichrist?'

'Excuse me?'

'It's a simple question.'

'Well, the Antichrist is supposed to be ... Jesus' adversary,' I said.

'Yes. Mysteriously mentioned in the Bible only as the "Beast" and prophesied to appear just before the end of the world. Well, he's coming. In fact, he'll be here any time now.'

'And how could you possibly know that?' I scorned.

'Raphael told me.'

'Oh, I see. You're on speaking terms with the seven great archangels, are you? Tell me, do you chat with them often?'

'No, not often,' Stephomi said with a smile, ignoring my sarcasm. 'Only when necessary. They're very busy, you know. What with the War and all.'

'Angels don't go to war!'

'Of course they do, Gabriel. Theirs is the first War. God's team against Satan's. It's been raging for millennia.'

'Satan doesn't have angels, he has demons,' I said sharply.

'Whatever. It's all the same, really,' Stephomi replied with a shrug.

'It's *not* the fucking same!' I snapped.

Stephomi grinned, easing himself into a more comfortable position. 'You never did like the idea, did you? What's this grudge you have against Lucifer's angels anyway? Do you know what Samuel Butler once said? "*An apology for the Devil: it must be remembered that we have heard only one side of the case; God has written all the books.*" Come on, Gabriel, don't look at me like that. I promise you I'm not a devil worshipper. Just devil's advocate, perhaps. Did it ever occur to you that there may be good and bad devils as there are good and bad men? Devils are scapegoats, that's all. Blamed by the angels for all of Earth's failings. We need scapegoats like we need oxygen, to ease the guilt and the shame of being human.

'Politicians seem to be the prime choice nowadays. Poor bastards. I'd sooner nail my own hand to a railway track than be the President of the United States at the moment. Can't win, no matter what he does, can he, poor sod? It's never black and white, although I admit that if it was, things would be a hell of a lot easier. What of Wladyslaw Szpilman and the courageous Captain Wilm Hosenfeld?' he asked, a ghost of a sneer curling his lip.

'And what of Hitler himself? He wanted to be an artist, you know. He tried, without success, to get into an art college in Vienna. An *art college!* If only they'd let him in, eh? He might have lived an inoffensive life of beauty then. He might have left paintings behind when he died instead of all those graves and slaughterhouses. Wouldn't that be nice? I mean, if there had been just one man at that art college who had seen something promising in Hitler's application and argued his case, Hitler might be remembered today for his contribution to the art world instead of for how many people he murdered. Should it really be so dependent on chance, where we deserve to go once we're dead? Hitler liked animals as well, you know. He befriended a little stray terrier while he was serving in the First World War, which he doted on, apparently. And when Hitler put a gun in his mouth, his new bride, Eva Braun, killed herself too rather than face a world without him. What do you think that means, Gabriel?'

I gazed at Stephomi feeling sickened. 'I can't believe you're really suggesting Hitler wasn't evil.'

'Evil is a tricky word,' Stephomi said with a slight shrug. 'Evil people don't scare me because I'm free to hate them. And hatred is so easy, isn't it? Much, much easier than love. Did you know that Hitler was regularly beaten by his father as a boy and was once even put into a two-day coma by him? Wouldn't it have been nice if he'd just killed him instead?'

'Well, of course,' I snapped. 'But what has this to do with anything? You're getting off the point.'

'It doesn't matter, really. What does matter is that the battle between the angels has escalated.'

'Why?'

'I just told you – because the Antichrist is coming. Did you know that Nostradamus predicted it would happen around this time? Devoutly religious man, Nostradamus. He published hundreds of prophecies, all in quatrains. I have to say the language of the Antichrist prophecy is a little vivid for my taste. It goes like this:

> *The Antichrist three very soon annihilates,*
> *Twenty-seven bloody years his war will last.*
> *The heretics dead, captive, exiled.*
> *Blood human corpses water red hail cover the Earth.*

'You know, it's that last line I really don't like the sound of, Gabriel,' Stephomi said quietly. 'The Antichrist War lasts twenty-seven years and after that –' he snapped his fingers '– blood. Human corpses. Red water. End of the Earth. All over.'

I glanced at him and, despite the lightness of his words, for once there was no amusement on his face. I even thought I caught a faint spasm of fear before he quickly hid it.

'But what makes you think that this will happen now?' I asked, hoping for reassurance. 'Nostradamus wasn't right all the time, was he? Or perhaps his prophecy has been misinterpreted?'

'It's a little difficult to misinterpret this one since, unusually for Nostradamus, he gives specific *dates*. The years 2007–2008 in *Century X*, quatrain seventy-four, as well as the 2008 Olympic Games, are highlighted by Nostradamus as marking the beginning of the end, so to speak. The last two lines of the quatrain refer to the end of the world, Judgement Day itself:

> *Not far from the great millennium,*
> *When the dead will leave their graves.*

'Chilling thought, isn't it? But anyway, forgetting Nostradamus for the moment, I know that this is all beginning to happen because Raphael told me so. Nostradamus believed the future was fixed, immutable, but luckily angels don't think that way. They're not ready for Judgement Day yet. They're trying to delay it. So are the demons.'

'*Delay* Judgement Day?' I repeated incredulously.

'That's right. Angels don't like being judged either, you know. But, er ... there is one little problem. Apparently, there's some uncertainty as to whether this person is indeed the Antichrist or, well ... effectively Jesus' second coming.'

'*What?* How can there possibly be any uncertainty over which it is when the two are so different?'

'Are they so different?' Stephomi asked sharply. 'It all comes down to greatness, doesn't it? Angels can sense greatness but they don't know what form it will take, that's all.'

'What *rubbish!*' I protested. 'Good and evil are *opposites.*'

'No, not really,' Stephomi said mildly. 'Hot and cold are so-called opposites, but haven't you ever touched something so scalding that for a moment you think it's freezing? When you get to extremes, the brain confuses the two, can't process them properly, mixes them up. Or perhaps it's just that they're really not that different to begin with.'

We lapsed into silence for a moment as I thought about what he'd said and tried to twist it into something I could make sense of. Devils ... angels ... wars ... prophecies ... I would have thought it was all some kind of practical joke if I hadn't seen the demon with my own eyes.

'How do you know all this anyway? Who are you that you can *talk* to angels?' I asked suddenly.

'Ah, well, that's the question, isn't it?' Stephomi sighed. 'Did you know that babies can see angels, Gabriel? They're innocent, untainted by the world. So they're close to angelic realms and can see angels all around them. They lose this ability as they grow up. The world strips people of their innocence before long, one way or another. But there are some rare adults who can see the angelic and demonic realms which overlay our own. You should count yourself lucky you live in this time. We'd have been accused of witchcraft in the past and been burned at the stake by a pious, Christian mob of killers. That fire you saw at Michael's church ... most people wouldn't have seen it. And they wouldn't have heard the bell ringing either.'

'Then why can I?' I asked, very much fearing the answer. 'Why can you?'

'Well ... sometimes it's possible to catch glimpses of angels and demons in places of the In Between. Graveyards – because they're places that belong to both the living and the dead. Churches – places of both the mortal and the divine. The moments before sunrise and sunset where the Earth belongs to both the night and the day. Mirrors that reflect reality the wrong way round and dreams that allow both the impossible and the possible all at once ...There are some people ... who are themselves people of the In Between, neither truly one nor the other. And this allows us to see things that others can't. As I understand it, the insane and the dying can see the devils around them, just as the newborn can see angels. But the reason is not always quite that extreme.

'Take me, for example. I used to give lectures on religious philosophy. Guest lectures at various universities and religious functions. Because of the ... passionate nature of my teachings, my lectures always seemed to be filled with either the zealously religious or the fiercely atheist. The clash of the two extremes between faith in God's existence and an equal faith in his non-existence caused a spark somehow, with me at the centre. My teachings themselves are a place of the In Between.'

'And what about me?' I asked fearfully.

Stephomi frowned. 'There are many professors of religion out there like me who aren't people of the In Between. Sometimes it happens, sometimes it doesn't. With you, Gabriel, who knows? You never told me and I assumed you didn't want to talk about it.'

I ran my hands through my hair in frustration, an unreasoning fear building from within me as I paced agitatedly. 'What is the Ninth Circle?' I threw at Stephomi, rounding on him suddenly.

'Ninth Circle?' he repeated in genuine bemusement. 'I ... well, according to Dante, the ninth circle of Hell was the—'

'Yes, yes I know the theology of it,' I snapped. 'But there's something more to it, isn't there? There's some other reference. Something of this world.'

'I don't know what you're talking about,' Stephomi said, gazing at me curiously. 'What makes you say that?'

I hesitated, but then shook my head and said it was nothing. I didn't want to tell him of the note I had received. 'Well? Is it true?'

'Is what true, Gabriel?'

'Are there really nine circles of fiery, torturous Hell?'

Stephomi gave a slight shrug. 'I have never been there, my friend, I couldn't tell you. Perhaps you should ask Keats.'

'*Keats?* The poet?'

'That's right.'

'What's he got to do with it?'

'Keats longed for Hell,' Stephomi said in a strange, soft voice that sent chills down my spine.

'John Keats wrote of beauty,' I snapped. 'He wrote of joy and life and—'

'Yes, yes, joy and life, very nice. But he also wrote of Hell,' Stephomi said, his mouth twisted in a smile. 'He rather seems to have enjoyed it.'

'I don't know *what* you're talking about!' I virtually shouted in an effort to drown out what he was saying. Why was I so angry? What was it about Stephomi's suggestion that frightened me so badly?

'*On a Dream?*' Stephomi prompted. I am sure there was something of maliciousness about the way he looked at me as he spoke. 'Aren't you familiar with that particular sonnet, Gabriel? Keats wrote it after he dreamed of visiting the Second Circle. I think I'm accurate in quoting the great poet when he said that, "*The dream was one of the most delightful enjoyments I ever had in my life—*"'

'*No!* No, no, you must be wrong! Keats was an artistic genius! He wrote of love and ... and beauty and—'

'Who's to say that Hell itself is not beautiful, Gabriel? Can you really be so sure it isn't?'

I could feel my mouth twisting in a grimace of revulsion at the disgusting suggestion and, turning on my heel, I started to stride towards the doorway but paused and turned back when Stephomi called out to me over his shoulder, 'I don't think I've said thank you.'

'What? What for?'

'For saving my life, of course,' Stephomi replied, twisting slightly in his seat to glance back at me, with that amused expression on his face once again. 'I think I might have been prematurely parted from my head had it not been for your fortuitous arrival. What where you doing on the island, anyway?'

'Oh. I couldn't sleep,' I said, staring back at him. 'Would that thing really have killed you?'

'Of course,' Stephomi replied with a wry smile. 'Did you not see the large, impressive sword?'

'What can we do about all this?' I asked.

He looked at me incredulously. 'Haven't you heard a word I've said?' he asked. 'This is an *angelic* war, Gabriel. There's nothing you or I can *do* about it. Oh, wait ...' he said, and I looked at him hopefully as a thoughtful look came into his eyes. 'Do you have a spaceship?' he asked after a moment.

'What?' I said blankly.

'A spaceship. If you've got one then perhaps we could pack some Kendal Mint Cake, go to another galaxy and leave the angels to squabble over this one. What do you think?'

I scowled my annoyance at him, irritated that he was mocking me at such a time. 'What were *you* doing on Margaret's Island?' I asked.

'I could not sleep either,' Stephomi said lightly, turning back in his chair.

The metro stations re-opened for the day at 4:30 a.m. so I was able to get one of the underground trains back to my apartment, stopping to pick up the morning paper from an early vendor outside.

I'd had less than three hours' sleep but I didn't feel tired as I let myself into my dark apartment.

I was not at all happy about what I had learned from Stephomi that night. The burning man that I had thought a product of my imagination was, in fact, real. And tonight he had tried to kill the one friend I had in the world – if I could continue to call Stephomi a friend, for he had been less than truthful with me from the very beginning. But I was not afraid of angels or devils, for I had nothing they'd be able to take from me. Except my memories, I suppose ... but that is why I have this journal.

What Stephomi had said about Keats disturbed me greatly. I don't know why I found the idea so intolerable. Perhaps because I respected Keats for his ability to recognise beauty; an ability that allowed him to see something beautiful, something of value, in misery itself. But to associate any kind of beauty with Hell disgusted me beyond words, and it seemed the most dreadful contradiction that Keats could have seen such a thing. For Stephomi was right. I found the poem the next day in one of the collections on my shelves. Keats did indeed dream of visiting the Second Circle after time spent reading about it in the fifth canto of Dante's *Divina Commedia*. The Second Circle: where the lustful are punished for their sins by being blown and driven about by fierce eternal winds of misery.

I was reminded forcibly of Giuseppe Tartini's *Devil's Trill Sonata* and his claim that it was a poor reflection of the beauty the Devil had been able to wring from the violin in his dream, for Keats too maintained that the inspired poem really was no comparison to the delight of the dream itself. Nothing but a pale reflection of the beauty the Devil had brought with him to the sleeping minds of artistic geniuses...

I don't know why the poem upsets me so much. It's true that Keats described the dream as one of the most 'delightful enjoyments' of his life, and expressed the desire to return there every night ... *Every night*, oh God, the grotesqueness of such a desire! At the end of Canto IV, Dante himself faints (the only occasion he does so during his whole journey through the Circles) out of horror and fear at the things he sees within the Second Circle. That anyone, much less a poet of the most astounding ability, would *wish* to visit this place ... I can't think about it, for it disturbs me too greatly and I feel that there must have been something, after all, quite flawed and twisted within Keats' soul.

But all this nonsense about angels fighting each other ... that can't be right. Surely Stephomi isn't *still* lying to me? Am I being paranoid now? Truth be told, I think I am predisposed towards paranoia. But as the saying goes, even the paranoid man has enemies.

I did not like the idea that a demon had invaded my home and my dreams. Stephomi had said that dreams themselves were a place of the In Between, neither truly one reality nor the other, a merging of the possible and the impossible. And I had seen the demon in mirrors too, I remembered. I had seen him and the mystery woman in the mirror of the bathroom, both of them in flames ... I started, appalled as I thought back on it. At the time I had dismissed it as a semi-waking dream, a nightmare, a hallucination. But now ... I realised what this must mean. The woman, the lost woman of Budapest had indeed been found. By a devil! A devil who had taken her straight to Hell! *Fuck!*

Horrified, I picked up the telephone and dialled Stephomi's number, very much relieved when he answered. I proceeded to tell him what I had surmised. And then noticed that he was very quiet on the other end of the phone and another truth burst savagely into my mind. 'You already know, don't you?'

'Yes, Gabriel, I know. I've seen her too.'

'What can we do?'

Stephomi sighed down the phone. 'We can do nothing, Gabriel. You must get this into your head. You can't *fight* angels and devils. It's not a question of taking kung fu classes – this isn't *Buffy*, you know. Look, lost souls have always been rich pickings for hunting demons, that's just the way it is. Have you seen the morning paper?'

I replied that I hadn't had the chance yet.

'Then I suggest you go and look at it. Now if you'll excuse me, I really must go—'

'Wait!' I said. 'I've been thinking about it and that day I came to see you in the morning at the hotel ... Your room was a mess and so were you. You'd had a demon in there, hadn't you?'

Stephomi hesitated. 'A demon, yes.'

'Well? What happened? Did you kill it?'

'No, Gabriel, I didn't kill it,' he said, patiently. 'That would have been a very foolish thing to do indeed'

'But ... why the *hell* did you have a demon in your hotel room anyway?' I demanded.

'Look, as I've already said, there aren't many people who can see them. Demons and angels know who we are and I think it unnerves them to have humans who can see into their own worlds. They don't like it. They preferred it when people like us were burned at the stake. But sometimes they need a human agent here on Earth, and that's when they come to us.'

I paused for a moment, a grimace of distaste twisting my mouth. 'You've *served* the whims of demons?'

'Angels too, Gabriel,' Stephomi said, an amused tone in his voice. 'Don't worry, I've done nothing I should be ashamed of.'

'But ... but, they're *devils*! They'll have ulterior motives!'

'Everyone has those, my friend. Even angels. Anyway, sometimes we mortal men have little choice in the matter. The world belongs to them, really. God gave it to them to squabble and fight over. That's why everything's such a mess. Anyway, I really have to go. I suggest you go and read the paper. Page six. And I assure you I had nothing to do with it.'

Nothing to do with it? Those ominous words still ringing in my ears, I hung up the phone, walked back to the kitchen table, sat down and spread the newspaper out at page six. And then my heart missed a beat and my breath caught in my throat as I looked at the photo and the caption on top of the small article. As I sat and stared, growing more horrified by the moment, there was a soft, slicing sound from just behind me and the page was suddenly covered with splattered drops of blood, blotting and soaking into the page, mixing and swirling with the black ink used to print the dreadful story.

In horror, I leaped from my chair and whipped round to stare behind me, half expecting to see some devil with a dripping carving knife. But there was nothing. The kitchen was completely deserted. I raised a hand to my face, wondering if a spontaneous nosebleed had caused the newspaper to become spotted with blood. But it wasn't me who was bleeding. At a loss, I turned back to gaze at the newspaper but, to my astonishment, the page was quite unmarked. There were no longer any swollen beads of blood staining the article. Cautiously, I picked up the paper and ran my hand over the surface. It was bone dry. Once again, I felt that terrible tugging sensation from within – as if laughing, mocking devils were tugging at my sanity, madly determined to have it from me.

With an effort, I sat back down at the table and re-read the article. The mystery woman now had a name. And she was also now dead. Her body had been found yesterday morning in a seaweed- and barnacle-covered crate left beneath the Holocaust Memorial during the night ... 'Neville Chamberlain's Weeping Willow is weeping still' ...

When people had noticed the box yesterday, bomb diffusers had been called for in the fear that the box contained explosives. But as soon as the crate had been prised open, a mass of water had rushed out and with it, the body of a woman. Her name was Anna Sovànak and she was a scientist working on developing new medicines in Budapest. She had disappeared a few months ago, back in June, while holidaying with her family in Italy. There had simply been no trace of her, not a single clue for the authorities to build a case upon. She had just gone for a walk on the coast after storming out of the villa, having argued with her husband, and had not been seen again. Eventually, it was assumed that she must have decided to go swimming and had been overcome by savage currents that had swept her out to sea.

The paper confirmed that the water from the crate had indeed been salt water and that the unfortunate woman had most likely been in this crate at the bottom of the ocean since her death, which was estimated to have taken place in June soon after her disappearance. She had died from a precisely applied stab wound to the neck, which would have killed her virtually instantly. Anna Sovànak was from a long line of Jews and, together with the fact that her body had been left beneath the Holocaust Memorial, police had officially concluded that this was a simple anti-Semitism inspired killing. An isolated incident of prejudice and hatred. They were following several leads and were sure to catch those responsible soon ... very soon ... How very comforting ...

I gazed at the article incredulously for some time. Why would anyone go to the trouble of concealing the body in the Mediterranean, only to bring it up months later and somehow transport it to Hungary, without anybody noticing, to leave it beneath the Holocaust Memorial? How could this even remotely be classed as a straightforward, isolated incident? Were the police utterly incompetent? And what of the journalists? Why was such a story toiling away on page six with no more than three or four paragraphs? Surely this was front-page news? Was I in the middle of some huge conspiracy that *everyone* else was in on?

And it was horrifying that she had been dead since June, for I had seen her just last month in Budapest. Was I truly losing my mind? I thought back over it all and realised triumphantly that I was not the only one to have seen her. We had both been attacked by muggers that night ... But had they seen her or had they just seen a man running through the streets on his own? I had seen men step out behind her. But I had not seen them touch her, or speak to her, or step towards her, or acknowledge her presence in any way. When it was all over, she had been gone, faded softly from the alley like some wandering ghost.

But, no, there had been one other. The boy at the Basilica. The dying boy, I realised with a sinking heart. The child whose body was disease-ridden, causing his hair to fall out and his skin to turn grey. A pale shadow like me, not even really here. A person of the In Between himself.

I took her photograph out of my pocket. The photo that had been stitched into the lining of the antique Italian volume of Hell and its devils with the reference to the Holocaust Memorial on its back. And now this Jewish scientist had turned up, stuffed into a box, beneath the Weeping Willow memorial created in memory of all those who had gone before. Had the reference to a weeping willow been a clue? A premonition? A warning? Who was it who was playing these games with me? Who tormented me in such a fashion? Sending me the smallest snippets of information with maddeningly cryptic quotations that could not be unravelled until it was too late.

I pulled out the second photograph – the one that had been hidden in the case of wine from France; the one that showed Stephomi and me facing each other across the hotel room, the vast, stunning cityscape of Paris spread out through the window behind us. And the quote from Robert Kennedy on the back: '*Forgive your enemies, but do not forget their names.*'... *Do not forget their names ...* The implication was clear – that Zadkiel Stephomi was an enemy and not to be trusted. That he must be kept at arm's length and closely watched. But whatever Stephomi was to me, he had been more forthcoming and open than this cursed letter-sender, and in those moments I felt a powerful, unreasoning hatred against that person. That unknown person, out there somewhere, deliberately taunting me, pushing me to the edge of madness itself. God, how I *hated* them!

And, whoever they were, they were now here in Budapest. They had pushed the last note under the door with their own hands rather than sending it disguised in the mail. They knew where I lived. They knew that I could read and understand Latin. I took this note out too and lay it on the table beside the photos and the newspaper article to re-read it:

> *The gates of Hell are open night and day;*
> *Smooth the descent and easy is the way.*

And then, added beneath:

> *The Ninth Circle will not hide you much longer.*

Yes. Someone was surely trying to drive me insane. The Weeping Willow reference on the back of Anna Sovànak's picture strongly suggested that this was the same person who had deposited the Jewish woman's body beneath the Holocaust Memorial. Which meant that I did indeed have a most dangerous enemy: a ruthless and twisted killer; a clever lunatic. But I wouldn't let him beat me. I'd set a trap for him – catch him like the rat he was.

I went into Budapest today and purchased a very expensive, top of the range video camera, so tiny as to be hardly noticeable to the casual glance, which I fixed over my doorway. If anybody puts anything else under my door, I will know about it. I will see, once and for all, who is behind these dreadful games.

I have always been a fervent and devout Christian. I know this because of the worn out, heavily annotated Bible by my bed, but I can also feel my faith burning inside me. I accept God in my soul. I know that the Bible speaks the truth and I need no miracles to persuade me of this. I have always known that angels and demons are real. But I didn't realise that they were so close to us before.

The knowledge alarmed me, for Stephomi had said that angels and demons didn't like us – we few who could see them – but nonetheless, when there was something that they wanted, they might come and ask things of us. I knew that I needed to be protected against such an event. If an angel asked something of me, I knew I would gladly comply; but I vowed that I would not follow in Stephomi's footsteps and acquiesce to any demonic request that might be put to me – even if the decision cost me my life. I meant it, too. A person has to have something of heroism in them to be prepared to die for what they think is right, don't they? I can be proud of my convictions. It's more than Stephomi is willing to do. Not that I can really blame him. I realise that there can't be many of us who have such an inner selflessness.

In order to prepare myself, I reluctantly took out my many books on demonology once more and read up on the fallen angels, from the Watchers to Lucifer himself and his seven Princes of Darkness. I read of Beezlebub, so called 'Lord of the Flies' because of the insect swarms that lingered around his bloodstained altar. I read of Belphegor – the champion of lust – and Moloch, who demanded the sacrificing of children in his honour. And so the list went on: Mephistopheles, Belial, Samael, Asmodeus, Mastema, Nisroch ... each demon with their own despicable tale of sin and wickedness. I learned as much about each of them as I could so that I might recognise them if they came to me.

I studied the repulsive paintings in the antique Italian book, noting with distaste the lunatic expressions on the faces of these demons. But there was one painting in particular that disturbed me more than all the others. It was a picture of Mephistopheles by an unknown artist. The book explained that the painting had been discovered in Italy in the 1500s and the precise age of the picture was difficult to estimate. What so unnerved me about it was the distinct lack of any madness in the demon's intelligent gaze. His thin, twisted form was undoubtedly that of a demon, but something of the angel hung about him still. The large, bedraggled wings that were curved round him like a bat had not quite lost all their white feathers. He was perched on the edge of a mountain, his feet gripping the boulder like claws as he stared down hungrily at the world spread beneath him.

It was thought that Lucifer had bitterly missed God and longed horribly for Heaven for many centuries after falling from grace. But not Mephistopheles, who had promptly followed Satan from the Heavenly realms, revelling in his newfound freedom without even the slightest twinge of doubt or regret or uncertainty.

I thought back to the way Mephisto had so cleverly turned Faust's thirst for knowledge and self-improvement against him, and felt disgusted by the demon and his methods – to twist something good and admirable in such a way that, in the end, it completely undoes the man who once entertained notions of nobility and integrity.

I closed the book then and moved on to another, finding of all the demons it was Mephistopheles I feared meeting the most. With the other demons, even Lucifer himself, I felt that as long as I was firm in my adherence to Christianity and Godly values, they would not be able to touch me. But with Mephistopheles, it was those Godly values themselves that turned into weapons in his masterly hands to be used against the helpless men who became so inextricably entwined in his grasp.

The other thing that disturbed me was the idea that some demons are the 'dark twins' of angels. Two brothers on opposite sides of the bloody War. I dislike anything that connects angels with such vile creatures. Of all the angels, I like Michael the best. Head angel after Lucifer's fall, Michael is often portrayed with sword and armour and is said to have led the heavenly army against the rebel angels and is destined to do so again in the battle that will take place at the end of time. It's also said that Michael fought Satan for Moses' body after his death. So I suppose Stephomi was right – angels do fight, after all. With such an infestation of demons, what other choice do they have?

The Cherubim, second highest choir of angels, were said to have been formed from the tears that Michael shed over human sins. It would seem indeed that he is a powerful force to be reckoned with, and his existence comforts me in the wake of hours spent reading of powerful, reckless devils.

I am glad that I started this journal. It is a focus; it grounds me in some sense of reality, of stability. It is an anchor for my soul, not allowing me to become too detached. I sometimes worry that all my research into angels and their fallen brothers serves only to further distance me from those around me; to further sever the already tenuous link I have to this world and bring me closer to theirs.

12th October

Last night I dreamed I was in Salem in 1692, on trial for witchcraft. The public gallery was full. There was malevolence ... everywhere. Pummelling me in waves from every person in the courtroom. And ill children sitting on a bench together with their parents, too frightened to look at me. The judge walked in and everyone stood up. The muttering died down into silence as the judge addressed me.

'Gabriel Antaeus, you stand before the court accused of witchcraft. How do you plead?'

'Not guilty,' I said.

The judge stared at that, as if my answer astounded him, and an excited murmur went round the court.

'But you have already admitted to talking to Satan.'

'No, no, I haven't,' I protested. 'I've never even seen him! It was Mephistopheles! He tricked me! He tricked me into talking to him!'

'So you admit to talking to demons?'

'Yes, but I never—'

'And what about these poor children?' the judge asked, gesturing to the ones sitting on the front bench. 'Isn't it true that you cast a spell over them to cause their illness?'

'No! That wasn't me, it was Moloch! Look, where is Zadkiel Stephomi? He will speak for me.'

Even as I spoke I saw Moloch standing beside the kids, touching them with his unnaturally long black fingers, leaning closer towards them to mutter words of sickness in their ears.

'For God's sake, get those children out of here!' I cried.

'How dare you threaten the children in a court of law!' the Judge roared, rising from his seat.

'I'm not! I'm not threatening them!' I shouted back desperately, raising my voice over the outrage of the public in the gallery. 'It's not me! It's Moloch, I can see him right there! He's cursing them! He's the one making them ill! Find Zadkiel Stephomi, I tell you, he'll speak for me!'

'Silence,' the Judge thundered, bringing his mallet down on the anvil until the noise in the room subsided. Then he looked directly at me once again. 'Everyone here knows that a witch is incapable of reciting the Lord's Prayer,' he said in a quiet voice. 'If you truly mean the children no harm, if you truly are not a witch ... then you will be able to recite it before us now. If you can do so, you will walk free. If not, you will be burned at the stake for witchcraft and communication with the Devil.'

I gazed at the judge, hardly able to believe my ears. 'If I recite the prayer, I walk free?'

'That is correct.'

Relief swept over me. I knew the prayer, of course, knew it perfectly by heart. I took a deep breath and began, '"*Our Father, who art in Heaven, hallowed be thy name ...*"' I got that far before I faltered at the sight of Mephistopheles, standing next to the judge and grinning at me. Unlike Moloch, Mephistopheles looked almost like a man, but I knew him instantly for what he was.

'Isn't this madness, Gabriel?' he asked softly. 'Nineteen men and women in the grave already because of this hysteria. These hypocrites are about to burn you at the stake. You do realise that, don't you?'

Hurriedly, I continued with the prayer, very aware of the silent court watching me. '"*Thy Kingdom come, thy will be done, on Earth as it is in Heaven—*"'

'Hell's not so bad,' Mephistopheles went on, glancing round the courtroom with a sneer. 'Better than here, anyway. I expect you'll prefer it.'

"'*Give us this day our daily bread*,'" I went on, desperately trying to ignore the demon. One slip up, just one tiny inaccuracy in my recital, and I knew these bloodthirsty people would string me up by my neck or tie me to a stake. I could see in their hungry eyes how much they wanted me to fail. They had grown to love the smell of burning flesh. I must not let the demon distract me. "'*And forgive us our trespasses—*'"

'This judge is a pious, hateful little shit, isn't he?' Mephistopheles asked, looking down at the man's face. 'You'll hang whatever you do, you know. One of the sick children is his son. Someone has to pay for that.'

"'*As we forgive those who trespass against us*,'" I went on desperately, closing my eyes to block the demon out. Just three more sentences. Three more and I would walk free! "'*And lead us not into temptation, but deliver us from evil. For thine is the—*'"

Suddenly I broke off, choking. Mephistopheles was by my side now, his hands clamped tightly around my throat. The court murmured with pleased excitement at my very evident distress.

'Don't be obstinate, Gabriel,' Mephistopheles said calmly as I clawed frantically at his hands. 'Your time is up. You're going to burn out there today, I'm afraid.'

"'*The kingdom,*'" I wheezed, my lungs burning with the effort. "'*The power—*'"

'No!' Mephistopheles snapped coldly. 'This is it, Gabriel. Time to go. Lucifer has sent for you.'

'Take him out and *burn* him!' the Judge was roaring.

No! I screamed at them in my mind. *I can finish it! I could recite it perfectly if only Mephistopheles wasn't strangling me! How can you not see him? It's not the prayer that's choking me to death, it's the fucking demon!*

I desperately tried to draw enough breath just to say the last few words, but I couldn't get any air at all now. There were tears running down my face – from the extraordinary pain of being unable to breathe and the awful knowledge of how I was going to die. The demon would never let me finish the Lord's Prayer. He wouldn't let me prove my innocence to anyone. I couldn't prevent my body from twitching, jerking horribly, desperate for oxygen I could not get. The agony of it was unbelievable. People were on their feet now, running towards me, roaring with glee and pious bloodlust.

My vision blurred alarmingly and my head went light, but no sooner had my knees hit the floor than I was being dragged up again by the mob and Mephistopheles' grip was gone, the air rushing back into my starving lungs, burning like acid. "'*And the glory,*'" I gasped at last, but it was far too late by then. They were going to tie me to a stake and burn me until there was nothing but dust and ash left. They dragged me out of the courthouse to the stake driven into the ground outside. It had been used before: the blackened body of a man was even now being taken down from it. And although most of his skin was gone so that I could clearly see the skull beneath the flaking flesh, it was quite clear to me that this burned out corpse had once been Zadkiel Stephomi.

'*No!*' I screamed, waking myself up at last. '*No, no, I can say it! "Our father, who art in Heaven, hallowed by thy name ..."*'

I wasn't a witch! I wasn't a witch! I didn't talk to demons! I could just see them, that was all. That was all! That didn't make me something evil, did it? I pushed back the sheets, switched on the lamp and stood before the full-length mirror in my bedroom, still reciting the Lord's Prayer. I recited it five hundred times, absolutely perfectly. I proved to myself I did not deserve to burn. It was only a nightmare. I could recite the prayer for ever and never make a mistake because I held God close to my heart and was loyal to Him. Indeed, it was only the sun coming up and shining through the windows that made me realise how long I had been standing there repeating the prayer, and then I broke out of the trance. I had already more than proved my point.

16th October

From the snatches of conversation I have had with Casey over the past week, I've learned that she moved to Hungary from America when she was twelve. She claims that she and her brother stayed behind when her parents moved back to America, but I'm not sure that I believe this. What parents would emigrate leaving their children behind? I suspect her parents disowned her when they found out she was pregnant, and perhaps she ran away, taking the brother with her. It's clear that she dotes on him.

From what I've gathered, she has several different jobs, both at night and during the day. I said one day that if she ever needed something to tide her over she could come to me, but she didn't look very happy so I quickly backed off. Did she think ... did she actually *think* that I was suggesting something improper? I was only trying to be *kind*, but we have to be suspicious of kindness now, don't we?

Sex complicates everything. I can't help thinking that there must be an easier way for the human race to continue, generation by generation. Children can be friends with other children of the opposite gender without it mattering at all. Perhaps, to put Casey at ease, I should lie and tell her I'm a eunuch. But I don't think that would be a very easy thing to slip into a casual conversation. It's not the kind of thing that normal people just come out and say, is it? *Oh, by the way, have I mentioned before that I'm a eunuch? Because I am, you know ...*

I've seen Stephomi a couple of times this week, but I didn't enjoy meeting him as much as usual. It was my fault, for I persisted in asking him questions and didn't much like the answers he gave. This battle ... this War, or whatever it is, troubles me greatly; yet Stephomi seems to be almost indifferent to it. Another habit of his which upsets me is his tendency to refer to angels and demons alike as angels, maintaining that demons are simply fallen angels who have lost favour with God. But there should be *rules*, there should be *boundaries*. There should be distinct, separate groups. Otherwise the labels become meaningless ... *angel, demon, human* ... different words for the exact same thing ...

'I don't know why you get so upset about it, Gabriel. Why does it matter if we're all the same? What's so awful about the idea that demons can sometimes do the right thing and angels can be narrow-minded selfish little shits?'

'Shut up!' I said sharply, unable to stop myself from flinching at his words. 'For God's sake, listen to yourself! Do you *know* what goes on in Hell? Do you know what the demons *do* to people down there?'

I decided it was my duty to enlighten him so I proceeded to explain the tortures of each Circle one by one; but when I got to the Seventh Circle and the centaurs that guarded the rim of the lake of hot blood, shooting any souls who attempted to rise, Stephomi *appalled* me by throwing back his head and *laughing* at what I'd said. Really *laughing*! I stared at him, speechless.

'I'm sorry, Gabriel ...' he said, trying and failing to stifle his laughter. 'It just sounds like such fun.'

'I *beg* your pardon?'

'Do you think the centaurs keep track of their scores? You know, like target practice. Perhaps on a really good day they even hold tournaments?'

I'd heard enough by this point so I threw up my hands and stood up, intending to leave. But Stephomi caught my arm as I walked by, and when I glared down at him, he was looking at me in an odd way, this strange smile twisting his lips. 'Do you know what I think would do you good, Gabriel?' he asked. 'I think you should reacquaint yourself with Lilith's story. Look me in the eye and tell me that angels are perfect beings and devils are nothing but monsters after that.'

'Lilith?' I repeated with a frown.

'Adam's first wife.'

'There's no truth to that legend,' I said dismissively.

'What makes you say so?'

'There is no mention of her in Genesis.'

'Ah. Perhaps, after all, there are some elements of our history that God would rather not have recorded?'

'Don't be ridiculous!' I snapped.

Stephomi sighed as he released my arm. 'Lately I seem to offend you whenever we see each other, Gabriel. I'm sorry about that. But take my word for it – Adam did have another wife before Eve. She does exist. And her name is Lilith.'

I felt a little guilty after that, for I realised I'd been blaming Stephomi for a situation that was not his doing. He's just a messenger in all this... I have decided that Stephomi's occasional outbursts – like this issue over the Seventh Circle – are nothing but a defence mechanism. He is scared too, but he does not wish to show his fear to me. So he covers it with highly inappropriate jokes. But I forgive him, for he cannot help it. I did some reading on the theories of Freud and Jung and I realise now that his behaviour is not his fault. He is a textbook example of a man who cannot cope with his fear; cannot meet it head on, as I can.

At Stephomi's suggestion, I returned home and read of Lilith's story. I think I might have been vaguely familiar with the myth before I lost my memory, but I'm sure that I didn't know the story in detail. Maybe I never bothered to look into it in any great depth because the Bible certainly doesn't acknowledge that Adam ever had a wife before Eve, and Genesis makes it quite clear that Adam and Eve were the first humans to be created.

Lilith's story is a dark, twisted, vulgar tale. I find the whole thing most distasteful and don't wish to believe in its authenticity. The Bible should be the last word on all such things. But Stephomi's words have been ringing in my ears ... *She does exist. And her name is Lilith.* And after all, he should know, shouldn't he? He who openly admits to having assisted demons when they've asked him to. For the legend goes that Lilith became a demon after rejecting Adam and leaving the Garden of Eden – an idea that clearly parallels Lucifer's rejection of God and flight from Heaven.

In the beginning, Adam was the only human within the Garden of Eden. After some time he tired of coupling with animals and asked God if he might have a female companion of his own. And God sent Lilith, and she and Adam were married that very day. How very nice. But then Lilith refused to take up the subservient position for Adam at his demand during sexual intercourse ... Yes, how very awful of her. So, naturally, Adam responded by trying to rape his wife.

But Lilith managed to throw her husband off and ran from Paradise, making her home instead in a cave by the Red Sea where she entertained hordes of demons, finding them kinder and gentler lovers than her estranged husband. She proceeded to bear hundreds of demon babies that went on to plague mankind for centuries before Satan's fall from grace. The story reminds me of the tale of the angelic Watchers, procreating with mortal women who gave birth to a race of giants, thereby bringing a terrible Apocalypse upon the world.

God was incensed by the First Woman's behaviour. How dare she be such a disobedient wife and refuse to submit to rape? The horror of it! Three angels named Sanvi, Sansanvi and Semangelaf were sent to order her back to Adam. Lilith refused, preferring the company of the demons to her human husband. As a result, God sent angels to murder many of her demonic children, causing Lilith great grief and pain, but still she would not return to the Garden.

God created a new woman for Adam, this time fashioning her from Adam's rib to ensure that she would be a passive and subservient wife. And for some time, they did indeed live together in peace and happiness within the paradise God had created for them. And Lilith sat alone in her sea-washed cave, surrounded by the twisted corpses of her hideous demon-babies, grieving and weeping for them. And in her forsaken isolation and misery, she swore vengeance on all the helpless newborn children to be born to mankind in the years to come.

The vile wickedness of her vow transformed her into a powerful demoness, flying through the winds of the world for all eternity, looking for innocent, defenceless babies to devour and consume. Jewish folklore maintains that the only way to protect babies from Lilith is to hang amulets in the four corners of the baby's room, each inscribed with the names of the three angels who first confronted Lilith in her cave beside the sea.

An extension of the myth is that Lilith is also a powerful Temptress, tempting mortal men to father demons upon her. Or, alternatively, seducing them in their sleep – the unacknowledged cause of embarrassing nocturnal emissions. She was said to take particularly malicious delight in having her way with pious, celibate Christian monks and virgins during their sleep. It became such a problem that, in the end, the unfortunate monks were forced to take crucifixes to bed, covering their groins with them, so that Lilith wouldn't dare approach while they slept. I think it would be unwise to repeat this grand solution to Stephomi, for I know that he would laugh, and it's really not funny at all.

Anyway, I can't believe Lilith's story is true. I'm sure God would never have allowed it. I mean, God would never condone a crime as disgusting as rape, would He? He would have punished Adam for what he'd tried to do, if the story really were true. It's just an unfounded and unsubstantiated myth, that's all. Adam was not a rapist and he did not have sex with animals ... And yet this story troubles me, picking at my mind and tugging at my faith in a most unpleasant way. Unable to get the story out of my head, I telephoned Stephomi to ask him about Adam's abandoned wife. 'Have you ever seen her?' I asked.

Why did I care so much about the answer? What did I want from Stephomi? Reassurance. I wanted him to tell me that Lilith somehow managed to put the misery of the past behind her. That she somehow managed to forgive men and angels for the great wrong they had done her.

Stephomi hesitated a moment before answering me, 'Yes, I've seen her.'

'Where?'

'By the sea. She haunts sea-caves. Beaches are places of the In Between – where land meets ocean. When God sent angels to destroy her children … she wasn't able to save them all. There were too many defenceless babies and too many self-righteous, avenging angels with large swords. She's still haunted by that.'

'What does she look like?'

'Why the sudden interest, Gabriel? Yesterday you were quite adamant that she didn't exist at all, that she was a myth. Because angels do not slaughter children, do they?'

I fell silent, not quite sure myself what it was about Lilith's story that had so affected me. 'Is she really a lascivious Temptress who comes in under the cover of night to seduce holy men in their sleep?'

'Ah, now, Gabriel, you're asking me questions that I can't answer. Although, just a passing thought … If Lilith did entertain fierce, passionate demonic lovers for so many years in her cave by the sea, don't you think there's a very slight possibility that slumbering, elderly monks would be a bit of a disappointment to her? For such an accomplished seductress, it seems doubtful to me that pious priests would be able to satisfy her apparently voracious appetite. In fact, it strikes me that the holy hypocrites were probably just looking for a justification, an explanation, a rather pathetic excuse. After all, if Lilith is to be blamed for every child's death, why not blame her for some old monk's wet dream as well, eh? Assuming that's what it was – monks are a horny bunch, you know.'

The bitterness in his voice surprised me. 'You're being vulgar,' I said shortly.

To my surprise, Stephomi laughed. 'Pardon me, Gabriel, but you asked a vulgar question, even if it was politely phrased. What is Lilith's sex life to you anyway?'

'Nothing!' I said, suddenly feeling flustered. 'I mean I … it's none of my business anyway and I … look I just wanted to learn more about her, that's all!'

To my horror, I have started to dream about Lilith. It's become so bad that I find myself fearing to go to sleep at all. Perhaps the Lilith of my dreams is real. Perhaps she isn't. How can I know for sure? But real or not, she is so incredibly beautiful. Actually, she's the most beautiful woman I've ever seen in my life. It's not natural for a woman to be that supernaturally stunning. She has black hair, reaching down to the small of her back. Hair that runs through my fingers like freshly-woven silk. And her white skin is marble perfect ... cool to the touch. But there is this sadness in her always, in her blue eyes and in the tears that fall silently from them ... salty tears that drop onto my skin ...

I forget, when I see her, that she is a demoness, for she looks like nothing if not a goddess. Beauty and eroticism and desire personified. She wears long black gowns that cling to her body, contrasting starkly with the whiteness of her skin. And she brings with her a velvety, soft heaviness that presses in all around with sweet, erotic promises that she refuses to fulfil.

I want to talk to her when I see her. I want to apologise for what Adam tried to do, for the threats the angels made and for the appalling way in which God punished her for not submitting to her selfish, disgusting husband. But her presence always pushes all nobler thoughts from my mind. And all I can think about then is how much I *want* her ... how much I want to touch her, to kiss her, to make love to her all night. I resent her for having that power over me. What worth is there in *lust*? I am sure she does it on purpose. She *teases*; she loves that she can arouse me just by *being* there, in the same room. She revels in it. But she never delivers, oh no, though she may push it to the brink when she chooses. Always at that crucial moment her eyes will turn cold, her lips will tighten, and she will hiss spitefully in my ear that no mortal man ever again will take satisfaction in her body, for she belongs to the demons now.

I wish to God that Stephomi had never brought her up, for she now haunts and torments my dreams, real or not. In the end, I had to buy some medicine from a pharmacy to aid undisturbed rest; and, to my relief, it seems that Lilith is unable to invade drug-induced sleep.

23rd October

Something very ... strange ... is happening. I left my apartment this afternoon and stepped into the corridor straight into this ... this golden *mist*, that's really the only way to describe it. I stopped dead in amazement, for one wild moment thinking I had somehow stepped straight into Heaven itself. I might as well start by saying that the mist was *ineffable* so I know that no matter how hard I try, I will not be able to describe it adequately here.

It wasn't just the fact that the mist looked like sunlight made more solid – it was also the *feel* of it. Like a pure, ethereal beauty gently surrounding me. It felt warm on my skin and was scented – a very faint dusting of vanilla that settled on me softly as I stood there. It started right outside my apartment and trailed all the way down the corridor towards the stairs. Even as I watched, the mist around me was fading and dissipating, and I walked down the corridor quickly, anxious not to lose it.

I don't know why I followed it. I guess I was just so captivated by it. It never really occurred to me that it would actually lead to anything, or anyone, and it wasn't until I walked into a coffee house not far from my apartment block and saw Casey that I realised.

It was clinging to her, surrounding her, moving with her every time she moved. Clearly no one else could see this but I was mesmerised, for I had never seen anything so beautiful. Perhaps this was an aura all pregnant women carried with them and it was just that no one else could see it, but I hadn't noticed it around her before.

She was stood at the till, four credit cards before her on the counter and a queue of people fidgeting impatiently at her back. I could see Toby nearby holding a tall glass of hot chocolate in one hand and a plate with a slice of cake on it in the other. He was stood unmoving at Casey's side, head bowed in silent misery.

'That one's been rejected also, Miss,' the waiter behind the till said, handing her back another credit card.

'Are you sure?' Casey asked, staring at the card he'd just given her. 'Look, would you mind trying it again?'

'Come on, lady!' someone called impatiently from behind her.

Casey ignored him. 'Please,' she said to the waiter, 'can you just try the card one more time?'

'Casey,' Toby muttered, putting his cake and drink back on the counter, 'don't worry about it. Let's just go.'

'I'm sorry, Miss,' the waiter said, 'but the cards have all been rejected so unless you have some cash—'

'Some of us have places to be, you know,' came another disgruntled comment from behind her.

'Shut up and wait your turn,' Casey snapped, turning her head to glare back at the sullen queue behind her. 'Fine. Please take these back,' Casey said, pushing the hot chocolate and cake back over the counter towards the waiter, 'and instead give us ...' She paused for a second, running her fingers through the change in her purse. 'One small low fat yoghurt drink, please.'

'Wait,' I called, pushing my way through the groaning queue to the front, my wallet already in my hand. 'Don't touch that,' I said, indicating the cake and drink on the counter. 'We'll take it.'

'Gabriel? What are you doing?' she asked, switching to English with that soft American drawl.

'Hi, Casey. What do you want?'

'What?'

'To drink. What would you like?'

'Oh, you really don't have to—'

'You might not have noticed but that queue behind you is

starting to get a little irate, so why don't you choose something now and we can argue about it later? I'm sure Toby isn't the only one here who likes cake.'

When there were at last three cakes and three drinks on a tray, I carried it to a table at the back of the shop, aware of the less than good-natured clapping coming from the queue behind us as we left it. Casey's cheeks were burning as she helped me move everything from the tray onto the table.

'Well – they're an impatient lot, these Hungarians, aren't they?' I said, rolling my eyes and smiling in an effort to lighten the mood.

To my relief, she grinned at me then, shrugging off the humiliation with a graceful laugh. 'I guess they are,' she replied, fishing the lemon slice out of her coke and handing it to Toby, who gleefully put it straight in his mouth. 'It's awesome to finally be able to talk to someone in English. Thanks a lot for helping us out back there.'

'No problem,' I replied.

I looked at her, puzzled that I'd never really noticed before how attractive she was. There was nothing at all sexual about it. Her beauty was not the seductive, dark, velvetiness of Lilith with her black hair and lace ... The golden aura that surrounded Casey tinted the coffee brownness of her skin and glinted in golden flashes from the many gold hoops in her ears and the silver nose stud, collecting in pools in the liquid brown of her eyes. The electric pink and blue streaks through her dark hair seemed all the more colourful for the aura, and I had never seen a person look so healthy – so radiant with a delicate innocence that took on a golden physical existence of its own, reflecting down the lengths of her eyelashes and clinging in golden droplets to her dark skin.

When I glanced at Toby, I was disappointed to see him look-ing distinctly uneasy in my company, so I made an effort to talk to him, to try and draw him out of himself; but he just looked doubtful and uncertain and only answered my questions with a brief word or two.

'What's got into you, Toby? You're not usually this shy,' Casey said, matter-of-factly wiping away a smudge of dirt on her squirming brother's face.

A couple of old ladies on the table next to ours caught my eye and gave me encouraging smiles. I smiled back, feeling puzzled. And then ... it *struck* me. They actually thought that Casey and Toby were my *children*! I glanced at the two of them. Yes, they had brown skin but it was of such a colour that I suspected one of their parents was white. And I was probably about sixteen or seventeen years older than Casey so I was just about old enough to be her father.

I was aware that when strangers looked at her, they probably looked no further than the many piercings, the tattoos, the dyed hair, and the painfully obvious fact that she was pregnant. She did, in fact, scream 'troubled teen' and anyone looking at her was bound to assume that she was a troublemaker. Believing me to be her father, the people around us liked me for taking her out to lunch, but they pitied me too for having such a troublesome child. How very ignorant of them. But I could be a friend even if not a father. I wanted something more than this fragile, cautious friendship that we had right now. But that kind of thing took time – I couldn't grab at it for she had to trust me first. And then a flash of inspiration struck:

'I don't usually eat desserts,' I remarked casually as I sank my fork into the marzipan gateau before me. 'But my partner has a very sweet tooth.'

'Partner?' Casey asked. 'Are you married?'

I saw her glance down at my hands, distinctly devoid of any wedding ring.

'No, she doesn't believe in marriage. We live in Italy but my brother lives in Budapest and he's had some family problems that I've been helping him with. Still, I'm hoping to be able to return home in a month or two.'

I could see straightaway that this was a good thing to have told her, for Casey relaxed visibly, reassured that my intentions weren't inappropriate and that I was just a normal person with a family of my own.

'Do you have children?' Casey asked.

'Two daughters,' I said.

'You must really miss them.'

'You have no idea.'

Already I was almost believing the story myself. I wished it were true. I thought of Nicky and Luke and felt that familiar longing rise up sharply. Hastily, I stuffed it back down again. I did not feel guilty for lying to Casey. All I wanted was to reassure her that I wasn't dangerous. That she had nothing to fear from me ...

'Is there something wrong with your cake?' I asked, noticing that she had been eating it very slowly and thinking that perhaps she didn't like it.

To my surprise, she laughed. 'No, there's nothing wrong with it at all. In fact, I think it's just the most delicious thing I've ever tasted in my life.'

I raised my eyebrows at her, puzzled by the enthusiasm in her voice. She gave me an embarrassed grin and indicated the banana cake on her plate with her fork. 'Cravings. I couldn't get them for some cheap, commonplace thing like rice, right? It had to be scarce, expensive banana cake. I've been lying awake at night just *obsessing* about banana cake the past few nights, so this really hits the spot, you know? I just want to enjoy it as much as I can. Thanks again.'

So why didn't you buy yourself a slice to begin with, I thought, watching her scrape carefully at a stray bit of icing on the edge of the plate. When I'd walked into the coffee shop, Casey had been trying to buy Toby a drink and a slice of cake, but she hadn't had anything for herself. She hadn't offered me any excuse or explanation as to why all her cards had been rejected, but I suppose the fact rather spoke for itself.

'When is your baby due?' I asked

'Oh ... around December, I think. I can't remember the exact day.'

'Where's the father?' I asked tentatively.

'I wish I knew,' Casey said with a wry smile.

'Sorry,' I said, feeling low for even asking her.

'Don't be. It isn't your problem.'

I wanted to discuss the matter further, to help her come up with some sort of practical survival plan, but I didn't want to mar the occasion by upsetting her. After we'd finished, I walked with them back to the apartment block. Casey was working in a few hours and just wanted to give Toby some fish fingers before dropping him at a childminder's and going on to her job as a barmaid. In the corridor outside the doors to our apartments, Casey paused and thanked me, urging Toby to do the same. I replied that it had been my pleasure to have some company other than my whiny, problem-riddled brother and then, after a brief hesitation, I spoke to her about the matter that was most pressing on my mind, 'Casey, look, I know it's none of my business but ... when the baby comes ... are you planning on keeping it?'

'Of course I will be keeping the baby! It's mine!' Casey said sharply. 'And you're right, it's none of your business!'

'I'm not trying to change your mind. I just wanted to say that ... if you want me to do anything ... If you ever want any help—'

'I thought you were going back home to Italy soon?'

'Oh. Well, yes, I am but until then ... And anyway, financially speaking you must have some kind of rights against the father. He must be under some obligation to you to pay maintenance or—'

Casey sighed and smiled gently at me. 'The truth is, Gabriel ... there is no father.'

I shook my head, confused. 'What do you mean there's no ...?' I trailed off, looking again at the golden aura that surrounded her and noticing for the first time how very like the golden halo around the Virgin Mary it was. Forgetting myself, I grabbed at her upper arms in my excitement. 'Is it a virgin birth?' I blurted out. I think I may have been grinning like a lunatic as I spoke.

But then I saw the alarmed way she was looking at me and I hastily let her go and wiped the insane grin off my face, horrified to realise that I was probably undoing all the good will I had painstakingly built up that afternoon. And I had been doing so well at appearing *normal* up until then too.

'Why would you assume that?' she asked, her voice almost a whisper.

'Just ... just a joke,' I said with a forced laugh. 'Sorry. So, er ... artificial insemination, was it?'

I held my breath, desperately hoping that she would accept my clumsy attempt to explain myself. But as I looked at her hopefully, my mouth dropped open in horror. Ever since seeing her in the coffee shop, Casey had continued to be surrounded by that breathlessly stunning, shimmering golden aura, glinting with flecks of liquid light, bathing her in an exquisite beauty.

But as we stood there, in the corridor of our shabby apartment block, the aura abruptly changed, turning to a thick, sticky black; clinging about her like tar, moving and swirling in the most sinister clouds of pure evil that I have ever seen. There was a faint burning smell too, and for all the world it smelled to me like human flesh. The hairs on my arms and on the back of my neck stood up as I gazed at her. She was clearly quite unaware of this depraved, undiluted malevolence that hovered over her and clung to her body.

She raised an eyebrow and said rather coldly, 'Well, my parents and the doctors didn't believe me either but at least they didn't make a joke out of it. They just shouted. It is an immaculate conception, Gabriel,' she said. 'Amusing though that may be to you.'

I gazed at her, desperately wracking my brain for what a normal person might say in this situation. 'Look, Casey ... It's ... it's easy enough to get pregnant by mistake. If the protection you used was faulty or something. And even if your boyfriend never actually ... well, there are other ways of getting—'

'I'm a virgin,' she said calmly. 'I haven't had a boyfriend since I was fourteen.' Then with a casual shrug, she added, 'There is no father.'

Then she turned away and went back into the apartment with her brother, closing the door behind her.

I have given much thought to the episode and have finally come to the conclusion that Casey simply must have been mistaken about what she said to me. Angels and devils running around on

Earth is one thing but a virgin birth is something else entirely and even though my mind automatically leaped to that assumption when she said there was no father, I have to be sensible about this. The odds are that Casey got pregnant by accident – that she is not touched by celestial strangeness as I am. That she is simply a normal teenage girl who made a mistake and that is all.

I must not allow what I know about angels and demons to touch every single aspect of my life. I can't let it affect the way I view reality. I mustn't let religion *consume* me. Otherwise I fear I will become one of those unstable people who fixate upon a thing until it takes over their life altogether. I am determined to remain balanced. Casey had unprotected sex with some boy. And that is why she is pregnant.

25th October

Do you know how hard it is to find banana cake in Budapest? They don't sell it in supermarkets or anything like that. They just have it in cake shops, but even then you can only buy it in slices and I wanted a whole cake. A huge, frosted, light and delicious, to-die-for banana cake. Hopefully with dried banana chips or something like that on the top.

I phoned all the cake shops in the city until I at last found one that could make me what I was looking for. A luxury (very *expensive*) banana cake with all the trimmings, delivered in a stiff white cake box to the address of your choice. I asked for the cake to be delivered today because I knew Casey would be home. I think she must have been listening out for me this evening, for I'd only been home a few minutes before she was knocking on my door. I have to say I was completely taken aback by her reaction as it was only a cake, but she was almost crying when she thanked me. In fact, she actually *hugged* me before she left, and asked me over to share some of it with her, so I'm going over there in a minute … I, er … ha … I almost feel happy right now. At last I know what it feels like.

30th October

Casey hasn't repeated her claim to me that her baby has no father. It's sad that she can't come to terms with what she did, but hopefully once the baby is born she won't feel the need to lie about it any more. The thought occurred to me that perhaps the father didn't know himself. I hoped she would reconsider and at least tell him about the child later. I mean, for all she knew, he might be pleased. He might want to marry her; he might want to help raise the baby. But it's not my place to say these things to Casey. The strange aura about her has not faded and continues to change from delicate gold to dripping black.

Tonight, I saw her in Heroes' Square. It was very late and there was no one else around. I was walking back to the metro station, having spent the evening in a restaurant nearby. I was alarmed when I realised the lone figure hunched up on one of the benches, head in hands, was Casey, for it was late and the square was deserted. I often go to Heroes' Square at night myself because I love seeing it floodlit. Really, I go there to see Gabriel. I suppose Casey was probably okay as the square was quite well lit, but even if she hadn't been pregnant, the city could be dangerous after dark.

She jumped in visible alarm when I came into her vision before she realised that it was only me. I could tell straightaway that, although her eyes were dry now, she had been crying before I arrived. I tactfully pretended not to notice as I greeted her.

'What are you doing here so late?' I asked, sitting down on the bench beside her.

She shrugged. 'Just on my way back from work. I'm taking the long route because Toby's staying at the childminder's tonight and ... well, empty apartments depress me.'

Tell me about it, I thought. 'Why Heroes' Square?' I asked.

'Because of him,' Casey said with a smile, pointing up at Gabriel so far above our heads. For the first time I noticed that she had prayer beads in her hand.

We sat in silence for some moments before she suddenly said softly, 'Did you know that once every minute a woman dies in childbirth? That means somewhere out there five women have died giving birth just while we've been sitting here.'

So that was what was upsetting her. I smiled reassuringly. 'The mortality rate is much lower for developed countries, Casey. And birth complications are less likely with younger women. I'm sure it's natural to feel anxious about it, but even if one woman dies in childbirth every minute, think about how many more give birth perfectly safely without any problems at all in that time. The death rate must be extremely low nowadays, especially if you're healthy to begin with.'

Casey nodded. 'You're right. But I'm ... I don't know, I'm probably just being stupid. But I can't shake this feeling that ... something ... something will happen ...'

Without thinking about it, I put my arm round her shoulders for a brief moment, quite touched by her naïve fears. 'The doctors know what they're doing,' I said kindly. 'They deliver babies all the time. You've got absolutely nothing to worry about.'

The soft, golden light from the floodlit monument gleamed off the many hoops in her right ear, and when she smiled at me I noticed for the first time that there was a little golden heart stuck to one of her upper teeth. Tooth jewellery, I realised, unconsciously raising my eyebrows.

'If you don't mind me asking, what do the tattoos mean?' I asked, to draw her onto another subject. 'What made you get all those piercings and things?'

Casey smiled and ran a hand through her dyed hair. 'Well, it must have been to rebel against my parents, right?'

'Er ...' I hesitated, aware of the odd tone in her voice. 'Was it?'

She smiled and I caught another flash of the gold heart on her upper tooth again. 'Believe it or not, some of us have piercings and tattoos and dye our hair because we think it looks pretty, not for any deep sociological reason. This isn't an act of protest against cultural or social repression. It's not a grand, deliberately defiant gesture against capitalists or feminists or any other social group. It's not even the fashion equivalent to sticking two fingers up at the world. The boring truth of it, Gabriel, is that I don't dress like this to hurt my parents or draw attention to myself or make a statement. I just do it because I think it looks nice. Disappointed?'

I shrugged, realising I had inadvertently touched a nerve. 'No, I agree with you. Sometimes an earring is just an earring, right?'

'Ha! Right. I have no interest in looking like any of those cold-hearted, Barbie-like celebrities who prance around wearing real animal fur and posing moodily for front covers of magazines ... Anyway, it's late. I guess I should head back.'

'I'll walk you home,' I said, standing up with her. The top of her head barely came up to my shoulder.

'Thanks,' she said, smiling up at me. 'You're not really an angel in disguise or something, are you, Gabriel?'

'No, I'm afraid not. Just share a name with one.'

'Are you sure?' She laughed.

We made our way back to our apartment block in companionable silence. It was almost one o'clock in the morning by this time, and I could see that Casey was tired. On the metro, she actually dozed off, her head resting against my shoulder. She apologised profusely when the train stopped at our station. 'I didn't drool on you or anything, did I?' she asked with an embarrassed smile.

I shook my head. 'No, but you do snore quite loudly.'

She rolled her eyes at me good-naturedly. I didn't mind looking after her. That was what God wanted me to do. In fact, to all intents and purposes, I *am* like an angel to Casey. Sent by

God to watch over her and protect her from any danger. We said goodnight outside our apartments.

'Oh, and by the way,' Casey said before disappearing into her kitchen. 'My tatts stand for tolerance, pluralism and broadmindedness.'

27th November

I know at last who's been putting notes under my door. And the identity of this person appals me. In fact, the sender is the one person I thought I could be absolutely and completely, one hundred percent sure was innocent.

These last few weeks seem to have passed so quickly. The temperature has dropped sharply, the leaves have all fallen, leaving the trees skeletal and naked, and it now truly feels like winter here. I have continued to meet up with Stephomi regularly and there have been no more distressing or disturbing revelations; and, much to my pleasure, I've found myself very much enjoying his company again. I've also seen Casey several times and she's always greeted me warmly. We are real neighbours at last. A familiar face right next door to me.

That's why I've neglected the journal these past few weeks – because I've been happy. Looking back through these pages, I realise that I tend to write in here when I'm unhappy. But lately I have been too involved with actually *living* to spend all my time whining about life in this book.

It's strange but the pages and pages of my writing in this journal really do comfort me. The paper has a different feel to it once it has been written on. The pages curl a little and do not stick together any more. And the paper becomes heavy with ink, taking on an uneven, crackly kind of texture. A book full of my words, my thoughts, my life. Perhaps that's why I'm so fond of this journal

– even now, I'm scared that I might forget everything again and this book is a safety net against that, for everything is here and written down and permanent, not to be lost again.

But something upsetting happened last week. I'd been dining late in the city and was walking from the metro station back to my apartment block. I was almost at the entrance when I stopped short in amazement. A woman had just walked out the doors of my building. The street outside was not very well lit so I couldn't see her clearly. All I could make out was that she was wearing a dark evening dress with black gloves that reached up to her elbows. I couldn't help but notice that she wore no coat, and it occurred to me how cold she must be, this late at night. Her long black hair was piled up on her head, and what looked like diamonds glittered at her throat and on her wrist. The stiletto heels of her strappy evening shoes clicked smartly on the sidewalk as she walked towards me.

She should surely know better than to come out on such a night with no protection from the cold, I thought. It was past midnight and no time for an attractive woman to be wandering around on her own. Streets that would be safe during the day could become dangerous at night. But there was something about the way she walked and held herself that suggested she was not afraid of the dark or what might be waiting in it for her. I drew breath anyway to ask if she had far to go, with the vague idea of offering to accompany her if her destination was very far. But as she passed me, she looked up, and weak light from a nearby streetlamp fell across part of her face, and the words died on my lips as she smiled slightly and carried on walking past me. For I was sure that this woman had been the Lilith of my dreams. Even as I turned and watched her striding away, I told myself I must have been mistaken. Stephomi had said that Lilith haunted places by the sea. Legend said that she flew though the night in search of her infant-victims. She would not have emerged from my shabby apartment block, dressed in all her evening finery, to walk the streets of Budapest.

But I had to know. I had to be *sure* that it wasn't her. So I turned back with the idea of catching up with her, but a frightened female cry from within the apartment block stopped me. I stood rooted with indecision for only a moment, watching the woman walk off into the darkness, listening to the click click of her heels, before I turned and ran into my apartment building, stopping short in the doorway in horror.

Casey was stood in the dimly lit lobby surrounded by three young men pressed in around her. One of them had hold of her bag and was trying to prise it from her grip but she was hanging on to the straps with both hands, pleading with her attackers while they laughed at her, delighted that she was making this so much fun for them.

Just give them the bag, I thought. *What does it matter?*

But the month's worth of rent she had in her purse meant that she wouldn't willingly be giving it to anyone. Was she really so naïve that she didn't think they'd *hurt* her if they had to? What good was a grotty old apartment if you were dead? Or if your baby was dead? What good would it be to you then? I could see tears running down her face as one of the men grabbed and twisted her arm, pulling it back roughly and tearing the bag from her hand while another mugger cupped a hand round her neck in a mocking caress, running his fingers through the dark strands of her hair.

'How about some sugar for Daddy, pretty lady?' he murmured greasily. Leaning towards her, he forced a kiss to her mouth, but then drew back sharply, his lip bleeding from where Casey had bitten him.

'You fucking bitch!' he snarled, spitting bloody spit into her face and then hitting her hard with the back of his hand.

And the desire to kill them all where they stood rose up within me, shaking me from the inside, and it took everything I had to fight the urge down. It is wrong to kill people. It is *wrong*.

'*Hey!*' I shouted, drawing their attention away from Casey. Rage boiling up inside, I strode forwards into the room and the three youths turned mockingly towards me, one of them still casually swinging Casey's bag from the straps twined round his arm. 'That was a mistake,' I said quietly, enjoying the promise for what it was.

I don't believe I seriously hurt them ... Well, there were no fatal injuries, anyway. They were cowards, so it didn't take much for them to turn and run. And I was prepared this time for the shocking, powerful surges of exhilaration that swept through me as soon as I hit the first attacker full in the face, relishing the feel of his nose crunching beneath my fist. I didn't let myself get carried away, even though hurting them filled me with such savage pleasure. This was even easier than it had been last time, for there had been five men then and they had been much bigger than these three teenagers.

The first mugger staggered back whimpering, blood pouring from his broken nose, while the other two came at me at once, one of them with a knife in his hand. But the problem with weapons is that they make people over-confident. It was so easy to take it from him that it almost seemed like he was *giving* it to me. If he'd just been another mugger, I would have thrown the knife down, but this was the kid who had hit Casey after kissing her and before I knew what I was doing I was pinning him to the wall, about to slice the knife straight through his throat.

His two friends had gone completely still, like statues, staring at us in the lobby. The blade was right there at his neck – one movement of my wrist and he would be dead. This was justice. He was despicable. He was prepared to steal from a pregnant teenager and then assault her. He didn't deserve to live. Cut the throat – nice and quick. I prepared to do so. And then suddenly caught myself.

He was looking right at me – brown eyes shocked and terrified. I stared at him, taken aback. How had I got here like this? What was I *thinking*? Casey was crying in the corner and it was this sound that at last snapped me out of it. I dropped the knife like it was burning me. Then I grabbed the boy's arm and gave him a shove towards his two friends. All three of them were staring at me like frightened rabbits and suddenly the three muggers were gone and I saw three children in their place, barely older than Casey was herself. I ran my eye over them anxiously but apart from the one with the broken nose they didn't seem too badly hurt.

I took a step towards them and they shrank back in unison. I stopped and when I spoke my voice sounded low and frightening even to myself. 'If you ever touch my friend over there again, if you ever *look* at her, if you ever come anywhere *near* her, I promise I'll track you down and I'll kill you.'

I could tell from their expressions that they knew I meant what I'd said. They knew it wasn't an empty threat. They knew I would kill them without even a second thought. Indeed I had almost done so just mere seconds ago. It terrified me. Perhaps, in that moment, I was even more scared of myself than they were. They were all still staring at me in silence as if too afraid to move but I needed them gone. The boy's brown eyes felt like they were boring into my soul.

'Get out,' I said, my voice barely above a whisper.

As if released by an invisible spring, all three of them scrambled for the door and a moment later they were gone.

I am a madman, lock me away. What had I almost just done? God, am I really that unstable? It was simply that he had made me so angry, hurting Casey like that. He was a threat to her so I wanted to get rid of him. But killing him was the first way I had thought to do so and that appalled me.

I think if I'd been by myself I would have run up to my apartment, locked all the doors, turned the lights off and just rocked back and forth for hours with my arms wrapped over my head, alone in the dark. But Casey was there and she needed me, so, with a great effort, I pulled myself together. Stifling the familiar nausea, I wiped the blood off my hands, brushed the hair out of my eyes and walked over to her where she was still sobbing in the corner by the stairs. She screamed when I touched her and lashed out at me instinctively, hardly seeming to know who I was.

'Hey!' I cried. 'Casey, it's me. It's Gabriel. It's okay, they've gone. They've all gone. They won't be coming back.'

I wasn't expecting her to turn and cling to me as she did, crying into my shirt, her body trembling against mine. I was taken aback for a moment but I recovered quickly and put my arms around her, speaking to her softly while the hysteria died down. She hadn't been badly hurt, although there would be a black eye later. But she had been frightened, of course, for herself and the easily hurt baby she carried. As I held her I instantly began to feel calmer about what had just happened. Casey had been in danger and I had protected her and that was all there was to it. None of those boys had been seriously hurt and, who knew, perhaps they would think twice about attacking anyone else in the future. Perhaps they would stay at home and do their schoolwork instead. Perhaps their lives would be *better* for what I had done!

The aura around Casey was golden today and, as I held her, it expanded to encompass both of us. I gazed in amazement at it, over the top of Casey's head, wondering how she could be unaware of such beauty. When she had calmed down at last, I picked up her bag from where the muggers had dropped it and took her back upstairs to her apartment. She had stopped crying but she was still shaking and when I asked if she'd like me to stay with her for a while, she accepted at once.

Casey still looked deathly white so I made her sit down at the small kitchen table. I boiled the kettle and made tea for her. I gave her a frozen bag of vegetables to press to her already swelling eye. *I* looked after her. She belonged to me and I was going to keep her safe. I put a mug of tea before her and sat down at the other side of the table.

'Why didn't you just give them the bag?' I asked quietly. 'Why didn't you just *give* it to them?'

'I don't know,' she said. 'I panicked. I just panicked. Our rent was in there.'

I sighed. 'Look, Casey, if anything like that ever happens to you again, just give them what they want and then run away as fast as you can. It doesn't matter if you're handing over your whole life savings; just give them what they want. It's not worth your life.'

Casey nodded. 'I know ... It's just that nothing like that's ever happened to me before. My parents have a lot of money. We always lived in a nice area ...' she trailed off.

'If I give you the money you would get in wages, will you stay here in your apartment at night?' I asked suddenly.

She winced at the suggestion. 'Gabriel, I can't do that,' she said. 'I can't take money from you.'

'The money doesn't matter to me,' I said quickly. 'I'm very well off, trust me, I won't miss it. Look, you can't just think about yourself now, you have to think about your baby too. Please let me help you. I really don't want anything in return.'

She hesitated for a moment, biting her lip. Then she nodded silently, tears welling in her eyes again, and told me the truth about how her parents had disowned her after finding out she was pregnant, and how she had panicked and fled to the city, taking her younger brother with her.

'We had all these screaming arguments,' she said miserably. 'I'll never be able to forget some of the things they said to me. My dad called me a liar and a ... a filthy slut. I mean, I've never even kissed a boy, not properly, not on the mouth ... unless you count what just happened downstairs. I did kiss Harry on the cheek once – you know, the boyfriend I had when I was fourteen – does that count? Does it? I couldn't even look at my Dad in the end because he didn't even *try* to disguise the disgust he felt for me, and I just couldn't bear to see that expression on his face when he looked at me.

'They said that me and my boyfriend had to learn some responsibility. They said he would have to support me even though I kept *telling* them there *was* no boyfriend. I had nowhere to go so I went to my grandparents and asked if I could stay with them, but they said they couldn't have me in the house. It wasn't their place to go against my parents' wishes, they said. Do you know what it feels like to get to the point where you can't ask for help any more because you know that if you get told "no" one more time by one more person you'll lose it?

'That's why I wanted Toby with me. He never blamed me and he was the only one who believed me. I never had sex with anyone but even if I had, would it really be so bad that they should all turn on me like that? I can't think of anything awful enough Toby could do that would make me stop loving him. And what does it matter to my parents if he lives with me? They were never around anyway! I was afraid that they might take him away and I'd never see him again. So I took him with me when I left. We stayed in a shelter for a while before we moved here … but I can't look after him. I have no money – my parents have cut me off from the accounts I had before, so I can't use my credit cards any more. It's just that I didn't want to be completely on my own, with no family at all. Can you understand that?'

Ah, yes, I could understand that far better than she knew.

'You're not going to turn me in, are you?' she asked, glancing up at me.

I shook my head. 'I just want to help you, that's all. I would never do anything you didn't want me to, I promise. You don't have to be scared to ask me for help.'

Casey smiled at me and I saw a mixture of doubt and hope in her face.

'Where did you learn to fight like that anyway?' she asked.

I hesitated, hoping she hadn't seen me almost cut that boy's throat. Should I tell her the truth? Could I risk undoing the trust I'd manage to build up between us?

'You have skeletons in your closet too, don't you?' she asked, smiling softy. 'It's okay, you don't have to tell me if you don't want to.'

And I had to tell her then because the way she'd said it and the kind smile she'd given me made me feel like a bastard for not trusting her enough in the first place when she had openheartedly trusted me with her secrets. And to my surprise and pleasure, she did not denounce me for a raving madman after I'd finished. She didn't shrink from me in uncertainty and fear.

'I'm sorry I lied to you … I just didn't want you to think I was crazy or something.'

'Yes, I understand why you did it.'

'Do you believe me, then? You don't think I'm making all this up?'

'A few days ago I told you that there was no father to my child,' she said wryly. 'The idea that you might be suffering from amnesia is not hard for me to believe, even if you don't trust my story.'

I hesitated, feeling guilty.

'It's okay. I know how it sounds,' she said with a shrug. 'Foolishly get yourself in trouble and then claim a Virgin Mary ... But, Gabriel, in this day and age, why on earth would I say such a thing if it wasn't true? When I know that people will denounce me for a slut and a whore as soon as I start claiming to be a pregnant virgin? I'm not stupid, although people often seem to think otherwise because of the dyed hair and the piercings and the tattoos. But for God's sake, if I was going to lie about it, I would have said I'd been raped. People would have believed that and pitied me then instead of scorning me and looking at me with disgust. I wish I'd told my parents I was raped now. Then I'd still be at home, with everyone I love fussing over me. I would never have had to realise how little they cared about me. I would have just gone on thinking they were the people I'd always believed them to be.'

She wasn't lying to me. I could see it in her face – not only did she think she was telling the truth, she *was* telling the truth. Perhaps I have known that all along. Perhaps I just didn't like to think that she was mixed up in all this too. I wanted better for her than that. I wanted her to have normalcy – even if that normalcy was as a struggling single mother with no family, no money and no one to help her.

'I'm sorry,' I said, trying to keep the weariness out of my voice as I accepted the idea. 'I do believe you.'

When I saw that she was doubtful, I told her a little about my own recent experiences. Not the whole of it, of course, for I had no wish to scare her. So I didn't tell her of the burning demon who had almost decapitated Stephomi outside Michael's church or of the strange notes I had been sent. I didn't tell her of the black fur and the claw marks and the cracked mirror in Stephomi's hotel room ... I knew that Casey was religious, for she had told me before that her whole family were Catholic. But most religious people, even if they do believe in a vague way in angels and their demonic counterparts, do not believe that devils and angels walk the Earth in a more physical manner – brandishing large swords, ripping hotel curtains to shreds, leaving black fur all over the cream suite, freezing wine solid in long stemmed wine glasses . . .

But I did tell her that I had known my share of strangeness since coming to Budapest. That I sometimes seemed to be haunted by strange dreams and waking visions that I couldn't shake. That something followed me through the days and nights . . . And she believed me. In fact, she seemed incredibly relieved that someone other than her had experienced things they could not explain. Things that haunted them and made them fear they were going mad.

When I at last got up to go, Casey pressed a string of prayer beads into my palm; the smooth feel of them and the soft click of the wood as the beads fell against each other was incredibly soothing and reassuring. I returned to my apartment aware that there were barriers between us that had been swept down beautifully that evening.

If I had ever had a daughter, I would have wished her to be just like Casey. Had I loved Luke like this? Was this what it had felt like? The conviction that you would do anything . . . *anything* to keep them safe from whatever might try to hurt them. I let Luke down, didn't I? A parent is supposed to keep their child *safe*. There should never *ever* be any need for those tiny little coffins. Not because of illness, not because of negligence, not because of accident . . . Children should not die. Old people die. Adults, sometimes. But not children. I don't know why God doesn't forbid it. I won't let anything happen to Casey. I'd die before I let anything hurt her.

After the incident with Casey and her attackers, life was uneventful for a week, and this lulled me into a false sense of security. The weather continued to cool and Budapest became laced with frosts during the night – frosts that melted away quickly as soon as the sun came up, shining down on the city with all the sharp, clear, freshness of a winter's day.

There had been no notes or visions or strange dreams. There had been no nocturnal visits from Lilith, even after I stopped taking the sleeping drugs. And life had seemed sweet to me, like nectar. But then, yesterday, I received another note. Like the first one, it had been slipped under the door and spelt out in block capitals but it was written in Italian rather than Latin:

> *PER ME SI VA NELLA CITTA'DOLENTE.*
> *PER ME SI VANELL'ETERNO DOLORE.*
> *PER ME SI VA TRA LA PERDUTA GENTE ...*
> *LASCIATE OGNI SPERANZA VOI CH'ENTRATE!*

This quote is from Dante and translated into English it reads:

> *Through me one goes to the sorrowful city.*
> *Through me one goes to eternal suffering.*
> *Through me one goes among lost people ...*
> *Abandon all hope, you who enter!*

The passage is straight from the *Divina Commedia* itself, *Inferno III*, which sees Dante and Virgil passing through the Gates of Hell on which the famous words are engraved. I can't say that the words did not chill me. But, unlike those passing through Hell's Gates, I did have some hope left. For now at last I would know who had sent me these notes.

After the initial twinges of foreboding, my first feeling was one of triumph. I had caught the little shit in the act. At last I would have the identity of my anonymous tormenter. I would know who had been sending me these threatening things. And then I would therefore also know who had stitched photos into the backs of antique books and hidden them in crates of wine. I would know who had stood in the hotel room in Paris and photographed Stephomi and me. And I would know who had killed Anna Sovànak. At last I would know what twisted man dropped her body into the sea, contained in a crate, and left her there for months before raising her to the surface, transporting her across Italy and Austria back to Hungary to deposit before the weeping willow memorial in the centre of Budapest for all to see when her ocean-bloated corpse washed out onto the street. This sick bastard had wanted her to be discovered in a public and sensationalist manner. Had he been trying to make the front page, perhaps? The story certainly should have made headlines and its banishment to page six was worrying in itself.

I had already drawn the uncomfortable conclusion that this man, too, was known to me before I lost my memory. He had been there with Stephomi and I in Paris, and he knew that I understood Latin and Italian and he had my address in Budapest. I very much hoped that we had been on bad terms, for I hated the thought that I had kept such vile company. When I took the camera down from the wall to replay the video, I half feared that the man might have seen the camera and somehow disabled it, or that there would be just blank, unexplained snow filling the screen. But the camera had not been tampered with and after watching it I did indeed have the identity of the note sender.

But I couldn't believe it. I must have watched and re-watched the tape at least a dozen times to be sure that I was not somehow imagining it. Even when I was quite certain what the camera showed, I still thought that there might be a mistake or another ex-planation somehow. That it couldn't possibly be what it seemed.

The only thing to be done was to confront him. And it seemed so unlikely and incredible that if he had told me he hadn't done it then I think I would have believed him over the evidence of my own eyes. But when I went round to Casey's apartment that evening and told her I needed to speak to Toby, and that it couldn't wait until the morning, she went and got him up and brought him into the kitchen and I could see by the guilt in his eyes as soon as I held out the note that the camera had not lied and that it had indeed been Toby March who had been putting these threatening things under my door.

*

I knew that Toby couldn't possibly have written the notes himself. Not unless he could read and write in ancient Latin. No, the deliverer and the sender must be different people altogether. Toby could be nothing more than an agent. Whoever the perpetrator of this scheme was, he had managed to find out who my neighbours were and had somehow bribed Toby to deliver these notes in secret. I remembered back to when I had received the first note a month ago, and had chased the fleeing footsteps down to the lobby where I had seen Toby loitering by the door before Casey found him and they left the building together. It was clear now why Toby had always seemed so nervous at the sight of me, and had been so uncomfortable in my company. It had never occurred to me that the nine-year-old might somehow be involved in all this – that the one responsible could be wretched enough to involve a child in this sordid mess.

'Can you understand what these say?' I asked, holding up the first note as well as the one I had received that evening.

Toby shook his head silently. Although my eyes were fixed on Toby, I could also see Casey out of the corner of my eye, gazing curiously at the notes, clearly puzzled as to what this had to do with her younger brother. She obviously could not read Italian either, for if she had understood the neatly printed messages, I am sure she would have been more visibly concerned.

'Why have you been putting them under my door?' I asked.

Casey turned sharply to her brother. 'I most certainly hope you haven't been putting anything under Gabriel's door, Toby!'

The boy stood there, hesitating, glancing anxiously at his sister then back at me and then at his feet, shuffling nervously where he stood.

I felt I couldn't bear the tense agony of waiting for him to tell me what he knew. My thoughts flew around chaotically, accusing everyone in turn: perhaps Stephomi had bribed Toby. Perhaps these things were his doing. Perhaps he was the unseen puppet master. Then again, perhaps there was no human agent at all. Perhaps the references to the dreaded Ninth Circle had come from some other thing's realm altogether. Perhaps it had been the burning demon himself who had convinced Toby to be the deliveryman of these ominous portents. To my shame, my suspicions even rested briefly on Casey, but I quickly rejected this. I would not ... could not believe that she had anything to do with this. I couldn't bear it any longer. The cold and fearful suspicions against all those around me; the distrusting of friends; the total, blind ignorance of the unseen agendas gathering around me. I felt if I didn't find out the identity of this contemptible, cowardly tormenter ... this wretched, disgusting excuse for a human being ... then I would surely go mad right there on the spot.

'Please, Toby,' I said, desperately, barely managing to resist the urge to shake him, 'please tell me who gave you those notes to deliver.'

The boy bit his lip, brown eyes troubled, before at last giving me the answer: 'You did.'

My thoughts collapsed in on themselves, leaving in their wake a deafeningly loud silence as I stood there staring at the kid.

'Are you *sure*?' I croaked at last.

'There are some more in my bedroom,' Toby said uncertainly. 'You said I had to put them under the door on the sixth of every month starting from October, and that you mustn't see me doing it or the deal would be off.'

'Deal?' I repeated blankly.

'Start from the beginning,' Casey ordered. 'When did Gabriel ask you to do this?'

'I dunno exactly when,' Toby replied. 'Some time in July. He said that if I delivered these notes when he said, without being seen, then he'd give me a thousand dollars.'

'He said *what*?' Casey repeated, looking horrified.

'And a thousand more when he found out I was the sender.'

'You mean I anticipated discovering your identity?' I asked, staring at him.

Toby shrugged.

'Toby, how could you accept money from a *stranger*? And that much? Where is it now? How have you been hiding it from me?'

'It's under my mattress,' Toby said, slightly sulkily, obviously realising that he was going to be in trouble over this.

'Go and fetch it right now,' Casey ordered.

'But Casey, you said we needed more money and—'

'Toby! Fetch the money now. I won't ask you again.'

With a scowl, Toby turned and stalked to his room.

'I'm sorry,' I said, turning to her after her brother had gone off. 'I ... I don't know what to say to you. I don't remember any of it.'

Casey flashed me a brief, worried smile. 'It's okay. We'll get to the bottom of it.'

When Toby returned, he was holding two black bags. The larger of the two he handed to his sister, who tipped the contents out onto the kitchen table and gasped involuntarily at the stacks of crisp, new dollar bills that piled up before us. There certainly looked like there was a thousand dollars' worth there. Thrusting the money back into the bag, Casey handed it over to me.

'You'd better take this.'

'But, if I promised, Toby—' I began, but Casey shook her head and cut me off.

'Look, I don't want to offend you, Gabriel, but we don't know where that money came from. It ... it could be stolen.'

I nodded bleakly and glanced apologetically at Toby. 'I can give you the same in florints,' I began, but again Casey rejected the offer firmly.

'Toby should know better than ever to take money in the first place,' she said. 'You're helping me out while I'm not working. I think you're doing more than enough for us already. What's in the other bag, Toby?'

'Gabriel said he wouldn't remember asking me to do this and, er ... he wasn't sure how long it would take for him to work it out, so he gave me copies and said to give whatever was left back to him when he found out. And you wanted this back too,' Toby said, drawing a computer disc in a plastic case from the second bag.

*

The other A4 pages Toby gave me all carried copies of the two messages I had already received. There were five copies of each message, making ten pages altogether. I must have been overly cautious, for there was no way that the anonymous letter sending would have gone on for ten months without my finding out who the sender was. It had been obvious and easy enough to fix a surveillance camera above the apartment door.

I gazed at the computer disc in its protective plastic packaging, clasped between my thumb and forefinger. It had been a complete dead end. As soon as the programme loaded up, I was presented with a black screen with one small central box requiring a password. There was only room for eight digits, and I had already spent hours and hours typing in all manner of words in an effort to crack the code. I was on the verge of losing my temper with it. Why bother to go to all the trouble of hiding the disc in such a manner if it wasn't important? What the bloody hell was the point of a disc I couldn't access?

Had I really been trying to *torment* myself with those notes? What kind of twisted and depraved man had I been before that I would spend time planning such madness? Had I also been responsible for the photos hidden in my deliveries? There had to be more than one person involved. I couldn't be responsible for all that had happened. For one thing, I couldn't have been the photographer who took the picture of Stephomi and me in Paris, because I was in the picture myself. Nor could I have possibly moved Anna Sovànak's body, unless I have taken to vast nocturnal journeys that I then have no recollection of in the morning.

In the end, I took all these things with me to the Hilton and confronted Stephomi with them when we met for a drink in the Faust wine cellar beneath the hotel that afternoon.

'You told me you thought you knew who was sending these,' I said, spreading the notes out on the table. 'I need you to tell me.'

Stephomi picked up the two handwritten notes he had not seen, and glanced at them in distaste before dropping them back on the table. Then he leaned back in his chair with a sigh.

'Tell me,' I repeated. 'Please, Stephomi. I think I already know but I'll confirm it on my own somehow if I have to.'

'All right,' he said, setting his wine glass back on the table. 'You sent them all yourself.'

'All of them?'

'Yes. I don't know about these notes but I expect you had the photos hidden in packages addressed to you, and then asked the sender to post them to your new address on a certain date, using some pretext or other.'

'And who is the photographer in this?' I asked, holding up the photo of Stephomi and I.

'You,' my friend replied. 'The camera was hidden and on a timer.'

'And why would I send myself a photo warning against you?'

The scholar smiled wryly. 'Because you know me too well, Gabriel. You wanted me to leave you alone and not try to befriend you after you lost your memory. You wanted to be alone. I didn't much care for the idea. You know the rest. I suppose you were trying to instil a wariness against me if I should happen to turn up.'

'Then what about Anna Sovànak? Did I know that her body would be left beneath the Weeping Willow?'

'How could you?' Stephomi asked, watching me carefully. 'Indeed, as I understand it, you hardly knew the woman.'

'Then why—?'

'Coincidence, Gabriel,' Stephomi said sharply. 'You couldn't have known that her killer would leave her body beneath the monument. I presume your reference to it on the back of the photo was simply because you knew she was Jewish. Take my advice, don't waste time looking for logic in what you have done.' He gestured at the things spread out on the table before us. 'You wanted to torment yourself. Nothing more.'

We were silent for a moment. Yes, surely Stephomi was right. I could not possibly have known where Anna Sovànak's body would appear. It was nothing more than a coincidence.

'My memory loss was a stupid accident,' I said at last, 'How could I possibly have known it was going to happen? How could I possibly have *planned* for it?'

Stephomi shrugged. 'I don't know, Gabriel. When I questioned you about it before, you told me to back off. You said you knew what you were doing.'

'Was I losing my mind?' I almost whispered. 'Was I different before? Was I this strange, twisted person?'

This was something that had been bothering me for a while. Was I really *me*? Or had my amnesia caused the reset button to be pushed so that I was just this blank slate once again? Starting from scratch ... having to rebuild my personality again through my experiences ... my environment ...

'No, you were much the same before,' Stephomi replied. 'But ...'

'But what?' I asked, latching on to his hesitation immediately.

Stephomi sighed. 'Well, Nicky phoned me about a week before she died. She was ... she said she was worried about you. She wanted to see me but I was in Japan at the time and couldn't get back.'

'Why was she worried?'

'She wouldn't tell me on the phone. I would've been in England within the next couple of weeks and I was going to go see her then.' He shrugged. 'To be honest, I expect it was just that you told her you could see devils and it freaked her out.'

'You mean she didn't already know?' I asked.

'No. It's not an easy thing to tell someone. But whatever your state of mind beforehand, you certainly weren't at all balanced after they died. So don't try to make sense of what you did. You won't find any. You wouldn't listen to reason and you wouldn't listen to me. To be honest, I really don't know the true extent of what you did and why.'

He sounded tired and I realised when I looked at him that there were bags of weariness beneath his eyes that he had not been able to disguise. When I asked him about it, he replied with an uncharacteristic impatience. 'It's starting, Gabriel. It's all about to begin. Can't you feel it? As a person of the In Between, I'm surprised you can't sense it. Have you not been having dreams? Mirror visions? Things like that?'

'I've had those from the beginning,' I replied, thinking of the recent appearance of Lilith in my dreams but not wanting to discuss it with my inclined-to-mockery friend.

'It's building like static,' he went on. 'It's been itching away at me, like nails on a blackboard, keeping me awake and filling my mind with ... disturbing images that I can't block out.'

I gazed at him in the dim snugness of the ancient cellar and knew that he was right. Perhaps it was my imagination, but even as we sat there I thought I felt power-surged currents brushing the hairs of my arms as they swept by. Rubbing my arm absently, I asked, 'What do you think will happen? Is there anything we can do that will make any kind of difference at all?'

I had expected Stephomi to give his usual brusque answer that, of course, as mere humans, there was nothing we could do to influence the centuries-old War that had for so long been raging between Satan's angels and God's. But for some time, Stephomi simply gazed thoughtfully at me, tapping the tips of his slender fingers on the edge of the wood-polished table.

'Shall we go for a walk?' Stephomi asked at last, standing up abruptly.

'I ... what? Where?'

'Anywhere.'

'But ... it's below freezing outside!'

'I need some fresh air,' Stephomi said. 'And I'd rather not have this conversation inside. There aren't so many people outside on a day like this.'

Feeling perplexed, I got up and followed Stephomi from the hotel and out into the savagely cold air. I was glad of the ankle-length black coat I had brought with me, and did the buttons up all the way to my neck. Still the cold chafed my fingers and face. How strange to think that warm autumn had been so short a time ago. The sudden descent into winter seemed unnaturally fast.

'It's colder than it should be for this time of year,' Stephomi remarked as we walked. 'Have you noticed?'

I nodded wordlessly. It was a strange kind of chill that seemed to settle over the city at night and couldn't be shaken off during the day. Several castle spires were visible as we walked further, the striking outline of the Hilton at our back. Our feet crunched on the frozen gravel path we were walking down. I noticed as we went on that the pressure of my weight was actually snapping the frozen pebbles in two, like brittle lengths of glass. The coating of frost over the buildings and the cobbled roads was only paper-thin, and yet still it had not melted in the slightly brighter warmth of day. And although there was neither rain nor snow on the ground itself, the air seemed thick with a kind of softened ice that blew into our faces and wetted our clothes.

'Feels like the air itself is freezing, doesn't it?' Stephomi said, echoing my own thoughts.

We soon reached the Fisherman's Bastion. It's so beautiful that if I lived closer I would go there every single night before returning to my apartment. It's basically something between a castle and a city wall, sprawling along the top of the hill overlooking the Danube, with great glassless windows and hollow towers you can climb into, each having open arched doors and the same windows carved into the rock. There are covered walkways with cobbled paths, and curved, sweeping wide staircases with white knights set into the walls and stone lions perched on top of pillars. It would have looked beautiful at any time of year, but when it's sparkling with glass beads of frost that cling to every spire and turret; every frozen knight and lion coated in pale blue ice, it is even more breathtaking and I really could sit there for hours. I *love* this city; I truly think it must be the most beautiful in the whole world, and I'm so thankful that I live here. If I had to live anywhere other than Budapest, I know I would be miserable.

We stopped in one of the covered towers and stood at an arched window overlooking the icy Danube. The view before us was incredible. Spires and towers rose up from the smaller buildings, and the whole city glittered in its winter coat of frost, like a vast enchanted ice palace straight from the pages of a fairytale. The Hungarians seem to revel in their adeptness at capturing elusive

Beauty in their churches, their monuments, and the angel-graced bridges that arch gracefully over the Danube.

'We have a little problem,' Stephomi said softly.

I glanced at him, eyebrow raised. 'Little problem as in "*The Antichrist is coming*" or little problem as in you can't find your house keys?'

'The first one, I'm afraid. I, er ... had assumed that all this fuss about the Antichrist was because he would soon be coming into a position of power where he would be able to do real damage ... You know, start wreaking havoc and so on. But ... apparently the dates Nostradamus refers to aren't to do with anything the Antichrist himself *does* as such.'

'Get to the point,' I said, aware that he was stalling.

'You won't like it,' Stephomi sighed. 'The dates refer to his *birth*. And Raphael told me last night that you know the mother.'

The vivid image of the conflicting aura surrounding Casey flew to the forefront of my mind at once. The aura that could at one moment be coloured in the most visually stunning shades of sparkling gold, and the next dripping with a wickedness so vile that all the senses screamed at the sight of it. It should have occurred to me before. I should have known. In all honesty, perhaps I did.

'So who is she?' Stephomi persisted.

'Casey March,' I said. 'She's my neighbour. I've been trying to help her. She's just a teenager and she hasn't got anyone. She says it's a virgin pregnancy.'

'Well, that's another point in favour of it being Jesus number two, I guess,' Stephomi said with a shrug. 'Poor little brat. He can be a Hitler or a Schindler but nothing in between.'

'Well, then, extra care must simply be taken with the raising of the child,' I said firmly.

Stephomi remained silent for a moment, gazing at the city before us, an expression of doubt on his face. 'Ah, well, that's the problematic thing, isn't it? People disagree about raising children as it is. Who's best fit to decide?'

'The mother, of course! It's Casey's baby, isn't it? She loves it already!'

'Yes, and I understand Clara Hitler was quite fond of her own little dictator,' Stephomi said impatiently. 'Come on, what has love got to do with it, Gabriel? If only she'd been one of those mothers who had starved and beaten her child. So many deaths might have been averted—'

'I'll help Casey,' I said, interrupting him.

'Oh, you will, will you?'

'Yes,' I said, nodding. 'I will.'

Stephomi glanced at me then, a wry smile twisting his lips. 'How nice to know that there is a hero here among us! I'm sure my dreams will no longer be plagued by visions of the Apocalypse now that I know you have put your name down for nappy-changing duty, Gabriel.'

I frowned, irritated by his sarcasm. 'You don't understand. I'm going to *save* Casey. That's what God wants me to do. That's why I'm here.'

Stephomi nodded wisely. 'So ... how do you know the big guy so well?'

'Big guy?' I said, trying to remember any fat men with whom I might be acquainted.

'The big man upstairs,' Stephomi clarified. 'God, Allah, Ganesh, Buddha ... whatever you want to call him.'

'Buddhists don't believe that Buddha is a god,' I said impatiently. 'And those other so-called "Gods" you mentioned are false ones.'

'Christ, why do you have to turn every question into a theological debate? I'll rephrase it for you, Gabriel: how can you be so sure about what it is God wants you to do?'

'I just know, that's all. Don't you understand? It's like one of those comic books. I'm like one of those superheroes. I don't *care* about myself, I just want to help other people.'

'Superhero, eh?' Stephomi said, looking me up and down. 'Yes, I can certainly see the similarities. I'd stay clear of the spandex costumes, though, if I were you. I don't think any man has ever looked good in spandex.'

'Oh, shut up about the fucking spandex!' I snapped, losing my temper. 'The spandex is irrelevant. The *costume* is irrelevant. Why do you have to turn everything into a fucking joke?'

'Sorry, Gabriel, it's a bad habit, I know. I just don't want you to forget while you're making these plans that you're not the only player in the game. The angels and demons might have plans of their own for the baby.'

'What the hell is that supposed to mean, Stephomi?'

Stephomi glanced at me, eyebrow raised. 'Don't worry. Budapest isn't about to be overrun by choirs of angels and hordes of demons. God and Lucifer frown on it.'

'Frown on it?' I repeated incredulously.

'Yes. Earth is a playing board for humans. Angels and demons can involve themselves in the game to a point. But the major moves must all be made by human players. Of course,' he added with a shrug, 'that doesn't mean that angels and their fallen brothers can't employ human agents. But there are so few people of the In Between in existence today anyway, and I believe you and I are the only ones here in Budapest.'

I glanced sharply at him and he returned my look with a slightly bitter smile. 'Don't look at me like that, Gabriel. I have no intention of taking the child from its mother. Children were never really my thing, you know. All that screaming.'

'They don't scream *that* often,' I said.

'No, I meant me. If I'm around them too long.'

I sighed and ran a hand through my hair. 'Am I the only one who feels like they're caught in a giant, invisible spider's web?'

'You mean God's web, don't you?' Stephomi said.

'It's a devil's web,' I said sharply.

'Well, it's a web that reaches down from the lowest layer of Heaven to the uppermost level of Hell, with Earth trapped in the middle. If God finds the situation so distasteful, one might wonder why He does not trouble to brush the web from Heaven's edge so that it might sink harmlessly down upon itself. Perhaps the Good Lord rather enjoys watching the insects that get caught in it, thrashing about, unable to free themselves. Entertainment is scarce when you're in Heaven, you know.'

'You must not doubt God,' I said, just about managing to control myself at his blasphemous words. 'You must have faith.'

'Where does your faith come from anyway?' Stephomi asked, glancing at me, a strange curiosity in his eyes. 'How can you believe in Heaven? I don't think I could take fat, naked cherubs plucking harps at me for any great length of time.'

I hesitated, trying to think of some way to explain, but I had no answer for him. You can't rationalise faith.

'Well, I'd better be getting back,' Stephomi said, glancing at his watch. 'You'd do well to keep an eye on this girl of yours, Gabriel. If nothing more, at least we've got a few more years than we thought while this kid is growing up before God comes down and starts dishing out justice like there's no tomorrow.'

It had become dark while we'd been standing there. The Chain Link Bridge was now lit up and I could see the outlines of the floodlit Basilica and Parliament buildings across the dark Danube. The old-fashioned lanterns had come on, lighting the sprawling fairytale white spires of the Fisherman's Bastion with a soft golden glow. It was so magical that I half expected to see a unicorn walking through the frosted arches, or snow faeries fluttering about the tall, glowing streetlamps as I made my way back towards the glittering Chain Link Bridge.

When I got back to my building late that night, I took the elevator up to my floor and walked along the corridor to my apartment, where I froze in sudden fear. The walls of the building were thin and poorly soundproofed, and I could clearly hear sobbing coming from Casey's apartment. Dread flooded through me as I thought of all Stephomi had said that afternoon as we overlooked the frostbitten Danube – things of an unborn child and the intense interest that angels and demons alike had in it ... *Don't forget you are not the only player in the game ...*

I knocked sharply on the door. When there was no answer, I called Casey's name. To my relief, she opened the door then, looking at me with red-rimmed eyes, clutching a grotty bit of tissue and sniffing pathetically.

'What is it?' I asked anxiously. 'What happened?'

'When I ... when I got back in today ... the social services and the police were waiting. They found me when I tried to use my credit cards ... They've taken Toby back to my parents.'

And then she burst into tears. I felt for her, even as relief swept through me. It had been bound to happen sooner or later. Casey herself had admitted that she couldn't look after her brother. I held on to her tightly while she sobbed against me, feeling painfully sorry for her as well as exasperated by my own helplessness to fix this for her.

'I was going to t-take him back anyway,' she gulped between sobs. 'But I was going to wait until ... wait until after Ch-Christmas. I've never been on my own at Christmas before. I just w-wanted someone from my fam-family ...'

I hated Casey's parents in that moment. Hated them. If I had been lucky enough to keep my family, I know I would never intentionally have hurt them or lied to them or betrayed their trust or made them feel worthless and unwanted. I think husbands who cheat on their wives are disgusting. And I think parents who throw out their children over pregnancies or sexuality or any other pathetic reason are a *disgrace*. They don't know how lucky they are to have each other to begin with.

'You won't be alone for Christmas,' I said softly. 'I know I'm no substitute for your family, but at least you won't be on your own. And soon you'll have a tiny perfect baby that belongs only to you that no one will be able to take away.'

30th November

Last night I dreamed I was back home with Nicky and Luke. I was in the bathroom of this beautiful old Victorian house, giving my son a bath before bed. He was splashing around with toy submarines, getting soapy water everywhere, and I knew Nicky would tell us off for making such a mess when she got upstairs.

Luke's pyjamas were on the side by the sink but I couldn't find his towel anywhere. I stuck my head out of the door and shouted down the darkened corridor, 'Nick, where's Luke's towel?'

But there was no answer – the large old house was silent. I turned back into the bathroom, frowning, and glanced at the white, fluffy 'His and Hers' towels warming on the towel rail. I grabbed my own and dried my son off with it, made rather a mess with talcum powder, and then managed to get him into his pyjamas.

I picked him up and walked down the corridor with him to his bedroom. There were soft toys on the shelves lining the room and trains on the wallpaper. I tucked Luke up in bed, brushed back strands of his dark blond hair, said goodnight to him, then turned the nightlight on and crept out of his room ... But no sooner had I shut the door than I froze at the sound of glass breaking downstairs somewhere. It was probably just Nicky dropping a wine glass while cleaning up our dinner, but ... something made the hairs on my arms stand up with this awful apprehension that prevented me from calling out to my wife and made me fetch the baseball bat from our bedroom before creeping down the stairs.

The house was dimly lit with only a couple of lamps still on, but I knew the house – it seemed very familiar even in my dream – and I had no trouble navigating the stairs in the half light. When I got to the bottom of the stairs I froze, cold dread making my heart beat painfully fast as I clearly saw the dark silhouette of a man standing in the next room. It was the living room and there was no light save for the moonlight shining through the French doors.

'Who are you?' I demanded, straining my eyes towards him, gripping my baseball bat harder. 'How did you get in here?'

Still he didn't speak, didn't even move. I approached slowly, aware that he was probably dangerous, that he might even be armed. I got to the doorway of the living room and then reached in and flicked on one of the spot lamps. The light shone directly onto Nicky's priceless baby grand piano in the corner, only softly illuminating the rest of the room – the bookcases, the beige suite, the box of Luke's toys neatly packed away. And the man stood in the centre of the room, staring at me.

He was tall, with dark hair combed back, black boots, navy trousers and jacket, white cravat and pale, waxy skin. But what alarmed me the most was that he held a long, thin sword awkwardly in his hand. And there was blood on its blade.

'Where is my wife?' I asked, my voice shaking slightly already.

The intruder looked at me and I saw that there were dark bags of fatigue beneath his eyes. 'Don't you recognise me?' he asked hoarsely.

'No,' I said, staring at him. 'Who are you?'

'I'm Valentine.'

'Valentine?'

'Gretchen's brother.'

'Gretchen? You mean the woman who was Faust's lover?'

'Mephistopheles is killing us,' he groaned, dropping the sword so it clattered loudly on the parquet wooden flooring. 'Once we're dead, he'll turn on you.'

'Where is my wife?' I demanded once again.

'She's upstairs. In the bathroom.'

'Look, why the hell are you in my house?' I said. There was something about his motionless posture, about his sunken eyes, that was making me feel increasingly alarmed. 'What's the matter with you?'

'I'm bleeding to death,' Valentine replied softly. 'That's what's the matter with me.'

And as I stared in horror, Valentine moved his jacket aside with one hand so that I could see the dagger buried in his chest and the blood soaking into his white shirt, running down the side of his leg to stain the parquet floor beneath his feet. With a yell, I dropped the baseball bat and raced upstairs to find Nicky, quite sure, even before I found her, that something really awful had already happened. When I burst into the bathroom, Nicky was already dead and our 'His and Hers' towels were dripping with blood. I couldn't scream, I couldn't even move – I just stood there, staring at the bloody towels, and when someone started to play the piano downstairs I somehow knew that it was Mephistopheles on my wife's piano, waiting for me to go down and face him.

It's lucky I know that my family died in a car crash or else this dream would really have upset me. As it was, it did, of course, scare me. But nightmares are only nightmares and I'm not going to make my usual mistake of attaching far too much importance to things that have no meaning.

15th December

Christmas is here now. Shops, restaurants and streets are decorated in all their festive finery and the snow has come to the city, making it sparkle and glisten in the fresh, clear light from the winter sun. Large Christmas trees and strings of lights have been put up around the squares and in the streets, and the artists' Christmas crafts markets have been set up outside.

For the first few days after Toby was taken away, Casey had been very down and, in an effort to cheer her up, I had taken her out to the three-storey Luxus Department Store in Mihàly Vörösmarty Square. The traditional huge bedecked Christmas tree had already been erected in the square, and the department store itself was lavishly laced and ribboned with festive decorations and displays.

In an effort to draw Casey's thoughts from her parents and brother celebrating Christmas without her, I had tried to focus her mind on the fact that soon she would be starting a family of her own. A few years from now, she would be celebrating Christmas with her own little son or daughter, making the season magical for them and enjoying everything anew through their eyes. To my relief, this seemed to cheer her up.

When we got to the large department store, I said I wanted to buy baby things for her as an early Christmas present. At first she protested, saying that I was already doing more than enough for her. But I insisted. I said frankly that there was nothing I needed or wanted for myself, that I had no one else to buy presents for and that, for the moment, we were both as alone as each other. I wanted to love the baby as much as she did. If she agreed to let me be part of her life, she would be giving me far more than I could ever give her.

So for a while she had walked around tentatively picking up the cheapest baby things she could see. But I continued to take these off her and put them back, picking up better quality items, until she finally gave in and started choosing nice things. We had everything a child could possibly want by the end of it. We had a cot, little feeding bottles, plastic bowls with matching spoons, a musical mobile to hang above the cot, soft toys to put in the cot, baby bubble bath with the unmistakable powdery soft scent of tiny, perfect newborn babies, and a set of yellow rubber ducks and other bath toys. We also bought a baby monitor and a highchair, an array of toys and books, and, last of all, we must have spent a small fortune in the clothes department.

Casey didn't know what sex the baby was going to be so we tried to stick to neutral colours and patterns on the baby-grows we picked out. We also purchased tiny, tiny socks and bibs and little knitted hats. I had never seen Casey so elated as she rushed round like an excited child, looking at the baby clothes on their tiny hangers, exclaiming in delight over some item or other. Perhaps it was just the first time that she had viewed her own pregnancy as anything other than an unmitigated disaster. She really was quite huge now, emphasised all the more by the fact that she had a small figure to begin with. It couldn't be much longer now. I even wondered whether she was carrying twins, she seemed to be so big.

There was far too much to carry by the time we were done so I paid extra to have it sent back to the apartment the next day. Casey voiced concerns again about the cost of everything, but I waved them away. To my utter astonishment, I heard a slight tremor in her voice as she said quietly, 'I'll find some way to repay your kindness one day, Gabriel, I promise. I can't tell you how much it's meant to me.'

Kindness? How could this be *kindness* when I was simply making myself happy? She made me happy just by being near me. Already I loved her so much that it hurt. But perhaps I was kind. After all, I was doing kind deeds – that must surely make me a kind person? I am a good person, aren't I? Look at all the good things I've done.

After the Luxus Department Store, we went to Gerbeaud's, the famous patisserie on the northern side of the Mihály Vörösmarty Square, and enjoyed coffee and pastries in the sumptuously rich interior made all the more splendid for the many Christmas angels and golden ribbons with which the patisserie was decorated for the holiday season.

It was the best day of my life. My time spent with Stephomi seemed to pale in comparison. Truly those days had been nothing to this one. To know that I had been responsible for the smile on Casey's face; to know that I was the one responsible for lifting some of the sadness from her eyes ... was utterly priceless to me. She would have been so miserable without me. She *needed* me. And I trusted her in a way I knew I would never be able to trust my more scholarly, evasive friend.

As we sat there in the warm, bright patisserie with golden chandeliers hanging from elaborate cream and gold ceilings, and alternating green and red velvet drapes sweeping to the floor from archways, I felt that even if my future was filled with one disaster after another, this day, this moment here with Casey, would provide me with enough happiness to last me until I died.

We were in the middle of a conversation and I had glanced down at my coffee cup for only a moment, but when I looked back up, the aura around her that had been soft with golden beauty only a second before had once again changed to thick, swirling clouds of black – the smell of burning flesh horribly pungent once again. Just the sight of it chafed horribly at my senses, instinctively warning of danger and the terrible potential for hissing evil ...

'What is it?' Casey asked, gazing at me, clearly quite unaware of the malevolence that clung about her.

'Oh, nothing,' I said quickly, and tried to continue with the conversation.

But I hated to have to look at her when the aura was this colour. It seemed to freeze my eyeballs in their sockets. And the sight was a crushing and brutal reminder, shattering the illusion that I had been so enjoying up until that point. We were not safe at all. This was not a warm and happy place, as it appeared. And I had just spent the whole day buying baby supplies for Casey for a child who was the focal point in an ancient War; a child who might grow up to be the next Hitler and inflict unendurable suffering upon hundreds of thousands of people in a battle that would last almost thirty years. And I one of the few people – really one of the only *two* people who could do anything about it – I was sitting here eating pastries and doing nothing.

'I, er … just have to go to the bathroom,' I said, needing a moment to collect myself.

The bathroom was empty when I got there, so I ran the tap and splashed some cool water on my face. I had told Stephomi sharply that the child would belong to Casey once it was born. But now, in the face of the burning black aura that clung about the teenager's body, I found myself beginning to doubt those words. What good would a demon child bring Casey? All day I had been telling her how happy she would be once the baby came, but what if that thing brought her nothing but further anguish? What if my decision was not being loyal to Casey at all? Suddenly, I wished I had not spent all day getting her so excited about her unborn child. *Christ, what the hell was I doing here?*

I looked up at the sound of the bathroom door opening. I expected the man who walked in to go over to the urinals, but instead he walked over to the sink next to mine and started washing his hands.

'I always wash my hands before eating,' he remarked conversationally.

I jumped severely at his voice, and fear shot through me when I looked at him. I recognised that American drawl and those heavy lidded eyes. It was the Judge. The Judge from the nightmare I had had several months ago in which I had been found guilty of witchcraft in Salem and been dragged outside at this man's command to be burned at the stake by a bloodthirsty mob.

'Hand me a towel there, would ya, fella?' the man said, indicating the paper towels by my side.

Wordlessly, I handed him one. He showed no sign of recognising me whatsoever. 'Do I know you from somewhere?' I asked suddenly.

The Judge looked at me for a long moment before shaking his head. 'I don't think so,' he said with a smile.

'We never met in ... Salem?' I persisted.

The Judge laughed. 'No, I've never been to Salem, son. My family's from there, though.'

'Oh.' I looked at him doubtfully. He didn't seem like he was lying, but it was definitely the same man. It was definitely him. If someone else walked into the bathroom right now, I wondered ... would they even be able to see him? Or would it just look like I was stood here talking to myself?

'We've never met before, then?' I asked again.

The Judge smiled good-naturedly. 'No, I don't think so.'

Perhaps I was just getting myself wound up about nothing after all. With a puzzled frown, I turned to go and rejoin Casey, but as I did so, the Judge's hand brushed my arm. And at his touch, flames shot up all around me, roaring with a frenzied heat. I could feel the stake at my back and the blisters around my wrists where the rope bound them together, and beyond the flames I could see the mob shrieking with pleasure as my clothes caught alight. I screamed, somehow managed to free one arm, and beat frantically at my clothes where they were smouldering, the acrid smoke stinging my eyes and making them water.

And then suddenly the fire was gone and I was in the bathroom of the patisserie again, panting, sweat running down my face. I wondered if I'd screamed aloud or just in my head. From the expression on the Judge's face, I guessed I'd screamed aloud. But the strange thing was that now he barely looked like the Judge at all. Perhaps there was a very slight physical resemblance, but it most certainly wasn't the same man.

'Jesus Christ, Mister!' the American exclaimed. 'What the hell is your problem?'

And he backed away from me and out the door, clearly glad to escape. But this doesn't mean anything. It doesn't mean anything at all. I felt in my pocket for the rosary beads Casey had given me, and quickly recited the Lord's Prayer through once to make sure. I . . . I think I might just have . . . overreacted.

I hurried us out quite quickly after that, anxious to get back to the safety of my apartment. We walked back across the square through the traditional Budapest Christmas Fair that always sets up there – a gathering of Hungarian craftsmen and artists selling their wares. I'd been a few days before and found it very festive, with the food carts selling hot wine and sausages and a musical carousel for the children. This time I just wanted to get home. The sudden craving for solitude was such that people's eyes seemed to burn into me like acid.

But as we walked back through the Christmas market set up in Vörösmarty Square, a young man hurried out towards us from behind one of the crafts stalls. He was slim and tall, although not as tall as me, with long blond hair tied back in a ponytail and a diamond earring sparkling in one ear. He wore jeans and a long-sleeved white top but no coat. I suppose he was good looking – he had high cheekbones and clear blue eyes, and he certainly had a nice manner – but . . . he gave the most extraordinary thing to Casey. We stopped when he approached us, one arm held behind his back.

'I'm sorry,' he said with a smile. 'I've just got to stop you for a minute.'

I stared at him in surprise, for he had spoken to us in English, although I couldn't quite place his accent.

'What's your name?' he asked Casey.

She told him before I could stop her. He smiled. 'I'm Raphael. There's something on my stall I think you might like.'

'Oh, I'm sorry but I really can't afford to—' Casey began, but the young man cut her off.

'I'm not asking you to buy anything,' he assured her hurriedly. 'It's Christmas. Please consider it a gift.'

He brought his hand round from behind his back and for a moment I thought he would be holding a flower or something equally presumptuous. But when he uncurled his fist, it was to reveal a small Black Madonna. It was without doubt a beautiful piece, carved from onyx and embellished with rich gold and red in the robe. There was a golden crown on her head and in her arms she held a black child, also adorned in a lavish gold and red robe with the same tiny crown on its head. This was no trinket he was giving her – this was an expensive and exquisite work of art. But for all its beauty, I couldn't prevent the grimace of distaste at the sight of the sinister looking thing.

Alongside Mary – the chaste, pure 'official' virgin, there exists an 'unofficial' virgin – black, mysterious and all-powerful – associated with beings that pre-dated Christianity ... Pagan goddesses and Ebony Ladies of the Underworld ... Of course, Black Madonnas are found in churches, but the Catholic Church does not officially afford them any special significance: black and white Madonnas alike are claimed to be the same. Black Madonnas are still depictions of the Virgin Mary; it's just that the artist chose to craft her from smooth ebony or Lebanese cedar wood or cold black onyx.

But there are rumours that the Black Madonnas were never meant to represent the Virgin Mary – that they stand for someone else altogether. And, unofficially, the church has taken to painting over their Madonnas with whitewash, to discourage the pilgrims who insist on affording them such an undue and inappropriate significance. For the Black Madonnas are associated with sexuality, fertility and procreation rather than chastity, and are credited by their followers with having supernatural powers. If the Black Madonnas are supposed to represent the Virgin Mary in some form, it is quite clear they represent something else as well – something a little older and darker – and I was not at all comfortable with Casey accepting this gift from such a stranger. He seemed harmless enough, but this was hardly normal behaviour, was it? I hoped Casey would refuse the Madonna, but I could tell she was flattered as well as delighted with both the gift and the good looks of the man who was giving it to her.

'Merry Christmas,' Raphael said. 'I wish you and your baby all the best.'

'Is Budapest crawling with angels?' Casey joked as we walked away, still beaming and examining the tiny Black Madonna in her hand as we walked.

'What do you mean?' I asked.

'Gabriel, Raphael ...' She laughed. 'I half expect Michael and Uriel to turn up on my doorstep any day now and tell me I've won the lottery.'

I glanced sharply back at the young man behind his stall, but then shook my head impatiently. Angels don't wear jeans and earrings. If every man with an angelic name really was an angel, then that would mean that Zadkiel Stephomi and I were not human either. I expect a feeling of Christmas spirit made that young man give Casey the gift. Or maybe he was hoping to get a date out of it. My eyes narrowed at the thought. If that was his intention, he could forget it – *I* was looking after Casey. She belonged to me now because I loved her the most. I am hers and I would do anything in the world she asked me to. But I expect my jealousy is unwarranted anyway. This Raphael guy was simply trying to be kind. I just wish that he could have picked a less inappropriate, less sinister thing to give her.

That night I had the dream that had so shaken me back in October. Once again, Casey and I were outside on the dome of St Stephen's Basilica, and once again snow fell around us. Again Casey gave birth to a perfect baby boy, and again I turned to pick up a blanket to wrap him in. But this time when I turned back, there was no writhing black demon on the ground. The baby was still there, but now there was a tiny pair of delicate feathered wings on his back – rainbow coloured, from emerald green to yellow to pink to sapphire blue. And the child glowed with golden light where it lay surrounded by snow at the top of the cathedral. It's said that it wouldn't be possible for a human to look directly at the angels of the higher realms without blinding themselves with beauty, much in the same way that directly looking at the sun would blind the naked eye with its brilliance. And in that moment, kneeling there in the dream world, I felt I could understand that; for this newborn creature on the ground before me was so enthralling, so utterly breathtaking, that I struggled to breathe with the joy of it.

But then the wooden doors behind us banged open and Mephistopheles was standing there in the doorway, smiling coldly, a woman on his arm. I knew the woman too, for she had visited my dreams before. It was Lilith, in all her dark, seductive, twisted sensuality. Horror suddenly froze me as I realised what dreadful danger the winged newborn baby was in. I reached out to grasp the child but Lilith was too quick for me and had swooped down to pull the crying baby from the ground by its wings. I winced at the roughness with which she handled him and tried to get to my feet to get him back, but Mephistopheles was holding my arms, freezing me solid with his demonic touch, so that all I could do was watch in horror as Lilith devoured the baby before its screaming mother's eyes.

'*God will forgive me*,' Mephistopheles murmured in my ear with soft mockery. '*He'll forgive us all eventually.*'

And with the demon's words still echoing in my mind, the dream scene tore away from me and I woke up sweating and shaking in my bed.

25th December (Christmas Day)

Today was beautiful to begin with. Casey and I went to a Christmas service in St Stephen's Basilica in the morning. The heavy snowfall during the night had dressed the city in a frozen, fine white robe of Christmas finery that sparkled at us as we walked through the streets to the cathedral.

People seemed more friendly than usual, and every family we passed stopped to wish us good morning and a merry Christmas. It was odd, really, and I wondered what made the day so special, so magnificent, for those who were not religious. For me the day was sacred for marking the time when Jesus Christ was born, but I couldn't understand what made the day anything other than ordinary for non-believers.

The sun shone radiantly through the stained-glass windows of the Basilica, the holy music of Christmas hymns lifted to the great arched roof, and sculptured angels gazed down upon us in virtuous approval. We ate out for both lunch and dinner, since neither of us knew how to go about cooking a Christmas meal. I didn't want Casey to be sat on her own in her apartment all day thinking about her family, so I tried to fill the day with things to keep us busy. I'm sure she appreciated the effort but I know she couldn't help thinking of her parents and her brother, and the Christmas she had been having with them just this time last year. But for me, having someone to share Christmas with was wonderful. I had not been condemned to spend the hallowed day sat in my apartment staring at the walls thinking about Nicky and Luke after all.

'Do you miss Luke?' Casey had asked me at one point.

I looked at her in surprise. 'I don't remember him.'

'But do you miss him anyway?' she persisted.

'Yes,' I said. 'Does that sound crazy to you?'

'No,' she replied with a smile. 'I love my baby and I've never even met him. I don't even know where he's *come* from! That's crazy, isn't it? How can you love someone so much when you don't even know them at all?'

When we returned to our apartment building late after dinner, Casey invited me in for a glass of hot mulled wine. Of course, I gladly accepted since I hadn't given her her present yet, not really wanting to do it in front of everyone in the crowded public restaurants.

We walked in to Casey's drab little apartment, and I thought as she heated the wine that I really should look into moving both of us to better accommodation in a nicer part of the city. She had decorated her apartment for Christmas even though she was alone. She told me that she had bought the few cheap decorations and strings of ribbon at one of the open-air Christmas markets with her last pay cheque. I loved her for the small, rather pathetic Christmas tree that stood on the kitchen worktop, decorated with grubby bits of ribbon, and for the cheap wreath she had hung on the door.

'I hope today hasn't been too hard for you,' I said, as I watched Casey arranging mince pies on a plate.

She shrugged. 'I really miss my family,' she admitted. 'All of them. Even though I know that the way I remember them is a lie. My parents ... hurt me so much that I know they couldn't have been the people I thought they were, because those people would never have dreamed of hurting me the way they did. So when I miss my parents, I know I don't really miss *them*, I just miss the people I thought they were. Does that make sense?'

'Yes,' I said. 'I'm afraid it does.'

'Thank you for being there,' Casey said, turning to look back at me. 'You don't know what a difference it's made.'

'I'll always be here when you need me,' I promised, and I had never meant anything more in my life. I would follow her to hell and back if I had to.

Casey smiled at me, handed over a mug of mulled wine and put the plate of mince pies on the table. Then she sat down herself and placed a small wrapped package before me.

'What's this?' I asked stupidly.

'A Christmas present, Gabriel,' she said, laughing. 'What do you think it is? I didn't use the money you gave me,' she added quickly. 'It really is from me. I sold a few things to get it.'

'You shouldn't have done that,' I said, upset by the idea.

'They were only things I didn't need any more anyway,' she said, brushing it aside. 'Open it, then. I hope it's okay. You're not very easy to buy for.'

In all honesty, if I had unwrapped it to find a slice of stale bread I think I would have treasured it like a holy relic until the end of my days. We had been strangers before. Look where I had brought us. Casey wanted me in her life now. She trusted me. I wanted to freeze this moment, for it seemed impossible that I could ever be happier than I was right then.

When I folded aside the Christmas wrapping and the white tissue paper beneath, a shining black object on a silver chain fell out onto my hand. It was a carved black onyx crucifix glinting with tiny flecks of gold. I adored it at once. Surely Nicky herself could never have bought me a gift so perfect.

'I got it from the Christmas market in Vörösmarty Square,' Casey said. 'People used to believe the crucifix would protect them from evil. You're going to think I'm being stupid but ... would you mind wearing it? Under your shirt or something? I know it's silly but I'd just feel better if I knew you were wearing it.'

I looked at her, a stupid grin on my face. 'You worry about me.'

Why did that please me so much?

'Of course I worry about you, Gabriel. We're both in this up to our necks, aren't we? Don't you feel frightened sometimes?'

Not for myself. It was clear that my own life had ended when my family had died. But here, now, this had become something more than friendship, hadn't it?

'We're all the family each other's got,' Casey said softly. 'I'm frightened that something might happen to you. You will look after yourself, won't you, Gabriel? Don't do anything stupid. Don't get involved in any fights or anything like that. Just ... stay here with me. I can't shake the feeling that something might happen to take you away, and I can't do this on my own.'

'Casey,' I said gently, unable to prevent a smile, 'I've already promised to be there for you whenever you need me.'

'But what if you recover your memories one day and go back to your old life?'

'You know I don't have one.'

'So no matter what you remember, you won't leave me?'

'No, I promise.'

'Don't make the promise lightly, Gabriel. People can get hurt that way.'

'I *promise*,' I said again, and with all my soul I meant it.

I already knew from Stephomi that I had nothing of any value to return to anyway – everyone I cared about was dead. But regardless of what Stephomi had said, I *knew* that there was nothing I could possibly remember – nothing anyone could possibly tell me – that would take me away from Casey. There is a limit to how much you can love another person, and I know I couldn't care for anyone more than I care for her. But if, for argument's sake, I did have to go somewhere or do something, then I would take Casey with me; and if I couldn't take her then I wouldn't go, simple as that. I told her as much, willing her to understand how deeply I meant what I'd said.

'And you don't need to worry about me,' I said. 'You know that I can take care of myself. But this crucifix is beautiful, Casey, thank you. And of course I will wear it. In fact, I'll put it on right now. Are you reassured?'

She nodded and gave me a grateful smile. When I took the present I had brought from my bag, and handed it to her, she told me with smiling exasperation that the shopping we had done at the Luxus Department Stores was supposed to have been her Christmas present.

'No, that was for the baby,' I said. 'I don't think those little woolly hats would fit you, somehow.'

I could see from Casey's face how delighted she was when she unwrapped my gift. 'She's perfect, Gabriel,' she said, smiling at me.

During one of my afternoons in the city, I had come across a tiny little shop, owned by an elderly Hungarian man, that was stuffed full of wooden carvings, most of them religious in nature. The old man told me he made them all himself with the help of his brother and nephew. Some of the carvings were painted, some were left as they were – the naturally pale golden hue of the wood the craftsmen used. Everything in there was extremely expensive due to the time and skill involved in making even the smallest piece.

The figure I had chosen for Casey was a small, unpainted statuette of the Virgin Mary, head humbly bowed, a long shawl clasped about her shoulders and falling gracefully around her slender figure to her feet. It really was a beautiful piece and seemed particularly appropriate for Casey because of her fatherless baby – and she had told me herself that she found pictures and images of the Virgin Mother comforting.

'What's that on your hand?' I suddenly asked sharply as I noticed the thin streaks of scarlet trickling over her palm.

'What?' she asked, glancing up at me.

I looked down at the white tissue paper lying on the table in which the figurine had been wrapped. It was stained with red.

'Can I see that for a minute?' I asked, snatching it from her grasp.

Then I gazed at the thing in horror. The tiny statue was weeping. Scarlet tears of blood were soaking into and staining the soft wood, and trickling over my fingers as I held the figure.

'What is it?' Casey asked.

I glanced at her and then held up the statuette. 'What do you think of this?'

'I love her, Gabriel, really. She's perfect.'

I felt my mouth twisting into a grimace as I realised she couldn't see the bloody tears, and my mind raced for an excuse. I could not possibly leave this thing in Casey's possession. It might be dangerous.

'I'm really sorry, Casey, but they seem to have given me the wrong one,' I said apologetically. 'The one I picked out for you was much better than this. I'll take it back to the shop as soon as it opens after Christmas and get them to exchange it.'

Casey protested that she really was delighted with the one I was holding in my hand, but I was firm. The fine lines and details of the carving's face were virtually imperceptible now, so covered was the figure in its own scarlet tears. Then I made the mistake of looking up at the kitchen worktop and saw Casey's hateful little Black Madonna standing there, also weeping tears of blood, and I knew I had to get out of the apartment fast. That same raw, desperate revulsion was rising up in me at the sight of the dripping blood, just as strong as the day I had sunk my knife into the rare steak, and it took everything I had not to leap to my feet with a cry of disgust and bolt from her apartment to the safety of my own.

I stood up abruptly, walked round behind Casey in the pretence of putting my mug in the sink, and snatched up the Black Madonna, stuffing it into my pocket without Casey noticing. Somehow I managed to thank my young neighbour for a lovely day and for the gift she had given me, before saying goodnight and returning to my apartment where I flung the Virgin Mary and her black counterpart onto the kitchen table and stared in trembling fear at the blood that was all over the palms of my hands. The sight stirred something inside me. It tugged at a memory that refused to come to the surface, for which I was grateful. But I knew in that moment that this was not the first time I had had blood on my hands. It wasn't the first time. This had happened before. Something really, really terrible ...

I didn't realise I wasn't alone until Stephomi spoke. 'You're late tonight, Gabriel. I've been here for hours.'

I spun round with a startled yell, making Stephomi jump himself. 'How did you get in here?' I asked hoarsely.

'I hope you don't mind. I just came to tell you, well, to warn you ... But I see you already know—'

'Know what?' I managed, willing my body to stop shaking. It was all the more disturbing because, even if something deep inside me remembered, I had no conscious recollection of what I was so scared of.

'It's begun,' Stephomi said, with a nod towards the furthermost wall of the room. On it was hung a painting of Jesus, and I could see even from here that he was weeping. Tears of blood ran down the canvas, staining and marking the picture horribly. 'Your neighbour will give birth this Sunday – six days from now. Every religious picture or statue in the city is weeping like that. Eerie, isn't it?' he said, with a glance of distaste at the carvings on my kitchen table, now floating in a pool of their own blood.

'What is this?' I asked, holding up my bloody hands.

Stephomi frowned at me. 'I just told you. Every painting and—'

'No, no, what is this? What is *this*?' I asked again, gesturing with my hands. 'Why do I remember *this*?'

'What do you mean?' Stephomi asked, looking puzzled. 'Are you okay?'

'Did I hurt someone?' I asked, afraid of the answer. 'I did something, didn't I? I did something really, really awful to someone.'

Something was tugging at me. I needed to remember something that had only happened a few weeks ago. Something that had been wrong though I hadn't realised it at the time ... Something Stephomi had said to me that hadn't been right ... He had contradicted himself; he had lied to me ... If I could just remember what it was, I could confront him with it and he could give me the logical explanation that I knew must exist. I glanced at the weeping statues and painting again, hating them. *They* were doing this to me! Along with those devils in my head. It wasn't me, it was them!

'Make them stop,' I pleaded. 'They hate me! They want me

to be insane like them! Don't you understand? They're trying to destroy me! They want me to forget again!'

Calmly, Stephomi picked up a kitchen towel and handed it to me. 'Clean that blood off your hands,' he ordered.

I did as he said; glad to have someone telling me what to do. At the same time, Stephomi turned the painting of Jesus round to face the wall, then took the towel from me and dropped it over the bloody virgins on the table.

'No more blood,' he said. 'All right? Do you feel better now?'

'*The rest of your family were there ...*' I said, remembering at last.

'What?'

'When I asked you if you came to Nicky and Luke's funeral, you said yes.'

'What of it?'

'And then you said that the rest of my family went to support me.'

'So?'

'So I don't *have* any other family. I said so in that letter I wrote my aunt before she died. There wasn't anyone else apart from Nicky and Luke. You're not still lying to me, are you, Stephomi?' I was almost begging him.

I saw him hesitate and then I knew for sure, and it made me feel sick. With myself as much as with him ... I was so tired of having to rely on other people to tell me who I was. How many times was I going to have to go through this miserable uncertainty? It was starting to make me feel like a shadow rather than a real person.

'Why did you lie about the funeral?' I demanded. 'How much of what you told me about that day was true?'

Stephomi sighed. 'None of it.'

'*None* of it?'

'Gabriel, you have to understand; I lied only because I knew the truth would hurt you. You weren't all that stable and I thought these stories might help you to become more grounded. Make you feel more normal.'

'More normal?' I almost whispered.

'If I'd told you the truth, you might have done something stupid. You hated yourself for everything that'd happened.'

'I killed them, didn't I?' I said, almost to myself, realising what Stephomi was going to say. 'I killed my wife and son somehow. That car crash was my fault, wasn't it?'

'There never was any car crash,' Stephomi said quietly.

I stared at him, felt my heart begin to lift. 'You mean … Nicky and Luke …are alive?'

'No. They, er … they never existed.'

Never existed … ? After a moment I laughed, sure that he must be joking. But Stephomi didn't laugh. For once, he wasn't even smiling.

'Don't be ridiculous,' I said, staring at him. 'I have the documents that *prove* they existed. I have their death certificates and our marriage certificate and—'

'Forgeries,' Stephomi said.

'Rubbish! If they never existed then why do I miss them so much?'

'Because you love the idea of them,' Stephomi said, with a shrug.

I shook my head, torn between amusement and irritation, 'All right, humour me. Where is my *real* family?'

'You don't have one,' Stephomi said simply. 'You've never had one.'

'Oh, I see. You mean, I was miraculously conceived as well?'

'You were orphaned.'

I gazed at Stephomi – for the first time realising what a pathetic person he was. How could I ever have relied on him the way that I had? Well, I had Casey now. I didn't need him any more.

'I don't think we should continue to see each other,' I said stiffly. 'It's quite clear to me that you have a compulsive lying disorder. It probably relates to some kind of repressed childhood trauma. I've read about these things, you know. It's all psychological. I would advise you to seek help. All you've ever done is lie to me. Come to think of it, I haven't heard about this so-called religious War or the Antichrist from anyone but you; I'm half inclined to believe that you were making it all up to impress me.'

'That would be a very dangerous thing to do,' Stephomi warned, quietly.

'You're jealous of her, aren't you?' I said, realisation dawning.

'I beg your pardon?' Stephomi asked, watching me with a strange look on his face.

'You're jealous of Casey.'

'Why should I be jealous of her?' he asked me patiently, like someone humouring a madman.

'Because of *me*!' I said gleefully. The thought gave me this happy, selfish little glow inside. 'I really needed you before I met her, didn't I? You just loved it, didn't you? All that attention. I relied solely on you for companionship, advice, answers about my past ... And then I started spending more time with Casey and less with you, and you decided you'd come round here and tell me another story about my past to get me interested again. It's not a dead family this time, it's a lonely orphan. How stupid do you think I am? You need me far more than I need you now. I'm not interested in the past any more, Stephomi. I know that my family were real. I can *feel* it. I don't need anyone to prove it to me. And there's nothing you can say that's going to make me doubt that.'

'Have it your own way,' Stephomi said, shrugging easily. 'But don't be too quick to dismiss me, my friend, for you might need me in what's to come, and then you might regret what you've said.'

'What's to come!' I repeated derisively. 'Assuming that there *is* anything to come, I will just pray to God if I need help.'

'*Prayer!*' Stephomi practically spat the word. It was the first time this evening that I had seen him show annoyance. 'Christ, Gabriel, how can you be so naïve? When has prayer ever worked? Do you know what happens to people when they pray? They draw attention to their own sins and God *punishes* them. He sends plagues, He sends *floods*—'

'You're still doing it! You're still lying!'

'I don't need to lie about God to make Him sound like a cruel,

selfish bastard!' Stephomi snapped. 'People suffer and die point-
lessly every day, Gabriel, every day! I tell you it would be a relief to
go to Hell after this; it would be a *relief*! What about Noah's Ark?
The whole world had been praying for salvation and how did God
reward their prayers? By drowning them *all*. Apart from Noah, of
course, but then he had to live with what he'd seen and done for
the rest of his life, and he ended up wishing he'd died with the rest
of them. It's the same tired old story – you pray to God, you get
kicked in the fucking teeth. Anyone who can pledge allegiance to
a God like that *disgusts* me! You're just a lot of fucking brainless
sheep! You can't even *conceive* of the possibility that God's a sick,
selfish bastard, can you?'

'Shut up!' I said angrily, finding my tongue at last. 'Shut up,
shut up!'

To my surprise, Stephomi fell silent – breathing deeply, collecting himself, as if he'd said more than he'd meant to. I'd never seen
his control waver like that before. It unsettled me. What kind of a
person could talk about God in such a way anyway? Just hearing
it made me feel like twisting his damn head off.

'I'm ... I'm sorry, Gabriel' he said with an effort. 'I didn't mean
to be disrespectful to your faith. I'll go if you want. But I'm telling you the truth about yourself, however much you might have
preferred the lies. Nicky and Luke were a beautiful dream, but
that's all they ever were.'

'All right, all right,' I said, waving my hand dismissively, just
wanting to be rid of him. 'Look, you were there for me when I
needed you and I won't forget that. So I'll help you with this,
okay? This lying disorder you have. We'll go and see a psychiatrist
or something. Together we can ... we can ...' I faltered, my attention caught by the large mirror on the wall across from me. The
burning man was there, staring out at me, his blue eyes blazing
as fire rained down about him. And then, in another moment,
he was gone and a name appeared written in fiery gold on the
mirror's surface: Stephomi. Unable to help myself, I glanced at my
friend, who turned his own gaze sharply towards the mirror; but
it seemed that Stephomi was not a party to this particular mirror

vision for he turned back to me with an exasperated, 'What is it now?'

I forced my gaze back to the mirror and, as I watched, the letters of my friend's name rearranged themselves until at last there was an altogether different name burning like fire on the mirror before me: Mephisto.

I turned back to the man standing in front of me, horror written all over my face, determined to speak, to question, to demand an explanation as to why the letters of his surname were an anagram of the name of one of the most notorious demons of all time: one of the Seven Princes of Hell, and the Devil's second in command himself. But the expression on my face must have given me away, for it was Mephistopheles who spoke first.

'Oh dear. I believe Michael might have just taken matters into his own hands and exposed me. I wish you wouldn't look at me like that, Gabriel, as if you hardly knew me at all.'

'Why?' I managed, staring at the demon with revulsion. 'Why the pretence and the lies and the deceiving? Why pretend to be my friend like that?'

'What deception?' Mephistopheles asked pleasantly. 'There has been no pretence or lies from me.'

'Get away from me, you filthy ... you *disgusting* creature!' I spat, instinctively staggering back a few steps.

I saw the demon's mouth tighten angrily. 'Now, Gabriel, let's not react too childishly about all this,' Mephisto said coldly. 'I'm the same person I was before. I like you, you know – even if you can be a self-righteous, pompous pain-in-the-fucking-arse at times – always whining about morality or Godly *virtues* or Lucifer or anything else you can fucking think of. But to my surprise, I have enjoyed keeping you company. I kept Captain Hosenfeld company too – you remember him, don't you? Szpilman's brave rescuer. Do you know how God rewarded his bravery, Gabriel? By sending Russians to capture him and torture him for years and years after the war ended, until at last he died in a cold, miserable little cell, broken, alone and unwept for. That's hardly fair, is it? The only kind words he ever heard during those seven years were spoken by me.

'As for this imminent apocalyptic problem we'll soon have, I'm sure you'll do the right thing when the time comes. I've never known a person so constantly inwardly preoccupied with morality. I will just remind you, though, that the disgust you feel for me now didn't exist before you found out I was one of Lucifer's angels. I had nurtured a faint hope that if you came to know me with no prejudices clouding your mind from the outset, you might come to feel a little differently about the angel/demon divide. After all, if my kind really were so vile, you would think you would have seen through me, whatever form I happened to be in.

'You were forsaken by God and his army. When you were here in Budapest, friendless and alone, did any of God's angels come to your aid? Did they make any effort to take the edge from the loneliness that was tearing at you from the inside? Like it or not, Gabriel, it was Lucifer, not God, who sent an angel to you to pull you back from the brink of madness. You owe the Devil your sanity, my friend. How does that feel?'

I stared at him, feeling like I was going to be sick. How had this happened? *How* had this happened? How had I let myself be tricked by him? The idea that I had eaten and drunk with a demon; that I had welcomed a demon into my home as a friend ... The very *idea* sickened me and my stomach shrivelled nauseatingly at the horror of it.

'Get out!' I whispered – a mixture of shame and disgust making my whole body shake.

Mephisto narrowed his eyes at me and for a moment I could clearly see the demon there – the malice, the hatred and that dreadful cold nastiness ... Then he flashed me a sudden smile and gave an easy shrug, striding towards me.

'Oh, well, all friendships must have their final goodbyes. No hard feelings?' he asked, holding out his hand.

I shrank back from him in instinctive revulsion. 'I will *never* shake hands with a ... with a—' I began, but even as I spoke, Mephistopheles grabbed my arm with one hand and gripped my hand with the other, forcefully shaking it in a terrible charade of friendship. I flinched at the coldness of his touch but was too afraid to try and resist him as he stood there shaking my hand, gazing at me with an amused expression on his face, one eyebrow slightly raised as if in challenge.

'Goodnight, Gabriel,' he said suddenly, dropping my hand abruptly. 'Merry Christmas.'

I remained where I was, rooted to the spot as Mephistopheles strode from my apartment, the door banging shut behind him. Silently, I held up my shaking hand and saw that the demon's handshake had left glistening splinters of ice embedded in my palm, a raw frost burn outlining the shape where his long, slender fingers had touched my skin.

I should have known. I should have worked it out for myself long before this. Stephomi ... Mephisto. It was right there before me, a flaunting arrogance and recklessness that was in itself astounding. And I had been too stupid to see it. Even his stolen first name, Zadkiel, was a taunting clue, for Mephistopheles is the dark twin of the archangel Zadkiel.

And the burning man ... Mephistopheles had called him Michael. As in archangel Michael? Leader of the angelic armies and God's most trusted servant? When I had prevented Mephistopheles from being beheaded by him, it had been at Michael's church. The angel had been dispelling the demon from his own church. I'd thought that Stephomi's wound had healed so quickly because the sword had been abnormal, not the man.... Oh, God, why did I intervene? It had been the fire. That was what had thrown me. It's surely understandable to associate fire with Hell and its devils. But now that I look more closely at the books and paintings I own, I see that angels are indeed often associated with the blazing brightness and warmth of fire, while demons are connected with cold, blistering ice. I recall too that in Dante's *Divina Commedia*, the Ninth Circle of Hell – the one reserved for the most depraved and wicked of sinners – consists of a perfect sphere of ice in which these sinners are condemned to eternal, freezing agony, inwardly cowering at their hideous proximity to the Devil himself.

The Ninth Circle ... I know that the Ninth Circle is responsible somehow for all my misery. After Mephistopheles left my apartment, I stood rooted to the spot for some moments until I looked up and glanced over at the mirror again to see more letters written on its surface in shining fire: CIRCLEIX. Circle. IX. Roman numerals for the number nine. Circle 9. I glared in mounting anger at the mirror and in a sudden outburst of rage, I picked up the kitchen chair and threw it into the glass, smashing it with a grim, deeply pleasing satisfaction – showers of glass exploding out towards me and skittering across the floorboards in sharp, sparkling pieces.

Right now I feel I hate all angels, whether God's or Satan's. They're a bunch of bastards, the lot of them, and the terrible bitterness of it was that Mephistopheles was right. The one person to be a friend to me over these past months was one of Lucifer's devils. No merciful angel of God had come to explain what was happening to me, to comfort me, to be a friend to me, to take away my fear. On the few occasions that Michael (if that really was the identity of the burning man) had appeared to me in dreams and visions, his appearance had served only to frighten me ... He hadn't *helped* me. Stephomi ... that is ... Mephisto had come to me like a man, speaking in clear words, coming to my world rather than exploiting the fact that I could see through to his. And now once again Michael was being cryptic, ambiguous, enigmatic, and I could not even guess what the message written in fire on the mirror meant. Surely the angel must *know* that I had no idea what the relevance of the Ninth Circle was? He must *know* that I had asked Mephistopheles about it and researched it and wracked my mind for hidden memories but to no avail. The Ninth Circle surrounded me, trapping me with lies and agendas and my own self-imposed ignorance.

But I won't be used as a puppet. The strange message – CIRCLEIX – continued to appear as I prepared for bed. I saw it blazing above me in the bathroom mirror and scorched into the wooden footboard of my bed. But I ignored it. I didn't understand it anyway, and I wouldn't do anything about it if I could. I felt I hated the angels – or whoever was responsible – for tormenting me, for forsaking me and for putting some truth into Mephistopheles' words by refusing to explain clearly to me what the hell it was they fucking wanted.

26th December (Boxing Day)

I've disgraced myself before God by letting Mephistopheles trick me in such a way. I hope that one day I will be forgiven. The CIRCLEIX message is still appearing around my apartment, but I am ignoring it.

27th December

Mephistopheles. *Mephistopheles!* All this time it has been *Mephistopheles* I was talking to! How did this happen to me? How did it happen? How did it? How? Mephistopheles – the one known as 'He who destroys by lies' … Can I believe a word that demon said to me? Can I believe a *word* of it? Was he lying when he told me Nicky and Luke died in a car crash? Or was he lying when he said they never existed? They *must* have existed once! You can't love a dream.

29th December

I have drawn pictures of them to stop myself from worrying. I'm carrying them around with me in the apartment. Casey has been banging on the door outside, but I've pretended to be out. I can't see her right now. I can't see anyone. I want to spend the time here with Nicky and Luke. They're not much more than stick men, for of course I can't remember precisely what they look like. But that doesn't matter. When I talk to Nicky, it helps calm me down. Of course, I know that it's not really her. I'm not losing my mind or anything distasteful like that. I know my wife is dead. I'm just talking to a crude drawing, that's all.

It's all right, though. Nicky herself has told me that she's real, and she ought to know. Her death was an accident, like Stephomi said. There was nothing I could have done. I loved them. They were everything to me. I would never have hurt them. I wish this CIRCLEIX message would go away. It's burning into the floorboards as well as the walls now.

31st December (New Year's Eve)

My name is not Gabriel Antaeus. What a fucking surprise ... At long last, I know the full disgusting truth about my past. I know why I took pains to punish myself, for if any man alive deserves punishment it is me.

I have committed the most wicked acts and they haunt me now as they did then. It is necessary that I isolate myself entirely from those around me. But now, of course, I have a problem, for Casey's life is already quite hopelessly entangled with my own. Despite my promises I must cease all contact with her. I have made arrangements for her to have her baby in a nearby hospital in the city centre, with a private room and every comfort she might need. I have also deposited enough money in a bank account, set up under her name, to see her through for at least several years.

'But why?' she had asked, trying not to cry when I had told her. 'Why aren't you going to be there with me yourself?'

'I can't explain,' I said stiffly. 'That's just the way it has to be.'

'My Black Madonna's gone,' she said suddenly, giving me an accusing look. 'Did you take it?'

I hesitated for a moment before replying, 'Yes, I did.'

'Well, can I have it back?'

'No.'

'But it *belongs* to me!' she raged. 'That man in the marketplace gave it to *me*! How dare you steal it from me like that? How *dare* you? It was a present! You know how much I love it! I feel like I don't know you at all. You got your memories back, didn't you?'

'Yes.'

'So you're leaving Hungary?'

'Yes.'

'When are you coming back?'

'I'm not.'

'But you promised me, Gabriel. You *promised*! You said that no matter what you remembered, you and me would stay together. You said, if you had to leave then you'd take me with you, and if I couldn't go then you wouldn't either! You said it was as simple as *that* and I *believed* you!'

She started to cry then. I hated to see her so upset, but what could I do?

'I don't want to go,' I said. 'I'm sorry, Casey. I don't want to go. I love you. I always will. But I can't be around you.'

'*Why not?*' she sobbed.

'I can't tell you,' I said, feeling helpless. 'Look, Casey, do you trust me? I mean, do you really trust me?'

She nodded, tears running down her cheeks.

'Then you've got to believe me when I say that you'll be better off without me in your life rather than in it.'

'That's *bullshit*!' She tried to shout at me through her tears. 'What could *possibly* be worse than being on my own? How am I supposed to do this by myself, Gabriel?'

'I'm afraid you'll just have to find a way, Casey.'

And then she slammed the door in my face and I sighed and turned back to my apartment to pack for the flight. My plane leaves for Washington tonight. Arrangements will be made for my possessions at a later date. I don't know how long I will stay in the United States. I simply purchased the first plane ticket I could. I have had some money changed into US dollars, and packed a small bag of essentials. The important thing is simply to be away from Hungary, the focal point of the mounting tension of this religious War. I know that God won't let anything happen to Casey. Mephistopheles said himself that neither angels nor demons will be able to directly affect her or her child, and I believe him. If there were no need for a human agent, then why go to such lengths to pose as a friend and try to obtain my trust and loyalty in the first place?

I'm afraid that, as the only person of the In Between nearby, if I stay I might be compelled to act for the demons somehow. I fear that Stephomi ... that Mephisto will find some way to trick me into doing something that could hurt Casey. And I will never hurt her. I've hurt so many other people, but I won't ever be responsible for hurting Casey. I love her too much for that. So I'm removing myself. With no human agent available, Casey's baby will simply be born tonight, grow up and turn into whatever it is destined to be. Nothing good will come of my interference – that I know for an absolute certainty.

I leave for the airport in two hours. Meanwhile, I must make some record of all that has occurred since Michael's exposing of Mephistopheles. I must make some record of who I am. I want to ground myself. I don't want to feel myself slipping away. There must be a record. This is essential, *essential*. I won't go insane over this. People like me don't deserve the luxury of madness, although, God, I wish I *were* mad.

It was the messages. The fiery six letters and two numbers: CIRCLEIX. For five days I continued to ignore them, even as they increased in frequency and location – appearing in mirrors, on tables, burning into the spines of my books and the linings of my curtains. By the sixth day – yesterday – the message was all over every spare bit of space in my apartment: the furniture, the walls, the floor, the ceiling – everything, until all my rooms blazed with it. And then one of them burst, quite literally, into flames. It was one of the messages on the window in the living room. The fiery letters and numbers exploded into molten shards, shattering the window instantly with the heat and sending a shower of sparks over the room, where they started to smoulder on the rugs and on the furniture. Hastily, I managed to put them out with the fire extinguisher. When the last of the glowing embers had been stamped out, I threw the extinguisher into the corner of the room in frustration and tore my hands through my hair.

'What *is* it?' I shouted angrily. 'Circle 9! The Ninth Circle! I don't know what it is, you *fucking* idiots! If you don't realise that by now, then you really are the most fucking *useless* angels—' I broke off suddenly, my hands clamped over my mouth in horror. *Christ*, what was I *doing*? What was I *thinking*, swearing at angels? What a vile, disgusting, *unforgivable* thing to do!

'I'm … I'm sorry … I'm sorry. Forgive me, God,' I stammered, head bowed, half fearing that I might be struck down by lightning where I stood.

And then I froze, finally realising in a flash of enlightenment what the angels were trying to tell me. Cold fear prickled on my skin. The computer disc that I had given to Toby, with instructions for it to be handed back at a certain time … The disc that I had been unable to access because I did not have the eight-digit password … CIRCLEIX.

As soon as I came to this conclusion, the burning messages all disappeared from the walls and the furniture and the floor with a suddenness that made the ensuing quiet darkness seem strange and unnatural. I retrieved the disc from its hiding place in the cupboard, sat down at my computer and loaded up the programme.

And then I hesitated when the password box came up on the screen once again, tempted just to turn the computer off now and destroy the disc once and for all so that I might never know what was on it. But even as these thoughts filled my mind, the burning message appeared once again, with alarming ferocity, in the wood of the desk; and quite suddenly I found I was afraid of the angels and what they might do to me if I didn't do what they wanted. I already knew that they were not above violence, and that they were not above killing people when they had to.

'All right,' I said aloud and at once the message disappeared, leaving identical burn marks in its place.

I typed in the password.

The box disappeared and a message came up to replace it: 'Password Confirmed.' Then the screen loaded up, and I forced myself to look as a list of filenames appeared on the screen. They were people's names. Some of them were English, some French, some Chinese and Spanish, Korean and Australian ... And then my eye fell on one name that I knew. Anna Sovànak. Automatically, I double clicked to open the file. It was a video file, no more than thirty minutes long. But it was enough. Enough to show me what had really happened to that woman, and what my connection to her had been. And I knew that the video spoke the truth. That it was not fabricated or doctored in any way. I knew because suddenly I could remember it all.

I remembered my real name: Gilligan Connor. I remembered renting that isolated villa on the Italian coast purposefully because it was quite near to the spot that Anna Sovànak and her family were vacationing. I remembered striking up a friendship with Anna on the beach – a meeting that had nothing whatsoever to do with chance, despite outward appearances. I remember sympathising with her as she confided in me about her problems with her husband. His rudeness, the way he took her for granted, the way he never did anything to help round the house, the way he didn't romance her as he'd once done. And I listened patiently to her complaints about the problems she had with her children and her job and her friends.

I don't think Anna was a woman naturally given to whining and complaining, but people like to talk about themselves and probably find something freeing in talking with a sympathetic stranger they are unlikely to see again after their holiday.

We met a couple of times down on the beach when she had stormed out after arguing with her husband. It did make it very easy for me, but I would have found another way if I'd had to. I always did.

I asked Anna to come back to my villa for a drink one day and she happily accepted, clearly hoping for an adulterous sexual relationship and finding the idea of a holiday fling appealing after the family problems she'd been having. And, of course, there was also the fact that I was younger than her husband, with none of his middle-aged fat since my body was well-toned from years and years of disciplined training. When we got back to my villa, I made her a drink and we sat down on the couch on the veranda.

The private white beach stretching out before us, the salty tang of the waves filling the air, and the muffled roar of the surf made it the perfect romantic spot. She'd only had a couple of drinks before she was kissing me. I laughed at her eagerness as her cocktail glass shattered on the floor and buttons were torn off my shirt. She sucked in her breath in pleased surprise as she ran her hands over the toned muscles of my chest and abdomen.

'Aren't you lean?' she teased me. 'You must work out all the time!'

'Every day,' I acknowledged with a smile, speaking softly in her ear.

She giggled as I drew her away from the cream couch, towards the beach ... *What are beaches there for anyway?* She had asked me this bitterly one day while complaining of her husband's inaction. I had never seen the attraction of beaches, myself. But this was for Anna, not for me. So we went down together in the sand, her eyes shining in excitement at the vile deliciousness of cheating on the person you're supposed to love. I was aware of her hand caressing the back of my neck as, slowly, one by one, I teased the buttons of her shirt undone ... Then, while her hands were busy fumbling with my belt, I reached for the knife that was concealed at my ankle, and stabbed her in the neck with it.

We lay there, still for a moment, while she bled out under me. I knew where to do it so that her death would be relatively painless, almost instantaneous. The hidden video camera set up on the veranda caught everything. It was quite easy to wrap up her body in the plastic sheeting, put her in a crate, put the crate on board the little fishing boat I had rented, row out a little way and then drop the crate overboard into the Mediterranean.

I had planned for it all to take place on the beach because the ocean would wash away the bloodstained sand without my having to take any action to clean it up. The villa was filled with cream furniture and white sheets that would not have been so easy to clean – and it would never do to have mess. Mess was inefficient and led to too many questions.

I scrubbed and scrubbed at my hands in the bathroom afterwards so that not a drop of Anna's blood remained, not even traces beneath my fingernails. Then I took all my clothes off and dropped them into a bath full of hot water to soak. As the water slowly turned red in the tub, I showered and removed all traces from my hair and skin. I do this every time. I can't stand to be covered in someone else's blood and, as I said before, it just doesn't do to have mess.

Why did I kill Anna Sovànak? Why did I do it? Had she wronged me at some point in the past? Was she responsible for the death of someone I cared about? Was I in love with her? Was it jealousy? Envy? Spite? Was it a crime of *passion*? I believe I could have almost lived with myself if it had been a crime of passion. A crime of passion was still inexcusable, still inherently wicked ... but at least it was *understandable*. There was some human element in the act. But the truth was, I felt nothing for Anna. No like or dislike. Nothing. I killed her because somebody paid me to.

The government, to be more precise – as they had paid me to commit countless other murders. We were not like James Bond. It was made quite clear to all assassins from the very beginning that if we ever got into trouble we'd be on our own. The government would not formally acknowledge us in any way. The Queen was never going to pin medals on any of our chests ... We were the ones who got our hands dirty, and our superiors were grateful for that because it took the pressure off them, but at the same time – of course – it meant that they did not want to touch us.

I didn't dare to open any more of the video files, but as my eyes ran down the names, I remembered each and every one of them ... The poison, the guns, the knives, the strangulation, the blood ... My employers insisted on video cameras where possible to make sure we didn't back out as a consequence of becoming too attached to our marks. It had been known to happen, although never to me.

I couldn't prevent the memories cascading in with a force that dazzled me, blinded me. I am an assassin. Life and death within the same body. Truly, a person of the In Between. I stared at the computer screen for a moment, wishing I could doubt it. Wishing

I could deny what I knew to be true. But I *remembered* this. There was no Nicky. There was no Luke. They were just stories created to placate me, and then elaborated upon by a demon trying to manipulate me. I've only ever lived in grotty little flats or motels by myself. I am an orphan, as he said. I never got the chance to have a real family. After the incident at the orphanage, I had been almost overcome with the horror of what I had done, so far as my childish mind could truly grasp what had happened. It was not my fault he'd fallen. I was not to blame. But still it marked my life for ever.

And I had had no choice when the secret services had come to take me away from the orphanage. I had been six years old; I'd had to comply with the training I received as I grew up. But then, somewhere along the way, I realised I did have a choice. It was mine and I had made it. I would never be able to have a normal life now. Any friendships I might have would be built on lies, because any normal person would shrink away from me in horror if they knew what I had done – even though none of it was my fault. The government told us these people were dangerous, potential terrorists, threats to the safety of Britain. I think most of my co-workers clung to those reassurances.

Anna Sovànak, for example – I was told during my briefing that she had been designing a new kind of biological weapon, and there was fear that this might find its way into the hands of certain religious extremists with whom Anna supposedly had sympathies. I don't know if this was true, although I suppose if she really had been working on developing new weapons, then that might explain why the story of her discovered body had been quietly consigned to page six. Who's to say whether there were genuine reasons for my victims' deaths, or whether they were simply political murders? You can't think like that when you have a job to do. And it really doesn't matter to me, for I believe that all human life is sacred: that life, in any form, even the smallest, tiniest insect, is absolutely and inherently sacred. And I loathed myself for what I'd done. There could be no greater sin than taking a life. And I had done it again and again and again. But there had hardly seemed any point in quitting.

I killed my first person when I was six years old, although I did not mean to and no one paid me for that crime. It was at the orphanage; I remembered it now. The other children there had taken a dislike to me right from the beginning, for whatever arbitrarily childish reason. But there was one in particular who really hated me. Aaron Thomas. He was older, about nine, and would bully me whenever he got the chance – and the nuns who ran the orphanage never troubled to do anything much about it, for it was all character building, wasn't it?

Then, one day, while playing, Aaron fell through a third-storey window and was left gripping the window ledge, screaming for help. I ran to assist him. I didn't hesitate for a moment, didn't even think about all those horrible things he had done to me. But as I ran towards the window, I tripped on a child's toy left in the middle of the floor, stumbled, and instinctively tried to right myself by grabbing on to whatever I could. It was unfortunate that my hands landed on the drawn up window, my weight bringing the pane of glass down hard on Aaron's fingers. The boy let go at once with a scream of pain and fell to his death. One of the nuns had come in to the room in time to see me 'leaping' for the window to pull it down onto my former tormenter's fingers, causing him to fall three storeys to the stone courtyard below. And that was what the other children there saw too. The nuns believed that, after quietly taking the pain and humiliation of being bullied for so long, I had finally lost my mind and committed murder with a coldness shocking in a child.

I never told anyone that I had been trying to help the boy. I never cried. I never showed any remorse, although I too was appalled by what had happened. *Why didn't I speak out?* How different would my life have been if only I had acted as a normal child and not convinced the secret service, with my cold stoniness, that I was an ideal candidate for their children's training programme? Aaron Thomas – that childhood bully – had not only made me miserable as a child ... he had ruined my whole *life*! I felt glad in that moment that he was dead! I *hated* him! I was *glad* I'd killed him; I was *so glad*! He was responsible for *all* of this! Look what he'd *done* to me! Look what he'd *done*! If he hadn't bullied me so badly, the nuns wouldn't have been so ready to see me deliberately murdering him. Instead, they would have seen the truth of what had happened. If Aaron had been a good-natured boy without an enemy in the world, then the nuns would have *wanted* to believe that I had been running to help him. So that's what they would have seen.

I started off gentle, that's the irony of it. I used to sneak round the girls' empty dormitories during the day, catching spiders and putting them outside because I couldn't stand to hear the girlish squeals and the accompanying *slap, slap* of slippers flattening any spider that was discovered there later.

'Why don't you like spiders anyway?' I'd asked them. 'What harm have they ever done you? What harm have they ever done anyone?'

It had seemed incredibly arrogant to me for those stupid, twittering girls to find the mere *existence* of these creatures offensive. Unfortunately, Aaron overheard me talking to the girls one day, and thereafter took great delight in killing spiders in front of me whenever he could. I hated him for that. I understood the importance of being kind to animals ... of being kind to insects ... of being kind to anything that was smaller than I was. I understood that all unnecessary deaths brought God pain. I didn't wish suffering on anyone – not even on Aaron, who I hated. So I ran to help him when he was hanging from that window, and in doing so I condemned myself to a lifetime of violence and horror and bloodshed. I should have just stood back and done *nothing* – just *watched* him fall, for no one would have condemned me for that, even though it would have been just as blameworthy.

I could remember once, when I was little, wanting to grow up to be a fireman. It probably had something to do with the bright red fire engine toy I'd adored before Aaron took it from me... Assassin had certainly never been on my list ...

What do you want to do when you grow up, Gabriel ... ?
Kill people ...

But for the whole of my adult career, I was a merciful killer.

Obsessively merciful. I went to great lengths to kill in the most painless way possible, and I would always pray for the victim's soul afterwards. I discreetly attended their funeral every time, out of respect, and left flowers at the grave in acknowledgement of the life they'd led. I went to Anna's funeral and watched her children – Max and Jessica, about whom I had heard so much – crying for their mother, and I wished that I could feel something for them ... pity, sadness, shame ... but there was nothing. It was as if my profession had burned out all emotions inside me so that I couldn't feel anything at all. It was this kind of behaviour that led my co-workers to mockingly bestow the name of Gabriel on me. Angel of Mercy, they'd said. Angel of Death. The assassin who sat and prayed for his victims' souls after coldly murdering them ...Gabriel ... what a logical choice ...

But these people were marked for death anyway, and if they were not assigned to me then they would be assigned to some other assassin within the programme. If I left, the government would pick someone else to fill my place and, in that way, another man's soul would be lost for ever. The way I saw it, I was doing the right thing by staying in the programme. There is logic in that, isn't there?

But now the true horror of what I had been crashed through me dizzyingly, and pain twisted inside as I fully realised how terribly isolated I would always be from everyone around me, by the very nature of my past. I could never have friends or a family. My profession had lost me that right. I had seen parents, lovers, siblings, spouses and children weeping at the funerals of my victims. I could never have people in my life when I had spent so much of it taking loved ones away from their families. Besides, I didn't know how to love people. Love was dangerous – it set you up for the worst kind of agony. I had seen it. So I was going to remain alone and I had always known that. Accepted it right from when I'd been six and the people at the orphanage had stared at me with unconcealed horror; loathed me for what I was ... a killer ... something you can't take back ...

But for the last four months, for the first time in my life, there had been hope that I might somehow manage to belong to other people. Because that's what we all want, isn't it? That's what we are all constantly striving for. I know what love is now, because I love Casey – but I shouldn't. Assassins can't have loved ones – can't have anyone at all – because you have to be able to kill anyone you might be assigned to. I'd learned that the hard way some years ago. How can you let yourself love someone when you know how easily they might be taken away from you? And now I'd found out that, not only were Nicky and Luke not real, but they never would be either.

To have all my illusions ripped away from me like that … I think I actually *tasted* madness for a second there. I am Wladyslaw Szpilman, hiding in my self-imposed attic, wishing, *longing* for human company but knowing that if anyone comes my way, I must distance myself from them, for their safety, for my safety, and for the sake of what is right. I'm so dirty now that anyone who gets too close to me will surely be tainted as well. I hurt people just by being near them. I couldn't stop the images of all those people from going through my mind – laughing, happy, relaxed – as I had seen them all at some point or other before murdering them. Now they were all lying in graves because of me.

I staggered into the bathroom … threw up again and again until my vomit became tainted with blood, and it felt like I had torn something inside. When I at last got unsteadily to my feet and turned around, I could see him there behind my mirror. If anything, his image scared me even more now that I knew what he was. Michael's face was turned towards me, though I could hardly make out his features for the light from his flames was so bright, blinding me, scorching my skin, suddenly choking the whole room with heat and smoke and the smell of burning flesh.

'Am I … am I going to Hell?' I asked, raising my voice above the noise of the spitting fire.

For a minute the angel didn't answer, but when he did, it confirmed everything I had tried so hard not to believe:

'One day.'

There was this horrible, helpless dry sob, which I suppose must have come from me for the angel had spoken without any emotion whatsoever.

'I'm sorry,' I said desperately, taking a step back, trying to find some relief from the immense heat. 'I'm sorry for what I did.'

'Too late.'

Too late ... yes ... it was too late, wasn't it? ... I might have started off gentle, but there must have been something wrong with me even then. Few men had it in them to kill again and again and again as I had done ...

I couldn't breathe any more. The flames were roaring now – pounding in my head, blistering my skin, stinging my eyes. I tried to look at Michael, but he blurred in the wavering heat haze. I staggered, clutched at the door handle, tried to get out ... but the heat took the air right out of my burning lungs so that I sank to the floor, blinking sweat out of my eyes and choking on the smoke. And then – at last ... at long, *long* last – my eyes rolled back in my head and I fell into this silent, cool, beautiful darkness.

I opened my eyes some time later, staring at the bathroom tiles, listening to the steady drip, drip from the leaky tap, wishing I could get my amnesia back. At last, I dragged myself upright, turned around and saw Michael standing in the doorway, watching me. There was a bright aura about him but he no longer dripped with flames. He was clearer, more sharply defined than I had ever seen him before. He had bright blue eyes, glossy blond hair, and was wearing plain, simply cut white clothes. Although physically he looked like a man, he still seemed incredibly *bright* ... illuminated – as if he was close to something so blinding that it lit him up as well.

'Can you see me now?' he asked in a deep and resonant voice, looking straight at me.

'Of ... of course I can see you,' I stammered.

'We're in need of your services,' Michael said. He looked anything but happy about it.

'Why didn't you come to me sooner?' I asked, and then flinched at the anger that flashed across the angel's face.

'Your ignorance and lack of desire for the truth distanced you from us, and placed you closer to demons. That's why you were such *pathetically* easy prey for Mephistopheles and why you couldn't see us. Do you remember the Ninth Circle now?'

I nodded. Oh, yes, I remembered it. I remembered it clearly. At some point, all assassins became too old and were required to retire. Or they cracked up and had to be quietly dealt with. When I told my handler that I had started seeing angels and devils, he decided that the work was getting to me; that I was one of the few who could not compartmentalise as we'd been trained to do, not dwelling on the crimes we'd committed. So he put me down for the Ninth Circle. It was an experimental programme designed to protect state secrets and help ex-assassins rehabilitate themselves back into civilian life. The process had not yet been fine-tuned enough to allow the removal of certain memories while leaving others intact. So the assassin's entire memory had to be repressed by blanking out everything, right down to early childhood. I have no idea why the programme was called the Ninth Circle. I'm sure there never was any kind of theological connection but, back then, the name seemed utterly profound and significant to me – like a warning from God that I must find some way of circumventing the effects of the procedure.

Careful preparation was made beforehand – with the willing co-operation of the assassin. They were given a new home, a new identity – false records were made up and stored in the bank. I even remembered copying out the letter to my non-existent aunt as my handler dictated it to me, and the hours and hours I had spent signing my new name so that the false signature might become automatic.

After the procedure, a blow was carefully applied to the head, causing a nasty looking bruise and some bleeding but hardly enough to cause any permanent damage – we'd all taken much worse during the course of our careers. The assassin was then left in their new home amid a set-up that would lead them to believe that an accident had caused them to lose their memory. I had had my doubts about the programme, sceptical that any man would be content to simply accept such a strange scenario.

But it worked. It really did. I had been sure that it wouldn't work on me, however. That, even with my memories temporarily gone, I would realise something was not right; and that I wouldn't rest until I'd found the answers. But it did work. And it would have continued to work, had it not been for the failsafe I had installed – there was that to my credit, at least. It was just that I had so *badly* wanted to believe that all I saw was true and that there were no hidden horrors. The scientists at the Agency believed it was a subconscious thing. That, on some level, the brain prevented assassins from delving too deeply into the set-up and instead urged them to accept the superficial 'truth' that they themselves had helped create.

And as an extra precaution, there was always the money. The cash was always left in the assassin's home as an added incentive not to go to the police. Human greed never failed. They didn't want the money to be taken from them. This was also why I had so much cash in my bank account, for assassins were handsomely paid – as if anything could pay the price for what we do.

The memories were repressed, not deleted, and could be recalled again with the careful application of timely prompts. I thought back to the clues I had sent myself. They had had to be cryptic. A sudden revelation would have recalled my memories only for a moment before being rejected by my subconscious and then becoming even more deeply buried within my mind. Hence the ambiguous clues … to instil uneasiness, to instil suspicion, but to postpone the final revelation until some time had passed. The photos alone would have been sufficient for that. There had never been any *need* for the quotes, but I did it because I wanted to feel fear. It was a curiosity thing. I had never felt fear before and I wanted to know what it was like. I couldn't have known that my plan would work so spectacularly. Fear of losing friends … fear of losing a normal life … And fear when I had read the accusatory notes written in Latin and entrusted to Toby … Fear that I might have committed wicked, terrible sins, of which I had no memory. Now I knew what that emotion felt like at last. It was only fitting, for I had been the instrument of fear for so many, even though I tried to make it as quick and painless as I could.

I always took pains to make sure my victims were unsuspecting, but ... sometimes, it couldn't be helped ... they *knew*. Not for very long, of course. But for moments, they knew what was about to happen to them. You cannot avoid fear completely – you cannot always kill people without scaring them first. I *detested* strangulation and avoided it, even though many of my colleagues favoured it because of the lack of blood. But what about fear? What about the agonising fear a person has to go through first? It is too slow, too drawn out. That is why I like weapons, for they are quick. They're merciful like I am.

Sex was an effective weapon and I'd used it before, in varying degrees, depending on the circumstances. It was useful for building up trust, and so on. But we were forbidden to have sex with a victim just before a kill because, of course, that would leave biological evidence that could connect us to them. I no longer had emotions by then, but lust is hardly an emotion, is it? Lust is nothing more than a base animal instinct, like hunger. It was only ever a job to me, and I never went further than I had to. That would have been wrong.

The *Neville Chamberlain's Weeping Willow* reference on the back of Anna Sovànak's photo makes sense to me now, for I had felt very strongly about appeasement. I'd felt that standing by and doing nothing while crimes were being committed was just as bad as committing the crime yourself. It was all to do with *self-loathing* – I had allowed myself to be pushed into becoming an assassin when I should have resisted it. I'd regarded the Weeping Willow memorial as belonging to Chamberlain and Churchill and Roosevelt just as much as it belonged to Hitler. I had been as much to blame for Anna's death as the person who gave the order. I remembered writing out the sentence on the back of the photo with a malicious smile on my lips, delighted at the prospect of frightening my future self.

And the photo of Mephistopheles ... We had never been friends, in spite of his lie. He had been no more than an acquaintance of whom I was suspicious. He had claimed to be from a rival agency. He had tried to tell me that I had nothing to be ashamed of because my job was a necessary evil that must be performed by someone. He had spoken to me of moral ambiguity. One man's terrorist is another's freedom fighter. I had a role to play, that was all. I had been working on a case in Paris when he came to my hotel room to see me. He spoke of another kind of career, serving under a different boss. But he was vague about the nature of the work I would be expected to do, speaking only of my 'special talents' and their need for someone like me. I had turned him down, of course. The higher salary he offered was of no interest to me; I couldn't spend the money I earned as it was. I had purposefully taken the secret photo to warn my future self of him should he approach me again, for he had known that I was booked for the Ninth Circle procedure when we last spoke and I was worried then that he might try to exploit my ignorance. The problem was that I had been so eager to latch on to any friend that I had not heeded the warning, and Mephisto himself must have been quite delighted with the change in my attitude.

I had not wanted the Ninth Circle procedure. But I knew I would ultimately have no choice and the safest thing to do was to pretend to go along with it. Most assassins were delighted to accept since it meant a fresh start for them. A life untainted with the guilt that all of us carried but none of us admitted. Like I said – it's not like James Bond – you can't really casually kill twenty men in a day and then not see each and every one of their faces that night, no matter how many beautiful women you might have writhing around in your bed to distract you. It just doesn't work like that. James Bond is a fallacy – killing has never come so easily to anyone, and that holds true even if you do believe you're doing it in pursuit of a just cause. It's still *killing*. It's still *death*. Someone who existed that morning no longer does because of you ...

I'd felt that I deserved no fresh beginning or second chance. I wasn't fit to live and circulate with other people. So I set about laying clues for myself, a trail of black and shrivelled breadcrumbs. I chose the name of Gabriel Antaeus because I knew I would try to find out more about the name and I knew the disturbing connotations I would find. I concealed clues in packages and paid Toby to hold on to the disc and deliver the notes, written in Latin so that he would be unable to understand them. I had to be careful, for I knew that the organisation would search the apartment and my belongings to ensure that there was nothing there that would trigger my memories to return. But they never expected to find anything really, because assassins were supposed to *want* the procedure. What kind of madman would reject the chance of a new life?

'If your memory has now returned,' Michael said, gazing at me coldly, 'then you are aware that you have committed the most wicked series of crimes.'

I nodded silently. I knew now why I had acted with such distinctive horror at having to kill the butterfly that the boy in the park had mutilated. I knew why the sight of blood, even from a steak on a plate, was repugnant to me. I wanted no more to do with death and dying, suffering and bleeding. I wanted to shut those things out from my mind and life for ever. I'd had enough to last me several lifetimes already.

'Do you know how Anna Sovànak's body came to be in Budapest?' I asked.

This was the one part I had been unable to figure out, for I clearly remembered rowing far into the Mediterranean before dropping the crate overboard.

'Yes, I put it there,' Michael said steadily.

'*You?* But I thought, Mephistopheles, or Lilith, or some other demon—'

I broke off in surprise at the sneer curling the angel's lips.

'*Mephistopheles!*' He spat the word, as if its very presence in his mouth was distasteful to him. 'Why do you think he never just came out and told you the truth when he had the chance? Why do you think he purposefully kept you ignorant about your past? Because ignorance itself brings you closer to demons, as truth moves you closer to angels. As your last victim, I had hoped that the sight of her photo in the papers might be enough to break through to your memories.'

Almost, almost, perhaps. But my subconscious mind had been working exceedingly hard to keep those memories buried for ever.

'She was lost,' Michael went on. 'Luckily I found her before Mephistopheles did.'

I thought back to the smashed violin and black fur in Mephistopheles' hotel room. An angry friend, the demon had said. *I've lost something of his ...*

My shoulders slumped with the bitter weight of guilt. Then Michael spoke, for the first time in a voice that was almost kindly, 'Redemption can only come in the service of God, Gabriel, not demons. It won't be easy. By its very definition, redemption must involve hardship and sacrifice.'

'I accept that,' I replied eagerly. 'I want to redeem myself. Please, just tell me what to do.'

'You must take Casey March away somewhere. She can't have her child in a hospital.'

I nodded, feeling a weight slipping from my shoulders as I gazed at God's angel stood before me. At last, no more demons, no more lies. Here was Michael, who would guide me.

'And as soon as the child is born, you must kill it.'

I stared at the angel, my mouth dropping open in horror.

'We can't risk the coming of the Antichrist at this time,' Michael went on.

'But it's ... it's just a tiny baby, for Christ's sake!'

'Who may grow up to be responsible for mass genocide on a scale never seen before,' Michael replied sharply. 'You must take action to prevent this abomination from ever getting the chance.'

'But ... but, Stephomi – I mean, Mephistopheles – said that the baby could be the Saviour too ... the Second Coming—'

'Yes, but it's an acceptable compromise,' Michael said. 'We have agreed it with the demons.'

'But I can't do it,' I said, desperately. Of all the things I'd done before, all the awful things I'd done, I had never come anywhere near the wickedness of harming a baby. Just think how tiny that coffin would have to be ...'I can't kill Casey's son. Oh, please, don't ask me to hurt her like that!'

Michael narrowed his eyes at me and I shrank back from the anger in his gaze. 'If the child turns out to be the Antichrist we've been waiting for, you will carry responsibility for his actions, because you have a duty to act now, while such action is still possible.'

'I'm sorry,' I said helplessly. 'I can't, I can't.'

'Can't or *won't*?' the angel snapped. 'You're an assassin. Killing and hurting people is what you *do*. This is just another job. I fail to see the problem.'

I stared at Michael for a minute. I had continued to work for the government because my soul was already consigned to Hell anyway, and I didn't want to condemn another innocent person to such a life and such an afterlife. And we were serving our country, the government said. Now the angels wanted me to save the world by killing a baby. My mind went back to something Mephistopheles had once said to me – '*Wouldn't it have been nice if Hitler's father had killed his son?*' ... '*Well, of course,*' I had replied tersely. If I had never lost my memory, the horror of killing a child would not have touched me in quite the same way. The justification would have come easier. And surely there were grounds for such justification here. But I could not bear to get any more blood on my already dripping hands.

'Look, I'm *through* with killing, all right? I don't want to *do* this any more! I'm trying to *repent*! For the last four months ... I've had a taste of what it is to be normal. I just want a *normal life*,' I said pleadingly.

'You can't have a normal life,' Michael said coldly.

'But if I ... if I dedicated myself to the service of God,' I said desperately, 'for the rest of my life ... He might forgive me eventually—'

'He would not.'

'Then what the hell's the point?' I shouted angrily at the angel. 'If that's the way you feel, then I might as well go and join the demon ranks right now!'

'You are flawed,' Michael said stonily. 'There's something twisted in your soul. I'm not asking you to help so that you might redeem yourself. I am asking you so that countless lives might be saved. This is not about you, Gabriel.'

'Oh, fuck off, if it's not about me then it won't matter if I sod off to America tonight, will it?' I snapped. 'I've had it with the lot of you, and I won't stay to be a part of any … any …'

I faltered, for suddenly Michael was no longer there. He was simply gone —vanished like smoke, so that for a brief moment I even wondered if I had imagined him. Had an angel really come to me and asked me to murder a teenage girl's baby? Or had I now become one of those people who heard the voices of angels or demons or aliens in their minds, believing they were being ordered to commit the vilest of atrocities? While I have been writing, Casey has left a message on my answer phone, saying that her contractions have begun and that she's on the way to the hospital. *'Please come if you get this message'* … But I can't. I can't risk the chance of some madness coming over me so that I kill her baby without meaning to … I am not a stable person, perhaps I never have been …

Perhaps, after all, I am already mad. A wandering madman with no idea of who or what I am, seeing things that are not there, hearing voices in my head … It's unbearable this sensation – as if the world has started to spin the wrong way round. Am I mad? *Am I?*

1st January (New Year)

It's done. It's done. I can't change it ... There's no way of going back and *fixing* it. For now at least, it's over. I'm still here in Budapest, for I didn't make my plane last night. I'm still here. And I, at least, am still alive. I know that my mind is still numb from what happened last night, but at least now I know what I have to do. I'm not mad any more. Madness would be far, far too easy.

I got home in the early hours of this morning and I'm now at this journal, even though my clothes and hands are stained once again with blood – angel, demon and human. One might think that, really, it should not be so very hard to go through life without getting blood on your hands again and again and again. Why don't I seem to be able to avoid it?

After finishing the entry I made last night, I walked back into the bathroom looking for Michael in the mirror, but he wasn't there – just my own reflection staring back at me. For some while I gazed into the mirror, trying to convince myself that I wasn't insane. Eventually, I sighed and raised my hand to massage my temple ... and then froze, for although my own hand was halfway to my head, my reflection hadn't moved an inch. He was still standing there motionless, both arms hanging at his sides. With a growing sense of dread, I lifted my gaze to meet that of my reflection's. As soon as our eyes met, a slow, nasty grin spread across my reflection's face ... More of a leer than a grin, really. I screamed at him and he stared back with that horrible grin fixed on his face, mocking me, scorning me, *despising* me. I stumbled backwards out of the bathroom, tripping over myself in my haste to get out of the apartment.

It was the final straw. I ran out into the streets like a madman. Celebrations were taking place all over the city to welcome in the New Year. As I ran, I saw many people dressed up for the night, and there were good-natured exclamations of dismay when the rain began to fall and thunder was heard in the distance.

I wasn't looking where I was going. I didn't really know what I was doing. I just had a vague idea of going to St Stephen's Basilica to get my answers. To find out if God was there or not. But when I got to the edge of the square, I cannoned into someone also heading through the rain towards the cathedral. I staggered back and glanced up straight into the face of Mephistopheles.

'Ah,' I cried, grabbing the demon by the shoulder and raising my voice above the rain. 'Tell me, Mephisto, my friend – are you real or am I dreaming you too?'

'What are you talking about?' Mephistopheles replied irritably, shaking my hand off and glancing over at the rising towers of the floodlit Basilica.

'I must *know*,' I said, clutching at his coat as I rambled hysterically at him. 'If any of this is real … if *I* am real, or if this is all something made up in my head or—'

I was not prepared for the punch in the face, and landed flat on my back on the wet pavement when he hit me.

'Sorry, Gabriel,' Mephisto said as he dragged me back up to my feet. 'But we don't have time for hysterics.' He turned slightly and pointed at the Basilica. 'You see the dome up there? That's where Casey is at this moment. She was attacked by Lilith on her way to the hospital.'

'*What?*' I said, horrified, one hand still pressed to my aching jaw. 'But you said demons and angels couldn't intervene! You said that a human agent would be needed if—'

'Lilith is different. She used to be human, remember? It's easier for her to interfere in human affairs. Besides, Lucifer cares for her in a way. And her madness prevents her from fearing him as she should.'

'What is she going to do?'

Mephisto raised an eyebrow. 'She wants the child, of course. Are you going to help, or would you rather fling yourself from the tower to see if God catches you?'

And with that, Mephistopheles turned from me and ran through the rain across the square to the Basilica. Gilligan Connor retreated to the back of my mind and Gabriel Antaeus came back as I sprinted after Mephistopheles. The floodlit Basilica had been locked up for the night and was deserted. I got there in time to see Mephisto tear the huge wooden door from its hinges in a shower of splinters. It was strange to see Stephomi do that, when mere weeks ago I had thought I had the upper hand when he was pinned to the floor of my kitchen. I had never been in control, I realised. As a demon, his strength had always far outweighed my own.

The elevator was shut down at the top so there was no alternative but to take the hundreds of steps to the observation level. By the time we were halfway up, I knew I couldn't go any further without my heart bursting from my body. But I kept running anyway, my lungs burning and head swimming, sure that I was going to throw up at any moment. I think I would have thrown up had it not been that, having spent most of the afternoon with my head down a toilet, there was simply nothing *left* inside my stomach. I tripped over several times, splinters from the wooden steps tearing at my hands, before scrambling to my feet in a desperate attempt to keep up with Mephistopheles.

At last we burst through the wooden doors out into the fresh air of the floodlit, snow covered observation dome. The loud rain had turned to hushed snow and was falling thickly, even as strange thunder rumbled in the distance. It was not far from midnight and celebratory fireworks banged and sparkled over the city below us. And there was Lilith, dressed in a velvet black ball gown, dancing dreamily on the low wall, just as beautiful and seductive as she had seemed in my dreams. Her long black hair was loose and blowing around about her as she danced, black silk scarves fluttering in her hands.

'Lilith,' Mephistopheles said quietly from the doorway.

He had spoken so softly that I didn't think Lilith would have heard him, but she spun round at his voice, jumped off the wall and ran over to him, her hair and skirts flying out behind her. She threw her arms round the demon's neck when she reached him, kissing him passionately, and I was unsettled to feel a stab of jealousy at the sight. There she was, the most stunning woman I'd ever seen ... and she was kissing a devil as if he was the only lover she'd ever wanted, when she hadn't so much as acknowledged my presence, and to my shame I couldn't help but feel jilted.

'I'm going to save them, Mephisto,' Lilith said breathlessly, eyes shining with a kind of mad joy. 'I won't let the angels get them this time. Not this time. I'm going to love the children as if they were my own.'

'Lilith,' Mephistopheles said again, his voice soft with an uncharacteristic gentleness. 'You must listen to me. Lucifer doesn't want this. He's angry with you already. The child could bring destruction on all of us.'

'They want to kill them! I won't let them! I won't let them kill any more babies!'

As Mephistopheles took Lilith by the hand and continued in his attempts to reason with her, I kneeled down on the cold stone beside Casey. When she realised it was me, she gave a dry sob and clung to me as I put my arms around her, thanking me over and over again for not leaving her alone.

Mephistopheles tried to restrain Lilith; he tried to calm her, but she lashed out at him and soon the two demons were savagely fighting each other, and Lilith's fine dress became dirtied and torn as she sought to escape Mephisto's grip and reach us. They only stopped when Michael appeared on the tower in a blaze of white light that burned my eyes with its brightness. Mephisto placed himself protectively in front of Lilith, and the angel and the demon each stood motionless at the top of the tower, glaring at one another bitterly.

Michael looked much the same as when I'd previously seen him, but for one small difference – this time he had wings. And with that addition I could clearly see the angel instead of the fiery demon. The wings were folded behind his back with an air of barely restrained movement. Each feather was snow white, flawless, perfect, and I could tell just by looking that the huge wings were powerful. These were not the tiny, just-for-show wings you saw in paintings on the backs of cherubs. These were great, feathered, muscled things that were clearly more than strong enough to take Michael's weight if he needed them to.

'You always did have a flare for the melodramatic,' Mephistopheles sneered, indicating the brightness of Michael's light.

'You are interfering in the forbidden!' Michael replied angrily, radiating with righteous hate the way only an angel could.

'Yes I know. It's a bad habit of mine.' Mephisto glanced over at me. 'Gabriel, I think you know everyone here? I am the madman and these,' he waved his arm to encompass everyone else, 'are my fellow inmates in Bedlam.'

'What is *that* foul whore doing here?' Michael asked, pointing over Mephistopheles' shoulder to Lilith.

Lilith didn't seem to be offended by what Michael had said. In fact, she hardly seemed to have heard him. She was staring at Casey hungrily. Then her gaze lifted to mine, and I could have sworn she winked at me. But if Lilith didn't care about the names Michael was calling her, Mephisto had more than enough anger for both of them. All traces of amusement had gone from his face, to be replaced with the most bitter loathing.

'It stings, doesn't it, Michael?' he hissed. 'That a woman who looks like that would come willingly to my bed but would scream and scream in disgust if you so much as touched her!'

And at that God's angel and Satan's went for each other with a savagery that I hadn't seen before even in the fiercest wild beasts – as if they just couldn't contain their hatred for each other a second longer. There were no weapons – instead, they were tearing at each other with their fingers, with their teeth, with their nails. Mephisto was much the smaller of the two, being far slimmer and shorter than Michael, and it was quite clear to me that he was physically outmatched even if he was supernaturally strong compared to me. He was doing everything he could to hurt the angel, grabbing fistfuls of feathers and pulling them out of Michael's huge wings, clearly delighted by the bellows of pain he got in response. He tried hard to reach the angel's eyes with his fingers, but he wasn't strong enough to do anything more than scratch at Michael's face.

And then – as I stared in horror – Michael managed to clamp the struggling demon hard around the shoulders ... and then twisted his head hard in one vicious movement, breaking Mephistopheles' neck with a loud, splintering crack, blood splattering on the snow around us. Casey screamed as Michael dropped the demon's lifeless body onto the snow. I whipped around to look at where Lilith had been, thinking she would fly into a grief-stricken rage at the sight of what Michael had just done to her lover. But she was no longer on the dome, and when I stared around I realised that she was sitting on the roof of one of the towers opposite us, idly swinging her feet against the stone, looking out over the city and clearly quite oblivious to everything that was going on. I saw her wings for the first time then – not leathery but feathered, each one raven black.

I turned back to the sight of Mephistopheles sprawled on the snow, blood running from his broken neck where the bone had pierced the skin, his head twisted at a horrible angle and his staring eyes completely blank. An odd emotion coursed through me then. Was it sadness? Remorse? Christ, could this really be *grief*? I couldn't see a dead demon at that moment – all I could see was Stephomi, who had been my friend. But I did not have long to dwell on it, for in the next second I almost screamed myself as Mephisto snapped his neck sharply back into place and stood up, swaying only for a moment before saying with a grin to Michael, 'You know, if I had a penny for every time you've broken my neck over the years ...'

And that was when he shook the wings out from his back – great, leathery batlike wings that stretched out, unfurling behind him as if they'd been stiff and confined before. Everything about him became darker: his hair and eyes became blacker; his hands suddenly looked like claws; and for wild moments I even thought I saw long, twisted *horns* on his head, and a black forked tongue in his mouth, with *hooves* at his feet – something truly *monstrous* … But my eyes screamed in protest at the awful change, refused to recognise it, and I can't be sure what I really saw.

The fight began again but this time Mephistopheles spread out his wings, kicked off from the floor, and rose up to the top spire of the bell tower with an excited laugh as Michael chased after him. I only tore my gaze away when Casey spoke to me in a frightened, shaking, but somehow quiet, voice: 'You're going to have to help me, Gabriel.'

I stared at her, still kneeling at her side on the ground. The aura that had constantly alternated between gold and black now seemed to be both at the same time – sometimes more one than the other, but always a combination of the two with the blackness spreading into the gold, swirling and mixing with it like ink in water.

'Help?' I repeated stupidly.

'Yes. Help me with the birth.'

'But I don't know how!' I replied, aghast.

Casey started to laugh, but quickly smothered it before it could become hysterical. 'Neither do I,' she said, through gritted teeth. 'But the baby is coming *now* so you *have* to *help* me.'

'No, no, I can't … I can't …'

Childbirth would involve blood. Just the thought of it brought back the vivid image of the blood that had stained the sand when I'd sunk a knife into Anna Sovànak's neck. Damp, bloody sand, crimson red … I felt like, if I saw just one more drop of it from anyone for any reason, I would scream until I was sick … be taken away in a straitjacket as whatever last shred of sanity I had was torn to pieces by vicious memories … I didn't know how to even begin to say this to Casey in a way that she would understand, but I knew I would not be able to help her.

'Look, I'm … I'm not a writer. My memories, you know I got

them back, and … I'm, I'm … I was a … an assassin. I've *killed* people … and I tried to repent, I really did *try* but the angels won't forgive me. They just *refuse* to even consider forgiving me. And if I can't get forgiveness then I'm still damned; I'm—'

I expected her to be looking at me with an expression of fear and horror at my revelation, but instead her expression was one of increasing anger, and the emotion seemed so out of place considering what I was telling her that I couldn't help but falter.

'Gabriel,' she said, in a harsh, low voice, 'I don't care if you're the devil himself – you are going to help me have my child!'

'You don't *understand*!' I pleaded, dimly aware that I was sounding rather whiny and childish. 'Seeing blood brings everything back to me, and I see the people I've murdered, and I don't want to see them! I don't want to see them ever again!'

Gritting her teeth against the onset of another contraction, Casey gripped my shirt and pulled me forwards so that I was dragged into a strange kind of kneeling bow over her as she hissed into my ear. 'If you leave me again now, I will *never* forgive you, Gabriel, *never*!'

Agonising indecision wracked me. I couldn't trust myself to make any kind of judgement on what was wrong or right. I was morally disabled – I didn't think my brain could tell the two apart all the time. This was never meant to have happened – just four months ago Casey had been a *stranger* to me! How was it possible to love someone *so much* when just four months ago I hadn't even so much as known her *name*? If only we had not been neighbours; if only I had kept to myself and not spoken to her … all this agony might have been avoided. I couldn't bear to see her suffer – that was what I had always feared would be the consequence of loving someone.

I hesitated – for a moment I was tempted to leave the Basilica as fast as I could, go to the airport and catch my plane for Washington. Fly further and further away from Budapest and pretend that none of this had ever happened; that I'd never even met Casey let alone loved her. I think I could have managed it – I'm quite good at ignoring things I don't want to think about.

Then with an involuntary cry of pain sharper than the others, Casey dropped my hand and turned her head away from me, tears streaming down her face, and I realised that she was going into the next stage of her labour – there was no more time to make up my mind. She had given up on me already – finally sensing the futility in asking an assassin for help. I don't think Gilligan Connor would have minded, particularly. But as Gabriel Antaeus, the thought of her believing I didn't care was *unbearable*, and I felt I'd rather kill myself now and have done with it than leave her here hating me.

'I didn't mean it!' I blurted out, appalled at myself, wishing I could take the words back. 'I didn't mean anything I said before, Casey, really! Look, I don't know anything about childbirth –' I made an open-handed gesture of hopelessness, '– but I'll do everything I possibly can to help, I promise.'

She tried to smile at me but ended up giving a dry sob, sweat running down her face despite the viciousness of the cold. I leaned over, kissed her on the forehead, and then moved round to help her, immensely relieved to see that the baby was positioned head first, for if it had been breach I just don't know what I'd have done.

Strangely enough, there was no time to feel any hint of awkwardness as Casey started to give birth. All my attention was focused on trying to prevent any part of the baby from touching the snowy ground. I instinctively knew enough to realise that such cold temperatures could be fatal to a newborn child. But as soon as I was touching the baby, there was blood on my hands, and I felt sick at the sight of it, even though it was not death this time that had put it there.

The image of Anna bleeding all over the beach exploded in my head, and I actually gagged with revulsion. For a long moment, the only thing I could see was Anna, eyes shining one moment with excitement and lust, and the next blank, staring, accusatory. Other people in other countries, various different weapons ... And always ending the same way – with me scrubbing and scrubbing at my hands in the bathroom. That last time, with Anna, I washed my hands until they bled, going round and round in a vicious circle, unable to remove the blood from my hands because it was my own; and the harder I scrubbed, the more they would bleed.

The memories of all those murders were like an unmerciful barrage, and for a moment I longed to be anywhere but the Basilica. I wanted to wrap my arms round my head and tremble in a corner until it was over. The sight of blood alone was intolerable to me, but worse still were Casey's involuntary cries of pain. I wanted to leave. But I just couldn't bring myself to.

I looked up sharply when ice and fire started to rain down around us simultaneously, splashing and hissing on the ground but somehow not touching us. Then I realised that there was no sign of Michael or Mephistopheles, and for a moment I thought they had gone. The sounds of fireworks and celebrations drifted up from the city, thunder rumbled louder than before, and the falling ice cracked and splintered as it shattered against the Basilica. The shower of fire lit up the cathedral, spitting as the molten drops fell into the snow. I thought of the fire I had seen covering Michael's church on Margaret's Island, and wondered if all the partygoers below could see the battle that was raging above the Basilica, or whether it simply looked its usual quiet and dignified self to their eyes.

And then I saw them – Michael and Mephistopheles – hovering just above the tower opposite us, biting, tearing, clawing at one another as if they would pull each other apart if they could. They were both almost unrecognisable to me. Their bodies flashed between the familiar human forms I was used to and something altogether different. Michael was once again lit up with a light so bright that I could hardly make out his features at all – as if he were simply too close to the sun or some other light-emitting force for me to look at him. But I could clearly see his powerful, feathered white wings spread out behind him as the two angels flew round, over and above the cathedral's towers, striking out viciously at each other. Every now and then, a white feather would flutter down from the sky to be stained by the blood already on the ground around us.

246

Casey was sobbing now, and I dragged my attention away from the angels and back to her. I must not let them distract me. I must stay focused. When, at last, the baby was born, I took a penknife from my pocket, cut the umbilical cord and shrugged off my coat to wrap the infant up in an effort to protect it from the freezing night. I was filled with relief as I looked at the baby in my arms. For she was human. A tiny, perfect, human little girl ... not angel or demon as I had seen in my dreams ... not one of those creatures fighting so viciously above us. And there was no aura around Casey or her daughter now. The swirling clouds of shining gold and dripping black had gone.

'She's ... amazing,' Casey whispered, gazing at her daughter in my arms. 'Isn't she *beautiful*, Gabriel?'

I couldn't believe how *fragile* she was, how *vulnerable*. I mean, she couldn't even hold up her own *head*!

'Do you want to hold her?' I asked.

Casey started to nod and then froze, a confused expression on her face, one hand trailing down to her stomach.

'There's a second baby,' she whispered.

'Second baby?' I repeated stupidly, gazing round as if expecting to see one lying on the ground somewhere.

'Twins,' she groaned. 'I never went to any scans so ...' She trailed off and then, to my horror, started to cry. 'Oh, Gabriel, I don't want to *do* all that again! I'm so *tired*! It's so *unfair*!'

'You're doing really well, Casey,' I said, equally horrified by the revelation that she was carrying twins but trying not to show it. I realised now that the aura I'd thought for a moment had gone, was still clinging about her. It was fainter than before but still that strange, unnatural mixture of gold and black. 'You're halfway through it now; halfway through.'

'But I didn't *ask* for this! I don't want to have children *like this*! I always thought there'd be a husband here with me or at least a boyfriend; someone who loved me, someone who was going to share this with me! Last ... last week I saw this young guy holding his baby in a ... in a restaurant, and when I got home I couldn't ... I just couldn't stop crying! I know feminists would hate me for this, but all I *ever wanted* was the white picket fence. A house and a family that loved me unconditionally. My ... my Mom and Dad ... didn't—'

'I love you unconditionally,' I said at once. 'And you can still have the house and the fence and the family. But first you have to have this baby. You'll love your children. And you'll find the husband later. But until you do, I'll look after you, because I really do love you unconditionally, Casey, and I promise I always will. You've got one beautiful daughter already and now you're going to have another. Just a little bit longer and then you'll be the mother of twins. Won't that be wonderful?'

I was relieved to see her start to try and smile as I spoke – looking at me through her tears for a moment like I was the most amazing person in the world. At last she nodded. 'Okay, Gabriel.'

'Good girl.'

I looked up sharply as the bell began to ring out loudly in its tower. Was this another phantom tolling that the celebrating Hungarians below would be unable to hear? Could all this really be invisible to their eyes? Could people really be so very ignorant of all that went on around them? The entire cathedral was being ravaged by the battle over our heads, and the bell continued to toll deafeningly. Half the building was on fire – including the tower nearest us. The other tower and the rest of the building was shining and glittering with a coat of ice three feet thick. Lightning, frozen from the sky by Mephistopheles, had fallen to the floor of the observation level, splintering into sharp, golden shards which crackled and fizzed with electrical energy as they slowly melted into the snow.

Although I didn't want to put the baby down, I needed both my hands and I was afraid of dropping her if I tried to keep her cradled in my arm. So I wrapped the coat about her more securely and put her on the ground beside me before turning back to Casey. Although the second baby was also correctly positioned, I could tell that this time something was wrong. There was too much blood, much more than there'd been last time, and I realised Casey must have torn something inside. It was clearly hurting her more and blood was pouring out over my hands, making it difficult to keep hold of her second baby. I couldn't think what to do, for there was no way to heal whatever had torn. All I could do was concentrate on the second child and try and get it delivered safely.

The bell ceased to ring the moment Casey's second daughter was born, and a rain of fireworks burst into the sky as cheers were heard from below, and I realised that midnight had come and gone: we had all just passed from one year into the next.

'Gabriel,' Casey whispered. 'I ... I don't feel so good.'

I didn't know what to say to her. It was painfully clear that Casey was bleeding to death. I wouldn't have thought she had that much blood in her to begin with. It was on my hands, my clothes, lying in glistening pools across the stone floor, freezing in the gaps between the flagstones. The aura had gone now. There was no black or gold, no beauty or repulsiveness around Casey or either of her daughters. I shifted her second baby so that she lay cradled in only one of my arms, and then took her hand with my free one, not wanting her to feel alone.

If I could only get her to a hospital for a blood transfusion ... But I would never get there in time. She would be dead before I'd even carried her down the Basilica's stairs. I had never in my life felt so helpless, and the frustration of it tore at me agonisingly.

'Can you see them?' she asked, visibly struggling for breath now. 'Those demons up there?'

The dying see demons ... That was what Mephistopheles had told me, wasn't it?

'No!' I cried with a sob. 'Not demons, Casey. Please not demons!'

I strained my eyes into the night and for moments I was sure I could see scores of them up there, vast armies both angel and demon, tearing and shredding at each other with their bare hands, fuelled by a truly limitless and ancient hatred.

'Gabriel ...'

I looked back down, Casey's second daughter still cradled in my left arm as Casey held my right hand and spoke to me for the last time – words that meant more to me than expressions of love or friendship or thanks ever could. 'I forgive you.'

She met my pathetic attempt at a smile for a brief, timeless moment before her grip went slack in my hand and she stopped breathing. I could see that she was dead even before I felt for a pulse. I know what dead bodies look like – after all, I've seen enough of them.

'*No!*' I screamed. '*No, no, no!*'

She still looked beautiful to me, despite the fact that her brown skin was streaked with sweat and her dark hair was disorderly, the lengths of coloured blue and pink hair shining brightly in the light of the fireworks and the fires that still clung to the cathedral.

The two angels above, realising that Casey's children had been born, fell back down to the observation level of the dome, one on either side of us. They each retained shreds of their human appearance but their clothes were torn and stained with blood, and I could see the ethereal outline of the wings folded back behind each of them.

'Is she dead yet?' Michael asked coldly, indicating Casey.

'*No, she fucking isn't!*' I screamed at him. 'I'm here to *save* her! She's *not* dead! She's *not!*'

'Of course she is!' Michael said impatiently. 'And the child must follow her.'

I covered my eyes with my trembling hand, trying to block everything out. But it didn't work. There was this terrible ache ... deep within me. Perhaps isolation, after all, was the better way in such a world ... I actually felt the moment when something snapped ... then I alarmed even myself with the raw despair in my sobs ... How very naïve I'd been to think I could feel no more pain. This was what it felt like to lose someone you loved. This was what Anna's children had felt because of me. This was what I had done to people every day. God was punishing me. Punishing Casey because He knew how much I'd loved her.

'It's because I don't have a costume, isn't it?' I wept. 'You can't be a real superhero without the spandex suit and the mask and the fucking cape! I promised her, I *promised* her. Why did I *do* that? *Why?*'

'*Don't make the promise lightly, Gabriel.*' That's what she'd said to me. '*People can get hurt that way.*'

And then there was a comforting hand on my shoulder. Someone kneeling beside me, talking consolingly in a soft voice. 'You kept your promise, Gabriel,' Mephisto said. 'You said you'd be there and you were.'

'I was supposed to ... save her ... at the last moment—'

'You're not still comparing yourself to a superhero, are you?' Mephisto asked. 'You mustn't do that, you know. After all, super-heroes only ever fought super-villains, not angels. If nothing else, at least you were there for your friend when she needed you.'

'But what difference does it make when she's *dead*?'

'All the difference, Gabriel.'

'I should have taken her to a hospital myself.'

'It wouldn't have mattered. She'd still have died.'

'How can I believe you?' I asked, turning to look at him at last. 'When all you've ever done is lie to me?'

'Oh, I don't know. There was the odd bit of truth in there sometimes, wasn't there?' he asked with a smile.

He shouldn't have been able to comfort me, he was a demon. But still, in that moment, I was grateful to him for trying.

'You didn't kill her, Gabriel,' Mephisto said softly. 'I know you quite enjoy blaming yourself. But not everything can be your fault all of the time. Sometimes God takes all the credit, I'm afraid. And maybe it's for the best. Life is about pain. Death is about the end of pain.'

My hands were so cold, up there at the top of the cathedral, so high above the city ... To think that I had come here before and felt *safe*, closer to God ... and now tragedy shrouded the icy cathedral, the bell was silent in its frozen tower, and bleak misery settled on me softly like ash – ash from the remnants of something that had once been so precious to me ...

'You must kill the child,' Michael said firmly.

'Yes,' Mephistopheles agreed, standing up. 'Throw her from the tower, Gabriel, and finish this.'

'Don't you mean throw *them*?' I snapped, looking round to

where the second baby was ... or should have been. I froze, staring at the empty bloodstained coat she'd been wrapped in only minutes before. 'Where's—?' I began, and then froze in horror as I saw Lilith dancing around on the wall once more, her black wings spread slightly, gazing down dreamily at Casey's first daughter wrapped in her arms.

Michael and Mephisto followed my gaze and I heard Michael's sharp intake of breath. 'There are *two* of them?'

Mephisto swore softly under his breath. 'Lilith,' he began, taking a half-step towards her. 'Please don't do anything stupid.'

I wanted to jump to my feet, run to Lilith and wrestle the baby back from her. But I forced myself to stay kneeling on the ground, somehow sensing that if I made any move towards her at all, she would leap from the wall, fly away, and I would never see that baby again. Michael, too, seemed to sense that the best chance of stopping Lilith was to let Mephisto talk to her, for he was still as a statue, the only movement coming from the steady dripping of blood from one of his wings.

'Give her to me,' Mephisto said softly. 'She's not one of yours.'

Lilith looked at him sharply. 'They're all mine,' she hissed. 'All of them.'

And then she stepped backwards off the edge of the wall. I was back on my feet with a cry of horror within moments, but in the seconds it took me to reach the wall, she and the baby had disappeared and I knew that Lilith had taken her back to her own realm. The guilt I already felt intensified so painfully that I was only dimly aware of Michael shouting at Mephisto behind me. My head was throbbing unbearably, like it was about to split open, and all I wanted was to crawl into some dark, silent place until this nightmare ended.

'*Shut up!*' I screamed, whirling back round to face Michael, who was still shouting unbearably loudly. 'Shut up, shut *up!*'

'Well said, Gabriel,' Mephisto remarked mildly, looked quite unruffled by the angel's anger.

'How *dare* you speak to me like that!' Michael snarled, looking very much like he wanted to hit me. I almost wished he would, for it would have given me an excuse to hit him back. But, of course, if he broke my neck, I wouldn't be able to snap it back as Mephisto had done – and there was no way that I was going to let go of Casey's second daughter, even for a moment.

I was pleased to see that Michael's wings were covered with streaks of slick scarlet blood, staining his white feathers and sticking them together where the blood had dried there. I inwardly applauded Mephisto for managing to physically hurt Michael. I hated that angel and I could only feel glad at the sight of him bleeding.

'You must *throw* that thing from the tower as you should have thrown its twin!' Michael snapped.

'I will *never*—' I began, pressing the baby closer to me.

'Give her to me, then,' Mephisto said. 'I promise I'll look after her, but not here. If I take her from this world, she won't be able to destroy it. Trust me, Gabriel.'

'No, you must give her to me,' Michael insisted. 'Demons already have one of them. It is only right that angels should have the other.'

For a few moments, I gazed at the two angels, paralysed by an awful uncertainty, as if I were a child again myself. When I gazed up at the night sky, I thought I saw those shadowy outlines of angelic and demonic armies, no longer fighting each other ... but simply staring down at me in silence from their ranks. Staring, staring, waiting ... All this over one tiny little baby ...

I was taken aback by the savagery of the desire when it rose suddenly inside me, as I glanced down at the city so far below us, and felt the strong longing to follow Lilith. To fling myself from the top of God's cathedral ... He would not catch me, oh no, I knew that now ...

... *Darkling I listen* ...

But it hardly mattered when everything precious to me had been shattered, even my illusions ...

... *and for many a time I have been half in love with easeful death* ...

How I *envied* Casey the ease of her death! Why did no such release come for me? I didn't want to do this any more. All there ever seemed to be was pain ... Hadn't I earned the right to die by now? I don't know where it came from, or indeed whether anyone else heard it, or if it was ever even really there ... but I'm sure I heard the sweet song of the nightingale there at the top of St Stephen's Basilica, even as further verses from Keats' ode to the bird flew unbidden through my mind:

Now more than ever seems it rich to die ...

What was there for me here now anyway? Nicky and Luke were gone, and their loss seemed no less painful for the fact that they'd never been real to begin with – they had been real enough to me. And now Casey was gone as well ... I was so tired of it all. I had tried; God knows I had tried to do the right thing. Casey was dead. I hadn't killed her. This one at least was not on my shoulders. But what difference did it make? What difference did it make to Casey? The dry sob alarmed me and brought my mind back to reality and the two angels watching me and waiting, waiting for my decision ... I couldn't make it. I wasn't fit to decide what was best for anyone, much less the entire world. I mean, Christ, if I made the wrong decision, that could lead to global *apocalypse* and I didn't want that kind of guilt. Wasn't it bad enough that I had spent my life *murdering* people for a living? I glanced again at the low wall round the edge of the tower.

'Gabriel!' Mephisto said with sudden sharpness.

But I had already scrambled up onto it and jumped over the edge ... almost seeming to hang there for a moment, like a bird in the night sky suspended high above the cathedral, frozen stars sparkling coldly in space above me, and frozen air blowing past me to grace the bell tower in so many thick ribbons of twisted ice, like candy canes ...

I began to fall and pure joy cut through me like blades – I've never known anything like it. This was it; soon it would all be over. At last I had taken steps to *finish* it. Cold air would dance around me, all the way to the last. The ground, the divinely hard, unyielding ground was waiting far below, and stone at least would fulfil its promise. *To cease upon the midnight with no pain ...* But the air went rushing past without me as a hand gripped hard around my arm and my body slammed against the cold wall of the cathedral, knocking the breath out of me, the tips of my boots scraping against the stone.

For a moment I just gazed out over the light-speckled city beneath me, wondering why I wasn't moving, thinking that I must have discovered some new superpower I hadn't known about before. Then I looked up and saw Mephisto, balancing on a ledge below the wall, clinging to the edge of the tower with one hand, the other gripped about my arm.

'What are you doing?' I demanded, irritated that he was interfering.

Mephisto grinned down at me. 'What are *you* doing?'

'Just let me fall,' I pleaded, even as he inched his way back up the wall of the tower and swung himself up onto the low wall. 'I deserve it. I've *earned* it! You've got no right to interfere.'

Mephistopheles paused, gazing down at me from his perch as I hung from the side of the tower, as if considering what I'd said for a moment before he spoke. 'The baby too, then, Gabriel?'

I glanced down. Casey's second daughter was still clasped in my left arm, warmly tucked into the folds of my jacket. How strange that I should have forgotten she was there.

'Well?' Mephisto asked pleasantly, gazing down at me with traces of that all too familiar amusement on his face. The shreds of his ripped black clothing were flapping about him in the glacial wind; leathery wings spread slightly to keep his balance on the low wall. I had truly liked Zadkiel Stephomi. If only he had been an angel instead of a devil. The ground below called to me still. Death himself was singing to me in the sweet, golden voice of a nightingale, and I longed for it like I'd never longed for anything.

'Let him go,' I heard Michael order from above. 'It is his wish. You must not interfere.'

'Isn't it rather unseasonable for nightingales?' Mephisto remarked conversationally, turning his head slightly to look at the angel.

The bird song stopped suddenly, leaving loud, melancholy echoes in its wake.

'Dear, dear, Michael. How very hypocritical of you,' I heard Mephistopheles say with a laugh.

I shook my head; confused, disoriented, feeling the mists of some strange trance evaporate from my mind. Then I made the mistake of looking down. 'Jesus *fucking* Christ!' I screamed, unable to stop myself from thrashing about instinctively as the city below me swung alarmingly. 'Oh, *fuck!*'

'Hold still, Gabriel, hold *still!*' Mephisto snapped, gritting his teeth as my weight pulled on the wounds he'd received from Michael that evening.

I felt his grip slip slightly and that panicked me enough to force myself to go limp, although it took all the willpower I had. I looked down at the baby. What had I been *thinking* to jump over the wall like that while holding her? She was so fragile, for all I knew my stupidity had already broken her neck. But, no she was blinking up at me. Lower lip trembling, she started to cry – which probably had more to do with the cold than anything else, for she couldn't understand that a demon's tenuous grip was currently the only thing keeping her alive.

'Pull us up!' I pleaded, looking up at Mephisto and, to my dismay, seeing him hesitate. 'For God's sake, Stephomi, pull us up *now!*'

Instinctively, I wanted to reach up with my other hand to grab onto his arm, and use him to drag myself bodily over the wall, but I couldn't do that without dropping Casey's daughter.

'This will go on, you know,' Mephisto said softly in a strange tone, gazing at the baby girl tucked into my coat. 'If you don't drop her now, while you can, it'll never end. It'll just … we'll all just keep going round and round in these circles … You can save us all from that. Do you really want this for yourself, Gabriel? Is it really something anyone would ever actually *choose?*'

I couldn't help but look down again as I felt his grip slip a little further. Fear of death. Here it was. I wouldn't have minded so much if I'd been atheist. If I could've believed that I would cease to exist once I fell. But I knew there was an afterlife, and I knew which Circle I would be going to, and I knew who was waiting to meet me there. It would happen eventually whatever I did. But not *yet*! Oh, Christ, not like *this*!

Without even realising it, I had started to mutter the Lord's Prayer under my breath. '*Our father, who art in Heaven, hallowed be thy name—*'

'Now, now, none of that,' Mephistopheles said angrily, shaking me – actually *shaking* me so that the city below swung madly as the horizons on either side of my vision went up and down. 'Now isn't the best time to offend me, Gabriel. Use your brain for once.'

I swore again, unable to stop myself from looking down, and feeling sick at the sight of Budapest so far below. The pressure of Mephistopheles' hand on my arm was excruciatingly painful by now, and I couldn't even feel my frozen hands any more.

'You were always going to drop me, weren't you?' I asked, loathing burning inside of me. 'You just wanted me to die unwillingly. You just wanted it to be as awful as possible, didn't you, you bastard?'

'Tut, tut, what a thing to say to the demon holding on to you for dear life,' Mephisto said with a leer. 'No, I really am saving your life, Gabriel. But I want to teach you something about the nature of *prayer* first.'

'What … what do you mean?' I asked, my teeth chattering together from the cold.

'Prayers to God have no effect on me,' Mephistopheles said coldly. 'So before I save your life … I want to hear you pray to Lucifer.'

I stared at him. Surely he couldn't be *serious*?

'I'm quite serious, I assure you,' Mephisto said with a grin. 'I serve Lucifer. So if you swallow your pride and pray to him, then you will see how much more effective prayer to the devil can be.'

I started to tremble, hating Mephistopheles with all my soul for this. I could feel the cold, heavy weight of the onyx crucifix Casey had given me just last week pressing into my skin. I couldn't hesitate for long – I was so cold by now that I was afraid Casey's daughter might slip right out of my numb arm, falling the whole height of the terrible Basilica on her own. The image was too awful – I would just have to pray to the Devil and hate myself for it later.

'Lucifer,' I said between gritted teeth, 'please … please … help me—' I bit my tongue to keep from crying out as a particularly savage gust of wind made me sway, the tips of my boots scraping against the old stone of the basilica, my coat flapping back from my body, tugging at my back. The baby wailed louder and I could feel her tears soaking through my shirt. 'Oh, shit!' I whimpered, trying in vain to tighten my numb fingers around Mephistopheles' arm. 'Lucifer, please, *please* don't let me fall! I don't want to die yet! Have mercy on us, I'm *begging* you!'

'That was very nice, Gabriel,' Mephisto said kindly. 'But there's no need to beg. You see what the Devil can do for you if you just ask him nicely. Trust me, he's much more reliable than God.' And with that, he hauled me up over the edge.

He tried to steady me as I landed shakily on the stone, but I pushed him away and stumbled over to the middle of the tower, desperately trying to erase that dreadful image of the city swinging crazily beneath my feet. Yet another memory to come back to haunt me in the middle of the night. I sank to my knees, closed my eyes and bent my head over Casey's daughter, who was still crying into my shirt. I wanted to cry myself but my eyes were painfully dry. This – all this – must be a dream. It was the only sensible explanation.

But when I looked up, Michael and Mephistopheles remained stood at the edge of the tower, watching me. I realised with a sudden jolt of fear that the baby had stopped crying. But when I looked down at her, she didn't seem to be hurt, except for a small scratch on her cheek where her face had grazed the Basilica wall. It wasn't a bad cut but the sight of it shrivelled my insides with guilt, and I knew I had to get her out of this freezing cold quickly. Still covered in her mother's blood, she was staring up at me with wide, brown eyes – as if she knew me, as if she trusted me, as if she really did love me already. Making up my mind in that moment, I looked up at the two angels and tightened my grip on the baby slightly. 'I'm not giving her to either of you,' I spat, glad to relieve some of the anger that was building up inside.

'Then what, precisely, do you propose?' Michael asked coldly.

I wrapped my arms more securely around my daughter and said nothing. Suddenly, Mephistopheles laughed, 'You plan to keep her for yourself! Well, well. You are a glutton for punishment, aren't you? But be very careful of little Adolf there, for she might come to haunt you in the years to come. At least the demons got one of them. A small victory for our side, Michael,' he said, with a mocking smile at the glowering angel. 'I'll never be too far away,' he said, nodding his head at me. 'I believe it was William Congreve who said, "*The Devil watches all opportunities.*" And so he does, my friend. So he does, indeed.'

Mephisto inclined his head at Michael and myself, and then turned and leaped from the dome as Lilith had done, spreading his great batlike wings behind him and fading back into his own realm. Michael was, of course, disgusted with me. He raged at me, shouted and cursed at me so furiously it made me tremble, but still I refused to give him Casey's daughter and eventually he left.

Once the angels and the demons had gone, the Basilica slowly returned to normal, the frozen half unfreezing and the fire on the other half smoking away into nothingness as the last of the frozen lightning crackled and melted away. And then it was just me, Casey and the baby. I stood there, wondering what to do, struggling against the great fatigue that was tugging at me. I felt I just wanted to crawl back inside the dome and curl up, to sleep there by the top of the stairs ... wait until morning for the police to arrive. But that was no good at all – there would be *investigations* and *questions*, and how could I give the police answers they'd be able to understand? So I had to leave Casey there. We said goodbye to her first, the baby and I, although I could hardly bear to look at her glassy eyes or the sweat that had frozen to her cold skin. At last I turned away from her, head down, shoulders slumped, and crept away into the night with her daughter.

*

Now I am back in my apartment, with my baby lying sleeping on the couch beside me, delicate eyelashes resting on her cheeks as she dreams. At the moment she is wrapped up in one of my jumpers, but later I will have to break into Casey's apartment and retrieve some clothes and other supplies for her. She'll be hungry – I'll have to feed her soon. Oh, God, I don't know anything at all about looking after her; I don't know how the hell I'm going to do this ...

I don't know what will happen about Casey. I suppose police will be called tomorrow morning when it's discovered that the Basilica was broken into. They'll find Casey's body, which will probably have frozen completely by then. It will be obvious that she died from natural causes. The mystery will lie in how she got there and what happened to her child. But that is a mystery for the police to deal with, and I do not think there is anything to link the scene to me.

I feel wrong – the world feels wrong. Everything looks different now, even my familiar apartment. I will grieve for Casey. But I can't do it yet and I'm grateful for the numbness. First I have to make plans. Where should I go now? Italy, perhaps? Or Holland? Oh, I know that what I flee from can't be escaped by moving to a different country. But I can't stay in Budapest now, after all that has happened, although I will always think fondly of the city that gave me the briefest taste of what life is like for normal people. I love Budapest like I'll never love anywhere else. But I can't stay here.

I have decided on a name for Casey's daughter. I thought of naming her for an angel, but my experiences with Michael turned me from the idea. He is not at all what an angel should be. He refused to forgive me my sins and, worse, he had wanted me to kill a newborn baby – had even tried to trick me into doing so when I refused. That nightingale's song – he deliberately put it in my head while I was holding Casey's daughter. He wanted the two of us dead and it was only the actions of a devil that saved us both. If I owe Lucifer my sanity, I now owe Mephistopheles my life and, to be frank, the speed with which I am clocking up debts to demons appals me.

I considered naming Casey's daughter for a saint or a leader or a hero. But finally, I decided to name her for a virtue: Grace. A man like me shouldn't be anywhere near this baby, or any baby. But I have to stay with her to protect her from the angels and the devils who might wish her harm. I have no choice. I must do all in my power to protect her, to save her, as I was not able to save her mother or her sister.

And so the question comes back to haunt me ... If you could go back in time to Adolf Hitler's birth, would you kill him if you had the chance? Would you kill him there and then – an utterly defenceless child? Would you have a duty to the world to do it if you could? Would you really be able to do such a thing to a baby who has yet to commit even the most inoffensive wrong? We all say '*yes*' but trust me, it doesn't seem quite such an easy question once it ceases to be purely theoretical.

As I sit here watching Grace sleep, I can't believe that anything bad could ever possibly come from her. In my dreams, Casey gave birth to both an angel and a demon. The angels themselves had believed that there was one baby, who would either be the Antichrist or the Second Coming of Jesus. But now the thought occurs to me that perhaps one of Casey's daughters will be a saviour and the other will be a destroyer. And if that is true, then which one did the demoness Lilith steal away with her back to her own demonic realms and which one is lying, content and peaceful in an innocent sleep, here on the couch before me? When I look at Grace, I *know* in my *soul* that those dark prophetic words Nostradamus wrote hundreds of years ago couldn't possibly apply to her.

I didn't kill Grace, or hand her over to the demons or the angels, because I wanted her for myself. It was pure selfishness. I weakened – the temptation was too great ... to have a baby who would grow up to love me automatically; to have some unbreakable bond between us because of my role in her life. A kind of bond that I would never otherwise know. I want to know how it feels ... to be loved like that, even if I will spend the rest of eternity paying for it in the Ninth Circle itself. To be loved in spite of what I've done … I mean, that's what family's supposed to be, isn't it? I want to keep Grace as I have never wanted anything in my life. I want her. She belongs to me now.

My name is Gabriel Antaeus. My daughter's name is Grace Antaeus. I know she will not hurt anyone. I know she will bring me happiness such as I have never known. And I know I am not making a mistake.

Acknowledgements

Many thanks to the following people who either contributed to the book or to the preservation of my sanity at some stage:

My agent, Carolyn Whitaker, for the first professional positive feedback I ever received and thus the first letter that I didn't tear up or viciously deface in some way after reading it. Thank you so much for all your hard work.

Simon Spanton and Gillian Redfearn - for taking on this book and for improving it immensely with all their comments and advice. And to Kustaa Saksi for the really beautiful cover artwork.

Christine Moffat and Qi Bao - for believing in the Ninth Circle before they even knew what it was about. The same goes for my grandparents - John and Joan Willrich, and Ali (1930-2007) and Joy Bell - who have all been so encouraging over the years.

Very special thanks to Shirley and Trevor Bell - the most supportive parents in the world - for bringing Mephistopheles home to live with us when I was six years old (even though it meant taking out a loan) and for graciously funding all on-site research in Budapest, including the essential visit to Faust's wine cellar!

Dad - thanks also for being the first to read this one and for the encouraging feedback at a discouraging time. And for letting me have Mephistopheles for the duration of the writing - he helped immensely with the difficult parts!

Lastly, thank you both for being such keen and avid travellers, providing me with a lifetime's worth of visits to different countries and cultures around the world before I was even out of school.

And finally, I duly acknowledge Cindy, Chloe and Suki because behind every writer there should always be three beautiful, rather perfect, if occasionally grumpy cats who dutifully keep the author sane.